THE GIFT OF HAPPINESS

A GORGEOUSLY UPLIFTING AND HEARTWARMING CHRISTMAS ROMANCE

HOLLY MARTIN

Published by Holly Martin in 2019
Copyright © Holly Martin, 2019

Paperback ISBN 978-1-9160111-6-8
Large Print paperback ISBN 978-1-9160111-7-5

Cover design by Emma Rogers

CHAPTER 1

RUBY MARLOWE BUMPED HER CUSTARD-YELLOW Mini along the country road, the headlights picking out the sparkling frosty leaves of the hedges but not penetrating much further than that through the velvet darkness. The moonlight lit up the sky, like a lighthouse welcoming her home, and, as she rounded a corner, she could see the turrets and towers of Harmony Castle silhouetted against the inky sky.

She pulled into the gates of the little village of Happiness and stopped in front of the castle, cutting the engine and listening to the complete and utter silence.

She peered through the steamed-up windscreen at the village that was going to be her new home. The start of the village was a little further down from where she was, the Christmas lights hanging above the street sending warm puddles of gold across the wet cobbles. There was not a soul in sight. It wasn't the warm welcome she'd been hoping for. But then what had she been expecting? It was two o'clock in the morning and everyone was tucked up in their beds.

Even her best friend Willow wouldn't be there as she'd gone to Paris with her boyfriend Andrew, although they were arriving back the next day. Or rather, later on that day. To be fair to Willow, Ruby was supposed to have moved to Happiness the month before, but last-minute complications with selling her home had caused a few weeks' delay, which was not ideal. As her job involved selling Christmas decorations and paraphernalia, December was her busiest and best time of the year. Moving into Happiness with just over a week until the big day didn't leave a lot of time to get her shop set up and some sales through the tills.

To make matters worse, there had been a flood in the shop she had been given. Kitty and Ken, the owners of the castle and the village, had promised her it would be fixed and cleaned up in a few weeks and assigned her a temporary shop in the meantime. It was double-fronted and one half was taken up by the artist Phoenix Blade who was apparently away at an exhibition. Kitty and Ken had been unable to contact him to ask if he would mind if Ruby moved into the other half for a short time but Kitty had assured her that Phoenix was lovely and probably wouldn't mind at all.

Probably.

That filled Ruby with all kinds of joy.

Kitty and Ken had offered free rent and accommodation for a year to anyone who could bring something to the rundown little village. They had been more than happy to give Ruby a shop to sell her Christmas decorations, which had been a dream of hers for a long time. But now, and not for the first time, she wondered whether she'd done the right thing. She played with the snowflake around her neck that Harry had bought her. He would laugh at her if he could see her now. Ruby had lived in the same town all her life, even after her parents had long since emigrated to the furthest shores of Norway. Her brother Cal had toured almost every country of the world before his thirtieth birthday, but Ruby had stayed put. Harry used to tease her that she didn't do change. She had been stuck in a rut, professionally, geographically, personally and emotionally, for too many years to count and when her best friend, Willow, had packed up her worldly goods and moved across the country to the little village of Happiness, Ruby had found herself yearning for a change exactly like that too. When she'd visited Happiness to see Willow, she'd kind of fallen in love with the place.

And that had absolutely nothing to do with Jacob Harrington, Andrew's sexy older brother.

Just the thought of Jacob sent a twist of desire through her stomach. He had been this glorious one-night stand – well OK, it had actually been three nights – and yes it had been incredible and he'd been lovely and made her laugh, but she had drawn a line under it when she had returned to her own home in St Octavia. He had texted and phoned a few times but she hadn't returned his messages and, when Willow tried to bring it up, Ruby had told her she didn't want to talk about Jacob Harrington. She wasn't interested in a relationship with him or anyone.

Not anymore.

She supposed she would have to face him at some point; he was Andrew's brother and would be bound to visit. But maybe if she got enough warning from Willow, she could make sure she was out the way those days, or at least try to keep her head down.

She looked around her. On the slopes leading up to the great castle was a tall Christmas tree with baubles as big as her head. Tiny lights twinkled in the darkness as they danced around the tree. It was an impressive sight with the castle silhouetted behind it.

There also appeared to be a life-size nativity scene set up in front of it with a large open-faced barn. Mary and Joseph were kneeling around the manger where presumably baby Jesus was wrapped up like an Egyptian mummy. There was no sign of the wise men or the shepherds but, as Ruby peered through the darkness, there was something moving in front of the barn.

She climbed out of the car and realised there was a real donkey and two sheep grazing in a small paddock in front of the barn. Well, that was certainly taking the nativity scene very seriously.

She knew Willow had been heavily involved in the decorations, although she hadn't mentioned a real-life nativity scene. Perhaps she'd done it to appease the older, more traditional members of the village.

Feeling suddenly mischievous, she opened her boot and rooted around until she found the appropriate bag and then walked up to the paddock.

She knew donkeys could be quite unpredictable and that some people used them as guard pets, but as Ruby approached the paddock the donkey immediately ambled over to the fence. She stroked his velvety nose and he seemed quite happy with that.

She shoved her hands in the pocket of her coat for the chopped carrots she had bought as a snack from McDonald's on her way over here and held one out. The donkey whiffled it up. The two sheep looked over with mild interest at the prospect of something to eat rather than grass or hay but they didn't approach. She tossed the carrots over the fence in their direction but they seemed scared by this gesture and quickly retreated to the furthest corner.

Ruby looked around; as no one was about she climbed over the fence. The donkey was unperturbed and she approached the nativity scene. Mary and Joseph were huge. If they had been standing they would have been seven or eight feet tall, but as it was they were kneeling down, leaning over the manger, which looked tiny in comparison. They looked creepy rather than realistic, and the model of Mary had very large hairy hands. In fact, it even looked like she might have had a beard at one point, which had been hastily painted over. Also, on closer inspection, Joseph was sporting an eye patch, although you wouldn't have been able to see that from the road as his face was turned to the side. Ruby laughed out loud when she spotted the hook instead of a hand. It seemed Willow might have got a cheap deal and found a couple of models of pirates to use for the nativity instead. The models had been dressed in real clothes and headdresses to make them look more authentic, so maybe Willow had thought no one would notice the pirate origins.

Ruby glanced down at the baby Jesus, who thankfully was just a large doll covered in a blanket and not pirate-themed like his parents.

She quickly looked around one more time and then swapped Jesus for a cuddly snowman, complete with top hat. She tucked the snowman under the blanket. She knew Willow would get a big kick out of this. Ruby and Willow had been playing jokes on each other every Christmas for many years so it was good to get in first before Willow could get back and start her regime of practical jokes.

Ruby made a move towards the fence just as one of the sheep started making a weird choking noise. She turned round and could see bits of chewed carrot on the floor in front of the sheep as the animal continued to hack and cough.

Bloody hell. Kidnapping baby Jesus was one thing but killing one of the sheep within minutes of arriving in the village was a new low, even for her.

She moved over to see what she could do,

wondering how she could do the Heimlich manoeuvre on a sheep. She'd done a first aid course a few months before and one of the sessions had been dog first aid and how to help a dog when it was choking – surely it would be much the same? The sheep didn't move away from her when she got nearer. It was quite a small animal so she moved behind it and wrapped her arms around its belly, squeezing upwards a few times, but it made no difference. She patted the sheep between the shoulder blades but still the animal was choking. She lifted the back legs up as if she was about to run a wheelbarrow race with the poor animal and somehow this did the trick. The piece of carrot fell out of the sheep's mouth and then the sheep gave Ruby a kick in the leg for her trouble.

Ruby staggered back a bit, rubbing her leg as the sheep continued to eat the carrots as if nothing had happened.

She glanced around and the donkey was watching her, almost as if it was afraid she would suddenly try to do the same manoeuvre on him. It was all rather embarrassing – her only saving grace was that no one had been around to see her manhandling the poor sheep.

She picked up Jesus and climbed back over the fence.

She watched the sheep for a few moments to make sure it wasn't going to choke on the carrots again, but it had now finished and had moved back over to a bundle of hay with its friend, who had barely looked up during all the fracas.

Ruby quickly hurried back to her car before she could get into any more trouble. She climbed back into the driver's seat and put Jesus carefully on the seat next to her, wiping the mud off his face from where she'd dropped him on the ground to try to save the sheep.

She looked at the map that Kitty had sent her marking where the shop was and where her cottage was. The village was laid out like a large triangle, with the only pub in the village,

The Welcome Home, at the top. Her shop and cottage were on the main high street that led down towards the cliff tops and the steps down to the beach. Along the cliff to the right, about half a mile down the coastal path, was Willow and Andrew's cottage and a little track from there led back to the village and met the pub at the junction with the high street.

She drove her little yellow Mini down the high street, passing small thatched cottages that had stood there for many hundreds of years, and shops that seemed to offer every-thing from bread, cheese, knitting stuff to some more items of the arty kind. The place had changed so much since Ruby had been there in the summer. The village had been practically a ghost town then but it looked like it had come alive in the last few months. There were Christmas lights hanging from the houses and lampposts, and it gave her hope.

She looked up at them as she drove care-fully underneath them. The lights were mainly laid out in vertical strings like icicles, forming a large curtain which was sort of triangle-shaped. She cocked her head and then slammed on the brakes. They weren't triangles at all, they were… knickers.

No, they couldn't be. But the more she looked at them, there was no escaping the fact these were illuminated knickers. In fact, the way the curtains parted in the middle made them look more like Y-fronts than knickers. Ruby sat there and stared at the Y-fronts that were hung incrementally all the way down the street and burst out laughing. She was never going to let Willow live this down. Nothing would top this.

But then she spotted the candles either side of the street. The candles had holly leaves and two large red berries at the candles' base, making them look like penises. Ruby was crying with laughter by this time. Penis and Y-front lights, these were the best lights ever!

Ruby carried on driving down the high street, chuckling to herself. She found the dou-ble-fronted shop quite easily; Phoenix Blade

13

had his name in gold writing above one side of the shop. She was just going to dump some of her stuff in the shop and then crawl into her bed.

Ruby got out of the car and stretched. There was a freezing chill in the air and the windows sparkled with a heavy frost, her breath coming out in little puffs of steam.

She wrapped her purple woollen coat around her and checked under the flowerpot near the door where Kitty had said she would leave the key. Sure enough, it was there waiting for her.

She picked it up and let herself in, closing the door behind her against the cold. She fumbled around inside and found the light switch, illuminating the whole room. There was an archway between the two shops and her side was empty, apart from a few boxes which seemed to have strayed over from the other half of the shop. She couldn't see much of Phoenix's side, as that half was still in darkness, but it didn't look particularly tidy.

Most of her stock was arriving tomorrow, so it wouldn't take her long to unload her car. She'd just taken the delicate things she didn't trust the removal men with.

She went back outside into the cold and started shifting the boxes inside the shop, but as she went back to collect the last one, she noticed a light on in the flat above the shop. She hoisted the box under her arm, closing the boot, and saw there was a tall shadowy figure peering out the window at her.

It seemed that Phoenix Blade had returned from his travels. He disappeared from the window and she wondered if she was going to meet her new neighbour. It probably wasn't the best time to introduce herself when it was two o'clock in the morning and she had been driving for what felt like eight hours.

She hoped to god he was nice and had been told she was coming.

She went back inside and closed the door, plonking the box on top of all the other boxes as she heard footsteps coming down the steps at the back of the shop. She dusted her hands down her coat, tried to straighten her hair and plastered a big smile on her face. And then suddenly a man was standing in the room with her and if this was Phoenix Blade he was not what she'd been expecting at all.

She felt a jolt of desire and shock slam into her as she stared at the man in front of her. His hair was dishevelled as if he'd just climbed out of bed. He was topless, showing a broad muscular chest and a smattering of hair disappearing into pyjama bottoms. His intense blue eyes showed shock and confusion. But mostly, what she hadn't been expecting was that Phoenix Blade was actually Jacob Harrington, the man she'd had probably the best sex of her life with just a few months before. The man who had touched places inside of her that hadn't been touched for over twelve years. The man she had blocked all contact with because she had been scared by how he made her feel.

Jacob stared at her.

'Ruby Marlowe, you're the last woman I'd expect to see here.'

Ruby found she still had no words to describe what she felt about seeing Jacob again.

She swallowed. 'I wasn't exactly expecting to see you either.'

He frowned. 'You're standing in my shop.'

Oh crap. This was *his* shop? Wait, no, Kitty had told her she was sharing a shop with Phoenix Blade, not Jacob Harrington. There must be some mistake.

'I was told the shop belonged to some artist called Phoenix Blade.'

'It does, and that would be me.'

He was serious. He was obviously living here in the village and now she was going to have to share a shop with him too.

'How was I supposed to know that was you?'

'It didn't come up in conversation between us?' Jacob asked.

'When you were giving me multiple orgasms, strangely not.'

A ghost of a smile appeared on his lips and she cursed herself. The last thing she wanted to mention was the magnificent sex they'd shared. She wanted to forget it had ever happened. In fact, she had spent the last four months trying unsuccessfully to forget those incredible nights she'd spent with this man, and now the memory hung in the air between them.

Her emotions fought a war inside her. There was a huge part of her that wanted to take him straight back up to his bed and rekindle that amazing connection they'd had a few months before. But her heart and her head knew better. If they were both living here now, she couldn't get involved with him again. That would lead to a whole load of complicated emotions and a road that she had no interest in going down.

'What are you doing here, Ruby?'

'Kitty didn't tell you?'

He shook his head. 'Well to be honest, I

haven't checked my emails and I've been away so I haven't seen her.'

Surely Kitty could have phoned him. And why hadn't Kitty mentioned to her that Phoenix was actually Jacob? Why hadn't Willow told her? Although Willow had no clue that Ruby had been given the other half of Jacob's shop for the next few weeks, she would have known he was living in the village. A little bit of warning wouldn't have gone amiss. Unless... There had been many villagers who had been rooting for Jacob and Ruby to get together when they'd both been there in the summer and anyone could see the chemistry between them. Had this whole flood debacle been part of a cunning plan to reacquaint her and Jacob again in a much more intimate setting than either of them would probably like?

'Well, I'm sorry to be the one to tell you this but you now have a roommate, at least until after Christmas,' Ruby said.

His eyes widened. 'You're living here?'

Ruby couldn't help but smile at the panic

on his face. He probably had a whole harem of women he entertained on a regular basis and he was now worried how this new living arrangement would affect that lifestyle. Even though she had her own cottage further down the street, she decided to tease him.

'Yeah, that's OK, isn't it?'

He looked around as if wondering where to stash her. 'I guess. I mean I have a spare room; it has a single bed for when Poppy stays over, you could sleep in there.'

She was surprised by that generous offer and that he wasn't throwing her out already. After blowing him off a few months before, she didn't think he would be welcoming her with open arms.

He fixed her with a mischievous look. 'Unless you want to share my bed?'

Ruby laughed. 'And there's the Jacob I know.'

She glanced down at his pyjama bottoms which had cuddly snowmen in various sexual positions all over them. She shook her head with a smile. They were funny, sexy, sweet and suited him to a T.

'I'm only messing with you, come on, let me show you to your room,' Jacob said.

She smiled. He was a good man. She certainly didn't deserve this level of kindness from him. She wondered if she had hurt him when she cut him off in the summer. But this was a man who had probably slept with more women than she'd had hot dinners. It had been a very casual, no-strings-attached arrangement in the summer and they'd both known that so he had no reason to be upset when she walked away. She sighed. She probably should have texted him back. They'd had fun, he had been really nice, they had parted with a really sweet kiss goodbye, she shouldn't have just blanked him. Although that kiss had probably been one of the main reasons why she had.

'I'm only joking too. I'm just sharing your shop. You don't need to worry about me cramping your style. You can continue to sleep with all the women in the village, I'm not going to be in your way,' she teased.

'You make me sound like some kind of Casanova,' Jacob said.

She smiled. 'We both know you're much worse than that.'

He laughed. 'You were the one who didn't return my calls. So does that make you the female equivalent of Casanova? Cleopatra maybe.'

'Maybe. Perhaps I should have delivered myself to you wrapped up in a Persian carpet rather than arriving in my little Mini.'

'Well that would have been a treat.' His eyes appraised her for a moment. 'Ah Ruby, I've actually missed you.'

He moved towards her and before she could stop him he wrapped her in a big hug.

She wanted to tell him it was ridiculous for him to miss her; it had been sex and nothing more. But she couldn't find the words to dismiss what they'd shared. This hug was everything she did and didn't need right then. His scent, his warmth, his body against hers. She took it all back, this was the perfect kind of welcome. There was a little voice inside her that was shouting at her that this was a terrible idea but she ignored that because being wrapped in Jacob Harrington's arms was the most incredible feeling ever.

She slid her arms around his back and held him close. Her heart felt tight in her chest, a lump of emotion burning a hole in her throat. She didn't want this but she couldn't let him go either.

Eventually she pulled back away from him.

'Come upstairs,' Jacob said, still holding her shoulders. 'We can… talk.'

From the way he was looking at her, talk seemed to be the very last thing on Jacob's mind. She absolutely could not jump straight back into bed with him as if the months they'd been apart hadn't happened at all. This was a dangerous road to go down. She didn't want this.

'Jacob, I need to go to bed. It's nearly half two in the morning and I'm exhausted.'

He hesitated before he spoke and something told her he knew she needed to get away from him.

'OK.'

'I'll see you tomorrow.'

'Come for breakfast,' Jacob said.

She really didn't want him to get any ideas about that hug or anything else happening between them. And although her plan for facing Jacob had originally been to avoid him at all costs, now it seemed she would need to talk to him, to explain that nothing was going to happen between them again. So if they were going to work alongside each other for the next few weeks, it would be better to have that conversation sooner rather than later.

'Breakfast sounds good.'

She wasn't looking forward to that conversation.

He bent his head and kissed her on the

cheek and she hated the way her heart leapt at his touch.

'I'll see you tomorrow then, Ruby Marlowe.'

She quickly hurried outside and locked the door, trying not to look at him as he watched her go.

She climbed back in her car and pulled off down the high street, bumping over the cobbles. The main shops fell away and out on the horizon the sea glittered under the moonlight. She could see a cluster of white cottages. She knew hers was on the right somewhere, so she slowed down and looked at the house names. Dragonfly Cottage, Butterfly Cottage, all with flowers painted around the door, which she knew had been done by her friend Willow's hand. And then she saw it. Christmas Cottage, with little holly leaves and red berries painted around the front door. She couldn't help but smile about that.

She quickly got out and looked at it. It gleamed in the moonlight. This was going to be her new home. She grabbed her suitcase, found the key under the mat and let herself in, stepping into the lounge. She switched on the light and looked around.

Ruby's heart filled to see the Christmas tree in the corner, tastefully decorated with a few baubles and tiny fairy lights. This would definitely be Willow's doing and she had left enough room for Ruby to add her own decorations. There was a gorgeous cherry-red log burner under a solid wood mantelpiece and a beautiful silver-grey rug on the floor that looked soft enough to sleep on.

She had a quick look at the kitchen before going upstairs and walking into the bedroom. Thankfully Willow had worked her magic in here too, making up the king-size bed with a super-thick duvet and squishy pillows. She quickly got changed, brushed her teeth in the tiny en-suite bathroom and peeled the duvet back ready to get in. She leapt back when she saw there was an ugly black spider the size of her hand waiting for her. But as she stepped closer to it, she realised it was plastic and no doubt placed there by Willow. Ruby laughed, removed the spider and climbed into bed. She switched off the light and looked at the stars twinkling above her through the skylight.

Jacob Harrington.

God, of all the people she had casually dated over the last twelve years who had meant nothing to her, why had the one person who had meant something make his way back into her life?

She closed her eyes, knowing if she did manage to sleep that night, then he would feature very heavily in her dreams.

CHAPTER 2

JACOB TURNED THE SAUSAGES OVER AND PUT them back under the grill. Ruby had texted him a while before and said she'd be over in half hour so he wanted to make sure that breakfast was ready for her.

It was somewhat ironic that that text was the first communication from her in around four or five months.

He'd read the emails from Kitty and Ken that morning explaining that Ruby was going to be in the other half of his shop until after Christmas. He wished he'd checked his messages before so he'd known to expect her. Although he still wasn't sure how he would have reacted if he had known.

He'd been here in Happiness for a week in the summer to help his brother, Andrew, get the dilapidated village ready for the open day and Ruby had been there at the same time. The connection between them had been instant, but she was only supposed to be a one-night stand and they both knew that. He'd never really had a serious relationship in his life and he was quite happy casually dating without any of the commitments or emotional attachments of a long-term relationship. They'd spent two glorious nights together, which normally would be enough for him, but when he'd left to do an exhibition, he'd thought about her constantly. He'd come back a week later to see the fireworks on the night of the open day and they'd ended up in bed again, making fireworks of their own. There had been something about Ruby that had got under his skin. And although he certainly wasn't looking for marriage or forever, Ruby had made him want something… more. He wasn't sure what that *more* would look like, but he knew he hadn't been quite ready to say goodbye to her in the summer.

But she'd left, returning to her hometown of St Octavia, several hundred miles away. Well, three hundred and thirty-four to be exact. He'd checked.

He'd texted her a few times, even called her, but there had been no response and so he'd let things slide. He'd put their time down to a wonderful couple of days and tried really hard to forget about her, although he hadn't been particularly successful at that.

He had moved to Happiness a few weeks later and life was good, he loved the little village with its colourful characters.

And now she was back and here to stay by the look of things.

He couldn't help being a bit thrilled about that.

Not that it meant anything. He wasn't entirely sure Ruby wanted to pick up from where they'd left off a few months before. He'd gotten some very mixed messages from her last night. She had held him so tight when he had hugged her, as if she didn't want to let him go, but when he'd simply suggested she come upstairs to talk she'd practically ran out of there.

He suddenly heard footsteps on the stairs and turned to find her standing in the room with him.

God, he wanted to walk straight over and kiss her but he wasn't sure that was allowed.

She smiled and cocked her head on one side to look at him. 'Jacob Harrington, you're looking pretty bloody spectacular as always.'

He moved towards her and wrapped her in a hug. She hugged him back. 'It's good to see you, Ruby.' He pulled back, holding her at arm's length. 'You're looking pretty amazing yourself.'

Ruby smiled and then moved further into

the flat, looking around. 'So you're living here now?'

He watched her, the winter sunlight catching her red hair. 'Yeah.'

'Funny that Willow never told me.'

'I believe she tried to bring me up in conversation with you several times but that you didn't want to talk about me.'

Willow had tried to defend Ruby's decision to not answer his texts and calls. She was obviously very protective of her best friend but in the end she'd told him that Ruby had her heart broken in the past and just wasn't looking for love anymore. It was more than a little sad that some asshole had destroyed Ruby's faith in men so much that she never wanted another relationship. But he wasn't looking for love either. He didn't want the big all-singing-and-dancing love affair so he wasn't sure why Ruby was shying away from him.

Ruby was clearly floundering at hearing this. 'That wasn't what it was, I was just busy.'

He made her coffee just as she liked it then

dished up the breakfast and carried the plates to the little table by the window that had distant sea views. The fields were covered in a thick layer of frost that sparkled in the winter sun. She sat down opposite him.

He watched her tuck into her breakfast. 'So you're moving into Happiness?'

'For a year,' Ruby was quick to clarify.

'And then what?'

She shrugged. 'Maybe some travelling.'

'That does sound good.'

'Alone.'

He suppressed a smile at the distinction.

'And we're going to be roomies,' Jacob said.

'In the professional sense. We're just sharing shop space.'

She was clearly trying to warn him off.

'So what's going on with you, Ruby?' Jacob asked, getting straight to the point. 'You practically hotfooted it out of here last night when I suggested coming upstairs.'

'Because I didn't want to sleep with you.'

He couldn't help but smile. 'Who said anything about sex? I just wanted to talk.'

She laughed. 'You're such a liar.'

'So what is it? Do you have some weird disease I should know about?'

She laughed in outrage. 'No I do not.'

'I know what it is, you got a tattoo with my face on it and you didn't want me to see it.'

She laughed again.

He smiled and took a bite of his toast as they watched each other across the table. He loved having this banter with her. She was so easy to get on with and he enjoyed flirting and teasing her. There was obvious chemistry between them, it practically crackled in the air. He had really missed this. He'd just never had this connection with any of the other women he'd been with.

'So what's going on here? I'm not proposing marriage and babies or even any kind of serious relationship. We had fun the last time you were here. I'm happy to have no-strings-attached fun again.'

'Wow,' Ruby said, dryly. 'What an offer.'

'I'm not sure why you're protesting so much. If I recall, you seemed to have a pretty good time in the summer,' he teased.

She smiled and shook her head. 'You're so cocky.'

'And I was under the impression that you didn't want a relationship.'

'I don't,' Ruby said, far too quickly for his liking.

'Neither do I.'

She stared at him for a few moments, maybe weighing up what was on the table. She picked up her coffee mug and took a big sip.

'I think it's best if we're just friends,' Ruby said after a while.

'Just to clarify, are we talking friends with benefits or…'

She laughed. 'Just friends, no benefits. We're working alongside each other, we now live in the same village, I don't want things to be awkward between us. If we start jumping into bed with each other every night, well that's starting to sound a bit like a relationship to me and neither of us wants that. And then when it ends, which it undoubtedly will, we'll have all this awkwardness between us. We really are better off just being friends.'

He stared at her. There was something going on here but he clearly wasn't going to get any straight answers out of her today.

He pretended he was giving it some serious thought but in reality he liked Ruby, and if the only way he was going to have her in his life was to be friends then he was more than OK with that.

'I've never had a girl as a friend before,' Jacob said. 'How does that work?'

'In the same way that it does with *boys*,' Ruby said.

'But no kissing or sex?' Jacob teased.

Ruby laughed. 'No!'

'OK, OK, Ruby Marlowe. I'm just messing with you. If you want to be friends then that's just fine. But just so you know, the offer of no-strings-attached sex is always on the table.'

She shook her head with a smile.

'So what brought you to Happiness?' Jacob asked, taking a sip of his tea.

'Oh, lots of reasons.' She paused for a moment as she thought. 'I don't know if I ever told you, my brother, Cal, is a Paralympian.'

'No, you never told me that,' Jacob said.

'He lost his leg in an accident when he was a kid and he went on to become one of the world's greatest athletes.'

Recognition dawned on his face. 'Callum Marlowe?'

Ruby beamed. 'Yes, you know him?'

'He's amazing, he won gold in running and hurdles in the last Paralympics. He was incredible to watch, he just flew down the track,' Jacob said.

'My brother is pretty bloody special. He's touring America right now, giving inspirational talks, and I just look at him and look at my own life and I wonder what I've done. I've lived in the same town all my life, had the same job. I just wanted a change. I just feel like

I've been stuck in a rut for so long and I wanted to do something different. Plus I missed Willow. When she lived in St Octavia, we'd see each other every day. The free rent is an attractive feature too, I can save some money for going travelling.'

'So I wasn't the reason you came back?' Jacob teased.

'You're so sure of yourself. It's not an attractive feature, you know,' Ruby said, although she was still smiling.

He focussed his attention on his food for a moment but when he looked up she was still staring at him.

'So you're Phoenix Blade?'

He nodded.

'I knew you were a scrap metal artist. I didn't know you went under a pseudonym.'

'Well that's where the name comes from. Phoenix as in something new from the old and Blade because of the metal.'

'Makes sense,' Ruby said.

'Jacob Harrington sounds a bit boring.'

'Trust me, there is nothing boring about Jacob Harrington,' she said, staring him right in the eyes.

He smiled. God, being *just friends* with her was going to be a lot harder than he thought.

'And what made *you* decide to move to Happiness?' Ruby asked. 'This place strikes me as a little bit too sleepy for you.'

He thought about that for a moment as he mopped up the last of the egg with his sausage. 'I grew up in Newquay. I've lived in Plymouth, London, Rome and Penzance. They were all wonderful places but none of them felt like home. This place feels like home.'

Ruby nodded. 'I know what you mean.'

'People look out for each other here, I like that. It feels like a good place to raise a family.'

Her eyes bulged; all humour now gone. 'Jesus Christ, is that what you want? I never thought I'd ever hear you say those words.'

'Oh no, I didn't mean me, just that there are lots of young families here now, and if Andrew and Willow have children it's a great place to raise them.' He felt like he was backpedalling and he sighed. 'I suppose one day I might want that.'

He surprised himself with that comment. Did he really want that?

She was still looking horrified so he decided to reassure her.

'You don't need to worry; I'm not talking about now. One day.'

'I'm not worried because I won't be the one marrying you.'

'Have you never thought about marriage, babies, the happy ending?' Jacob asked, realising how clichéd he sounded.

'Why does a happy ending have to include marriage and babies?' Ruby said. 'I'm very happy on my own. There are no arguments about what to watch on TV, my house stays tidy until I mess it up. I don't need to worry about shaving my legs for my boyfriend or husband. I can go out and do whatever I want without having to think about someone else. No drama or arguments, having the bed to myself. I have friends for company, and some-times wonderful men to spend the night with. That sounds pretty bloody happy to me.'

He'd obviously touched a nerve. 'I think you're right. Society puts a lot of pressure on us to get married, settle down, have children, when that life isn't for everyone. You need to do whatever makes you happy.'

Ruby visibly relaxed. 'I used to think I wanted marriage and children, when I was younger. I'd watched so many romance films, read so many books, and I expected that life. But that fairytale of the happy ever after doesn't exist. You need to make your own hap-piness in this world, not rely on someone else to do that for you.'

'To a certain extent I would agree. But just as marriage and children are not for everyone, there are many people that are very happily married, or very happy with a lifetime partner. Just because you don't want that lifestyle doesn't mean that other people won't find their happiness that way. Look at Andrew and

Willow. I've never seen two people so utterly in love and completely happy as they are together.'

Ruby smiled. 'I know. They are the epitome of the fairytale ending. You are right that, for some, they need someone in their lives to complete them, but I'm not one of them.'

'Some might say that the right man wouldn't complete you but complement you.'

'I don't need to be complemented. I'm pretty bloody fabulous as I am.'

He smiled. 'That you are, Ruby Marlowe.'

Jacob watched her finish her breakfast. He wanted to ask her what had happened in her life to make her so cynical but he decided that could wait for another day.

'So do you need a hand with settling in or moving boxes?' he asked.

'That's very kind. You're taking this friend thing very seriously,' Ruby said.

'If a job is worth doing, it's worth doing right.'

'Well, the removal van is arriving later, so

yeah if you can give me a hand with unloading stuff into the shop, that would be great.'

'I can do that.'

Ruby smiled at him and then held her coffee cup up. 'I think we are going to be very good at this friendship malarkey.'

He chinked his mug against hers. 'To friendship.'

CHAPTER 3

Ruby left Jacob's flat and stepped out onto the street, pulling her flowered knitted hat onto her head. It was freezing cold and the weather report had even promised a smattering of snow later.

She was glad she'd had the chance to sort things out with Jacob before it had got awkward and actually she was now looking forward to working alongside him for the next few weeks rather than dreading it. He was a lovely man and she knew they were going to be very close friends.

She decided to have a little wander around the village to remind herself of where everything was – she hadn't had a chance to have a proper look the night before when she had been distracted by giant underpants and penis-shaped candles. She looked to the left where, further down the street, her cottage was tucked into the last cluster of houses before the village ended and then there was only sea stretching out for miles into the horizon.

She turned right and wandered into the main part of the village. Villagers, wrapped up against the cold, bustled from shop to shop, either carrying bags of shopping or probably just popping in for a chat, while small children chased each other up the street or followed their parents around. The place felt so alive.

Little shops were dressed for Christmas, some with trees in the windows, some with lights curled around the window displays. It all looked very pretty. She took a few pictures of the more arty displays for her Instagram.

This was what a traditional Christmas was

supposed to be like. Her parents always flew over from Norway to spend Christmas with her and Cal, but this year they had opted to spend it on the warm beaches of Australia. They had invited her to come along of course, especially as Cal was likely to be working away from home over Christmas, but wearing shorts and flip-flops and having a barbeque on the beach just didn't feel Christmassy enough for her. And as the plan was to move to Happiness, she'd thought she'd try Christmas in her new home. Being here now, it felt like the right decision.

There was such an array of shops here, the practical grocery shops, bakeries, cafés, a chemist, interspersed with the more quirky touristy kind of shops with paintings in the windows, jewellery, pottery, and other arty things. It was the perfect mix.

Ruby peered into Willow's shop window, which was all in darkness now as she still hadn't returned from her holiday yet, but the

Christmas candles in the window glittered prettily in the lights from the street.

She walked on a bit further and smiled when she saw the gold hand-painted sign above one of the empty shops. *The Happy Little Christmas Shop.* This was where her shop was supposed to be until the burst pipe had put an end to that, well at least for now. She peered through the window and could see the shelves all ready for her Christmas decorations. It was a shame that her temporary shop was further down the high street, she would have preferred to be in the thick of it all. But at least it was only for a short while.

She turned around and saw what looked like a wanted poster on one of the lampposts. In fact, she realised, they were on every lamppost.

She moved closer and read it.

STOLEN! Baby Jesus was taken from the nativity last night, somewhere between the hours of 6pm and 7am. Reward of £5 leading to his safe return.

Then there was a photo of the doll underneath. Ruby stifled a giggle. What had started as a joke for Willow's benefit had escalated very quickly. She would be appearing on *Crimewatch* next. As soon as Willow had seen the snowman in the manger, Ruby would have to return Jesus to his rightful home. She was sure Pirate Pete and his wife must be missing him.

She decided to go into the post office, which also sold all the basic groceries, to get a few things. She remembered this place from when she had been there in the summer; it was a whole emporium of everything anyone could ever need, from inflatable paddleboards to ironing boards, from saucepans to pasta sauces, and everything in between.

Up at the counter, Julia Dalton, the postmistress, was deep in conversation with two other elderly ladies who Ruby recognised as Liz from the cheese shop and Dorothy who ran the little painting shop selling her wonderful works of art. They all stopped talking when they saw her.

'Ruby! Welcome back,' Julia said, coming round the counter and giving Ruby a hug. 'Or should I say, welcome home.'

Ruby smiled as she hugged her. 'Thank you, it's good to finally be here.'

'We were just talking about you,' Liz said with no trace of embarrassment. Ruby didn't know whether that was a good or bad thing. 'You're bunking with that gorgeous Jacob Harrington, aren't you? I think there's many a woman in the village that would like to be in your shoes.'

'I'm just sharing the other half of the shop with him, and only for a few weeks until my shop is ready. There's no bunking involved,' Ruby said.

'But it can't exactly be a hardship working alongside him every day,' Dorothy said, waggling her eyebrows mischievously.

Julia flapped her hands. 'Ignore these two, what can I help you with?'

'I was going to place a big food shopping order for later this week, and Willow has left me a few things in the house, so just a few basics to keep me going. Milk, bread, cereal, that kind of thing,' Ruby said, trying to ignore the beady eyes of Liz and Dorothy as they watched her astutely.

'No problem.' Julia handed her a little wire basket. 'Follow me.'

Julia marched down the aisles, tossing bread, milk, cheese, eggs, cereal, jam, butter, biscuits and bananas into the basket as Ruby hurried to catch up with her. She followed her into an aisle that was mainly toiletries and Ruby watched with amusement as shampoo, conditioner, shower gel, deodorant, razors, moisturiser and toothpaste went into the basket too.

'Thanks Julia, I think what we have there is more than enough, I really do just need a few basics,' Ruby tried.

'Of course dear, just the essentials,' Julia said, throwing in a few boxes of condoms and, to her surprise, a pair of fluffy handcuffs too. 'Just in case.'

Ruby suppressed a smile. 'The condoms really aren't necessary.'

'Oh, you need to be safe Ruby dear, safe sex is very important in this day and age.'

'I'm always safe, but I won't be having sex with Jacob Harrington or with anyone, so the condoms won't be needed.'

Julia nodded but didn't take the condoms back out. 'Of course not, but you never can tell when these moments might happen, those passionate, sex-up-against-the-wall, go-with-the-flow type moments. It's best to be prepared.'

'Who's having sex up against the wall?' Liz said, her eyes lighting up as they returned to the till.

'Ruby,' Julia said, simply.

'No I'm not,' Ruby laughed.

'But you plan to, judging by the number of condoms in your basket,' Dorothy said, picking up the fluffy handcuffs and giving

Ruby a pointed look over the top of her glasses.

Julia started ringing up the purchases.

'Those were what Julia considered to be essential shopping.'

'Quite right too,' Liz said. 'You don't want to have a baby unless you're in a serious relationship. Bringing up a baby alone can't be any fun. I see all of these single mothers raising their children and they just look exhausted. It's better to have a man there to help you.'

Ruby gave Julia the money. 'Well, I don't need a man to help me do anything and, as I was saying to Julia, I won't be having sex with anyone so—'

'Nothing wrong with a bit of casual sex,' Dorothy said.

'No, sex is perfectly natural,' Julia agreed.

Ruby decided to change the subject. 'So the decorations in the village, they look lovely.'

'Oh they do, don't they,' gushed Liz.

'So pretty,' Julia agreed.

OK. Obviously only Ruby's depraved mind

had made the rude connection. She decided to move on before she started giggling about it again.

'And I see from the posters around town that someone stole Jesus last night. Seems a bit odd, doesn't it?'

'It's very odd,' Julia nodded. 'I went up there this morning to feed Minty, Tatty and the donkey, Wonky, and he was missing.'

'Maybe an animal took him,' Ruby said.

'And swapped him for a snowman?' Julia said, sceptically.

Ah, that had been a rookie error on Ruby's part. She should have just stolen Jesus, not left a replacement.

'A snowman?' Ruby said, innocently.

Dorothy narrowed her eyes. 'You wouldn't have anything to do with this, would you?'

'Me? Of course not. I was too tired when I arrived late last night to do anything, let alone start stealing members of the nativity. I just went straight to the shop to dump a few things and then to my cottage. It sounds like something kids would do, not a full grown, mature adult.'

'I said it was kids,' Liz said.

'Well, that's why I offered five pounds for a reward. If some kid has got it, I thought five pounds would be enough to get them to bring it back,' Julia said.

Ruby nodded but inwardly thought that most kids today would barely get out of bed for five pounds. She wondered if she could prolong this somehow, maybe ask for a ransom for extra effectiveness. Maybe send postcards from Jesus on his holiday. She almost laughed out loud as she thought about all the fun she could have with this.

Ruby took her shopping bag. 'Well thanks for all this and for the… illuminating talk about sex. I'll keep my eyes peeled for Jesus.'

'Yes, please. And if you need any other… bedroom paraphernalia…' Julia lowered her voice but still spoke loud enough for Liz and Dorothy to hear her. 'I have whips, blindfolds and sexy lingerie out the back.'

Ruby smirked and nodded. 'I'll keep that in mind.'

She hurried out of the shop before there was any more sex talk or any more kinky essentials were added to her shopping basket.

Life in a small village was certainly going to take a lot of getting used to.

RUBY HAD JUST FINISHED UNPACKING the few bags of clothes she had brought with her when there was a hammering on the door.

She wondered if Jacob had changed his mind about just being friends and come to ravish her. She didn't know if she had enough willpower to refuse him if he had.

She went downstairs and opened the door and was met with a squealing whirlwind of brown hair. She smiled as Willow threw herself at Ruby and hugged her tight.

'I can't believe you're finally here,' Willow said.

Ruby hugged her back. 'It's good to see you too.'

Willow stepped back to look at her and then hugged her again. 'I'm so sorry I wasn't here to greet you.'

Ruby kissed the top of her head and ushered her inside. 'Don't be daft, you were in Paris, it wasn't your fault everything was delayed my end. Besides, you made my bed up for me, provided me with a Christmas tree and food in the fridge and cupboards. What more could I want?'

'Ah, it was the least I could do.'

'And thank you for the spider in my bed,' Ruby said.

Willow giggled. 'One point to me.'

Ruby smirked and decided not to tell her about stealing Jesus. She'd let Willow find that out for herself.

Ruby moved to the log burner and threw another log inside; the flames crackled and burned a welcoming glow of orange and gold.

'So what's going on with your shop? Andrew said there was a message left for him that there was some kind of flood?' Willow asked, throwing herself down on the sofa.

'Yes there was, but Kitty and Ken have temporarily rehoused me in a different shop, so Andrew doesn't need to bust a gut to get it fixed two seconds after he has come back off holiday.'

'Oh, you know what Andrew's like, always has to be doing something round here. And he has an assistant now, Lucas. He helps Andrew a lot. Anyway, which shop have they put you in, all the shops are filled?'

'I'm in the other half of Jacob's shop,' Ruby said and watched Willow's face light up. Then she frowned.

'God, that's got to be a bit awkward.'

Ruby thought again about the incredible time she'd had with Jacob in the summer, and the fact that she had gone back to St Octavia and completely cut him off. Being back here had the potential of being all kinds of awkward. He could have made things a lot more difficult for her, but in fact he'd been a complete gentleman about it.

'Actually, it wasn't as bad as I thought it would be. We talked it out and we agreed nothing is going to happen between us. We have to work alongside each other, live in the same tiny village, it'd just be awkward if it all goes wrong. Although, a little bit of warning from you that he was living here too wouldn't have gone amiss.'

'You didn't want to talk about him, I didn't think you would care,' Willow said, innocently.

'You mean you deliberately didn't divulge the information in case it put me off coming here,' Ruby said, sitting down on the sofa next to her.

'Maybe,' Willow said. 'So was there no spark between you two at all?'

'Oh there was plenty of spark,' Ruby said. 'I just don't think it's a good idea to pursue it. I think what we had meant something more to him than it did to me. He's talking about coming here, settling down and having babies, for goodness sake. How could I possibly fit into that picture? It's best to end it now, I don't want to hurt him by leading him on.'

'Oh, don't give me that crap,' Willow said. 'The way you looked at him, the way you talked about him when you were both here last. It was something very different to how you've been with previous men. You liked him.'

Ruby sighed, because there was probably more than an element of truth to that. She shook her head and pushed that feeling away. 'It was just sex, Willow. What we have between us is just lust, nothing else.'

'I don't think you're giving this a chance. What harm would it do to see where it goes? I'm sure if it doesn't work out you two can be mature enough about it to not let it turn weird between you.'

'I don't know if he really wants a relationship with me. Maybe he's saving the marriage and babies for someone else. He even said he was quite happy to continue with the no-strings-attached sex.'

'And what do you want?' Willow asked.

'I don't want a relationship either, you know that.'

Willow's face softened. 'Because of Harry?'

Ruby let out a hard breath. She didn't talk about Harry with anyone. Of course everyone in St Octavia knew, but they also knew better than to bring it up. The thing with Harry had happened before she'd met Willow but one drunken night at university she'd let it all pour out. Willow didn't bring it up very often but Ruby was glad she knew, it was too big a thing to keep inside. And at times like this of course Harry was going to come up. He had impacted on every emotional relationship decision Ruby had made for the last twelve years.

'Of course because of Harry. That asshole broke my heart, smashed it into smithereens, and I honestly don't think I've ever got over that. I couldn't go through that again.'

She was surprised she was still angry over

it. In the beginning it had been grief and pain but that had eventually turned to anger. Harry had promised her forever and then he'd left.

'I cannot even imagine what it was like to go through that but you can't spend the rest of your life avoiding love in case it happens again,' Willow said.

'Why not? It's worked pretty well for me for the last twelve years. Don't fall in love, don't get hurt. It's pretty simple to me.'

'You can't not fall in love because it's inconvenient. The heart doesn't work like that. It falls in love without permission.'

'Well, that's why nothing else is going to happen between me and Jacob, and then I won't get carried away and fall in love with him.'

'You think by not having sex with him you won't develop any feelings for him?' Willow said in exasperation.

'Yes. If I'm not intimate with him then we can just be friends,' Ruby said, even though she knew it was ridiculous.

God, was this all a terrible mistake? She'd thought that she had cleared the air with Jacob, laid down the ground rules and that was that. She hadn't thought about what it would be really like to work alongside him every day, to laugh with him, chat with him.

OK, it was just until after Christmas, then she'd move back to her shop at the furthest end of the high street from his and she wouldn't have to see him at all… In a village the size of a postage stamp.

Ruby looked at Willow's doubtful face.

'It's going to be fine. Now Jacob knows that any kind of relationship or sex is off the table with me, he'll find some other woman to while away his time with.'

'And how would you feel about that?' Willow asked.

'I'd be absolutely fine with it,' Ruby said, knowing that she absolutely wouldn't be.

What was with this man, why had he affected her so much?

Willow squeezed her hand and Ruby

looked down at the gesture, her heart suddenly leaping. 'Willow McKay, are you freaking kidding me, you're bloody engaged and you didn't think to mention it?'

'Oh.' Willow blushed, a huge smile spreading across her face. 'I just wanted to make sure you were OK first before I came in here and shouted my good news.'

'Tell me everything!' Ruby said, glad of the wonderful distraction.

Willow looked like she was going to burst with excitement. 'Oh god, it was so romantic, I had no idea Andrew was going to do it. It happened on our last night there. We went on a night-time river cruise of the Seine on this little boat and it was just me and him, and the driver obviously. The city lights were twinkling and we were cuddled up at the back under blankets and as we passed by the Eiffel Tower, lit up in all its splendour, he popped the question.'

'Did he use sign language to do it?' Ruby asked.

She knew Andrew was deaf, he could hear perfectly fine with his hearing aids in but not so much without them. Willow had been learning sign language so she could still communicate with him during those times, but when they had first met he didn't want to share that part of his life with her. As they had fallen in love, she had encouraged him to open up and trust her with it. If he had proposed with sign language Ruby knew that would be quite significant to Willow.

She nodded. 'He did. I wasn't sure at first what he was saying. I know most things now; I can hold a pretty decent conversation with him using sign language but I still struggle with a few words and phrases here and there. He asked me if I knew what this meant.' Willow signed something. 'And I told him I wasn't sure and then he did it again and said, "Will you marry me?"'

'This is amazing news, I'm so happy for you,' Ruby said, genuinely. Jacob was right, marriage wasn't for her, but she couldn't help but feel nothing but happiness at Willow's wonderful news. She hugged her and then pulled back to look at her. There was not an ounce of doubt that this was the right thing for Willow.

'I am so lucky to have found my soulmate,' Willow said. 'I love him so much. I just hope that one day you'll be able to find yours.'

Ruby smiled because now was definitely not the right time for her doom and gloom attitude to love.

'Maybe one day.'

Willow smiled at this and Ruby didn't have the heart to burst her bubble.

THE VAN with Ruby's stuff arrived just after lunch. She couldn't wait to get everything into the shop and make the place into a magical Santa's grotto with all of her decorations.

Jacob was banging seven kinds of hell out of a piece of metal next door as the removal men opened the back of the van and started unloading boxes. She didn't want to disturb him.

'Where do you want these, love?' the man asked.

'Oh, just inside the door on the left would be great,' Ruby said.

As they lifted one big box between them and took it inside, she was about to pick up one of the smaller boxes, when Jacob suddenly appeared at her side.

'Here, let me take that,' he said.

She passed him the box and took one herself.

'Is all of that Christmas stuff?' Jacob asked with theatrically wide eyes.

She laughed. 'Yeah, most of it is. All the boxes at the back are the ones for my house so I'll get them to drive down there when they're finished here.'

'You really like Christmas,' Jacob said, carrying the box into the shop.

Ruby followed him. 'Yeah I do, it's my favourite time of the year. I love the scents and the Christmas food. I love the Christmas films, the cornier and cheesier the better. I love silly Christmas jumpers and giving presents, but most of all I love the decorations, the Christmas trees, the twinkly lights, the streetlights. I love them all. I cannot wait to Christmassify this place. I'll do your shop as well if you want.'

'I'm not sure twinkly fairy lights wrapped around my metal sculptures are the best look but you're very welcome to help me decorate the flat,' Jacob said. 'My niece, Poppy, will be coming for Christmas so I need to make sure it's suitably festive for her.'

'Oooh, I'll take you up on that. I love nothing more than helping someone find their inner Christmas spirit.'

'I look forward to that,' Jacob said dryly.

'Actually, Poppy would probably like it more if she could help decorate your tree with you.'

He smiled. 'You're probably right, we could decorate it together, the three of us.'

Something like fear fluttered through Ruby's heart at that lovely rose-tinted family image.

They placed their boxes down.

'I'll leave you a box of decorations and order you a tree,' Ruby said, firmly. 'I'm sure Poppy would probably prefer it if it was just the two of you, she doesn't know me.'

'I can help you talk to her if that's what's bothering you,' Jacob said.

She knew Poppy was deaf and only communicated through sign language but Ruby definitely didn't want Jacob to think that was the reason she didn't want to decorate the tree with him.

'I've actually been learning a few words and phrases,' Ruby said and then regretted it when his whole face lit up.

'You have?'

'Yeah, it's not a big deal.'

He was smiling as if he thought it was. 'Why did you learn to sign?'

Ruby shrugged. She wasn't sure what had compelled her to learn sign language. She knew that it was partly to expand her skills and learn a new language and to be able to help understand people who might struggle to be understood. But she also knew that Poppy and Andrew had been in the back of her mind when she'd taken the course. She'd felt it was important that she could communicate with Jacob's niece and his brother, which was an odd thing to want to do since she'd never had any intention of seeing Jacob again. But with her best friend loved-up with his brother and Ruby moving to the village where they lived, she'd known she would cross paths with him again. Jacob had never introduced her to Poppy when she had been there in the summer – and why would he when they were only ever supposed to be a one-night stand? But if she was honest, she knew she wanted him to take her seriously

69

and not just see her as a flaky person he'd slept with a few times. She wasn't sure why that had been important when she had insisted to herself and anyone who asked that nothing was ever going to happen between them again, but clearly her subconscious had thought otherwise.

He was still waiting for an answer.

'I just thought that as Willow was learning to sign for Andrew then maybe I should too. Being deaf can be so isolating and I know he can hear just fine when he has his hearing aids in, but that's not always practical is it? And Poppy relies on sign language entirely and it must be frustrating for her sometimes that she can't communicate with everyone. I just thought...'

He was staring at her in awe and she regretted saying anything. Time to get the conversation back on track.

'Anyway, the point is, I'm not saying no because of Poppy. Decorating a tree is the kind of thing you do with family or a girlfriend, not some woman you had casual sex with a few times.'

One of the removal men coughed, awkwardly as he came back in to drop off another box. Ruby blushed but Jacob was unfazed.

'What about friends? Is there some rule that says friends can't decorate a tree together?'

'Yes,' Ruby said, with exasperation, moving back outside to get some more boxes and to get away from him. How had this conversation turned so quickly? The last person she had decorated a tree with was Harry. God, it hurt to remember that. 'Decorating a tree is romantic and we agreed that nothing was going to happen between us.'

'OK,' he said, slowly, as he followed her.

She passed him a box and saw he was fighting a smirk. She knew her desperation to avoid anything romantic was silly but she knew she had to keep some distance from Jacob, emotionally if not physically.

'So we can't decorate a tree together, is

there anything else we should avoid?' Jacob asked.

He wasn't taking this remotely seriously.

'I'll let you know if something comes up.'

He nodded. 'I'll make an anti-romance list.'

'You're so infuriating.'

He laughed. 'Sorry, let's change the subject. Are you ready for your welcome drinks in the pub this afternoon?'

She felt nothing but relief that he'd dropped it and she almost wanted to hug Jacob because of it.

'What welcome drinks?'

They stacked their boxes inside the shop and went back outside for some more.

'They always do it apparently, when there's a new resident. Well they started doing it after the big influx in the summer. I had mine a few days after I moved in. It's a nice way to meet all the villagers at the same time and for them to know who you are so you're not just some random walking around the village, although most of the villagers will remember you from the last time you were here. It starts at five, I think.'

'How do you know this?'

'It was on the village forum. It's where all the village info is, helps you keep updated with all the goings on. I'll show it to you.'

She stared at him. 'You have settled in here, haven't you? The Jacob I knew wouldn't be seen dead attending a village meeting.'

'This place sucks you in pretty quickly.'

He grabbed another box as the removal men took some boxes in themselves.

'So everyone will just be staring at me?'

'I think most people will be too busy eating to do much staring and I'll be there to hold your hand if you need me to,' Jacob said.

'There won't be any need for that.'

'Fine. I'll hold my own hand.'

She laughed.

'Besides, you don't want to miss Liz's cakes, they are to die for, and you have to meet Julia Dalton, the postmistress. She knows everything that is happening in the village.

I'm sure she'll know that you're here by now and what time you arrived last night,' Jacob said.

'Now that's a comforting thought, and not at all creepy. I've already met her actually, earlier today and in the summer, and I know exactly what you mean.'

'I wouldn't at all be surprised if there were rumours flying about that we'd already jumped into bed together.'

'I haven't even been here twenty-four hours.'

Jacob shrugged.

Ruby rolled her eyes – that would explain all the condoms Julia had made her buy earlier. Part of the reason she had left St Octavia was to escape from everyone knowing her business. And her past. She clearly hadn't thought moving to the little village of Happiness through.

Ruby placed the box down carefully. 'You're not that irresistible.'

'"The lady doth protest too much, methinks."' Jacob stacked his box on top of one of the others.

She smiled. She really bloody liked this man.

'Quoting *Hamlet* isn't going to impress me either.' Although the fact that he'd got it exactly right did impress her slightly.

'Would *Romeo and Juliet* do it for you instead?'

She wrinkled her nose. 'A romance that ends in joint suicide is hardly romantic.'

'Ah, do you see us more as Benedick and Beatrice?' Jacob asked.

She smiled. Of all of Shakespeare's couples, those two from *Much Ado About Nothing* were her favourite. And actually that Jacob knew of them rather than some of the more famous Shakespeare couples impressed her a tiny bit more.

'"Is it possible disdain should die while she hath such food to feed it as Jacob Harrington?"' Ruby quoted.

He laughed, not fazed at all by her words,

and went out to get some more boxes. She watched him go. It shouldn't be this easy between them. They'd slept together three times, and then she had put the brakes on anything happening between them again. She was backpedalling away from anything remotely romantic and he was here, helping her move her boxes, laughing and joking with her and chatting to her as if they had been friends for years.

She just never expected it to be like this with Jacob. She thought it might be awkward and she'd thought that there might be some unresolved chemistry between them but she hadn't expected it to be so... friendly.

And in many ways that was worse.

She really was in trouble with this one.

CHAPTER 4

JACOB WATCHED RUBY CHATTING WITH THE removal men as he sipped the hot chocolate she had made for them all. She was so bubbly and animated when she talked he couldn't help but smile. She was wearing a dress with Christmas trees all over it today. She really was the epitome of the festive season. She sparkled.

There was something about her that he found so... compelling. He enjoyed spending time with her, talking to her. He could laugh with her and he'd never had that with a woman before. But there was something much deeper there too. And to find out that she had started to learn sign language so she could communicate with his niece and Andrew when he wasn't wearing his hearing aids, that meant more to him than she could possibly know.

He looked around Christmas Cottage at the boxes stacked along the walls. There certainly was a lot of stuff, although he wondered if half of it was Christmas decorations.

There were just a few more boxes on the van, so he drained his cup and, as the removal men grabbed some, Jacob picked up the last one. God this one was heavy. He slid it to the edge of the van, climbed out and hoisted it up in his arms, just as the removal men came out and were saying their goodbyes to Ruby. Jacob walked into the cottage and was just about to stack it on top of one of the other boxes when the bottom gave way and the contents spilled out onto the floor.

Crap.

He tossed the useless box on the floor and

was relieved to see the contents were only books and not anything breakable.

He bent down and started stacking the books up but he stopped when it looked like one of the books was a photo album. It had fallen open and on the page was a photo of a much younger Ruby with a man... on what was obviously her wedding day.

His heart leapt. After her big speech about marriage and babies not being for her, how could she have forgotten to tell him that she had been married once? This couldn't be right, surely. He turned back to the front cover which had the words written in gold swirly writing, 'Our Wedding Album'. He turned back to the photos, Ruby with her brides-maids, Ruby and the groomsmen, Ruby and her husband in various different poses. But one thing stood out in every single photo: how completely and utterly happy Ruby was. The love she had for her husband, and how much he clearly loved her, shone from the pages.

Ruby came in and shut the door behind her.

'Jesus, Jacob, you had one job to do and you can't even do that,' Ruby teased as she caught him crouching over the fallen books.

Should he tell her what he'd seen? Should he pretend he hadn't noticed anything? If she'd wanted to talk about her marriage she would have, but Christ he had a million questions right then. No, it was none of his business. He quickly closed the album and made to hide it under the other books, but she was suddenly standing right there.

'Oh,' she said, softly, seeing the album in his hand. She touched the snowflake she wore around her neck.

'I'm sorry, the books fell out the box and this fell open. I didn't mean to pry.'

She knelt down next to him and took the album from his hands.

'I haven't looked at this for over twelve years. I couldn't. I had it stashed behind some other books on my bookshelf and I suppose I almost forgot it was there. My brother helped me pack and I guess he shoved it in here and…' she trailed off.

She opened it on the first page, a grinning one of the bride and groom, hugging and laughing together. It wasn't a posed picture, just a natural snap of two young people very much in love.

'God, I looked so ridiculously happy,' Ruby said, stroking a finger down the man's face. 'Harry was handsome, wasn't he?'

Jacob stared at her. 'You were married?'

'Yes, I was very young. We both were. He was my childhood sweetheart. We'd dated since we were eleven, got married at eighteen. Everyone said we were too young. Maybe they were right.'

'What happened?'

She stared at the photo for the longest time. 'By the time I was nineteen it was over.'

'That didn't last long. Was it another woman?'

Ruby shook her head. 'No, Harry would

81

never have done that. He went out to play football one day and never came home.'

'What? He just walked out on you? No explanation? Did you ever see him again?'

'I saw him, once. Called him every name under the sun. He didn't have a lot to say.'

'God, what an asshole.'

Ruby looked at him and smiled sadly. 'After, everyone always told me how wonderful he was, when all I could find in me was anger and hatred that he'd left me.'

'He doesn't sound wonderful to me,' Jacob said. What kind of dick left their wife just a few months after getting married?

'He was, in the beginning,' Ruby said, turning over the page. There was another of the two of them dancing by a Christmas tree. 'We got married just before Christmas, the twenty-third, because he knew how much I loved Christmas. The whole wedding was Christmas-themed; it was so beautiful.'

Jacob watched her as she reminisced. It

sounded like she still had some feelings for him.

'So this is why you don't believe in marriage anymore?' Jacob asked.

Ruby nodded. 'When he left me, I was so utterly heartbroken, it physically hurt. I don't think I could go through that again.'

'But you can't let this… cockwomble ruin the rest of your life. You can't avoid any kind of emotional connection with a man because this dick didn't know what an amazing thing he had with you.'

She didn't say anything for the longest time as she turned over page after page of gloriously happy photos.

When she looked at him her eyes were filled with so much emotion it completely floored him.

She reached out and stroked his face, making his heart leap in his chest.

'I really like you Jacob Harrington, but I'd really like you to leave now so I can have a good cry over these photos without you coming up with new and ingenious ways to insult my husband.'

He didn't understand any of this.

'You mean your ex-husband?'

She shrugged. 'I suppose you could call him that.'

And then suddenly everything was crystal clear. Everything. Why she was so scared of falling in love again, why she'd never had a serious relationship since Harry, why she didn't believe in marriage and happy ever afters. He swallowed the emotion that was suddenly clogging in his throat.

'He didn't leave, did he?'

She stared at him and then shook her head. 'Not by choice. He had a heart attack. He'd just turned nineteen.'

He swore softly under his breath. 'Christ Ruby, I'm sorry.'

'It's OK. It's been over twelve years since he died. I'm over it.' A lone tear slid down her cheek and she let out a little laugh. 'Mostly.'

He wasn't sure how you ever got over

something like that.

'Sometimes things like this bring it all back,' Ruby said. 'You should probably go, there's going to be a few more of these.'

'If you're going to have a cry, there's no way in hell I'm leaving you.'

'It's not going to be pretty.'

He got up from the floor and picked up the photo album, then he held his hand out for Ruby. 'Then we might as well get comfortable for it.'

She took his hand and he pulled her down on the sofa next to him. He grabbed a box of tissues from the nearby table and placed it on his lap, then he wrapped an arm round her shoulders and she leaned against him. As she flicked through the photo album once more he held her tight as she cried quietly into his chest.

RUBY STEPPED out of Christmas Cottage and

wrapped her coat around her. It was only a five-minute walk up the hill to the pub, but the day was still bitterly cold. She wouldn't be surprised if it snowed soon, which would be nice. Everything looked far more Christmassy when there was snow on the ground.

Jacob stepped out the cottage too, closed the door behind him and then took her hand as they started walking up the high street.

She looked down at where their fingers entwined. She hadn't held hands with anyone since Harry had died. Of course there had been men that she'd seen casually or had a fling with but it had never been anything serious with any of them, so she had never really had the hugging and hand-holding with them that she would have had in a more intimate relationship. She wasn't sure how she felt about this hand-holding either. There was a part of her that recognised this was a little weird. She wasn't in a relationship with Jacob, she'd made that very clear to him, and she knew he was only holding her hand to offer some comfort and support after she had cried on him for the last hour. But there was also a part of her that felt there was something very lovely about doing this with him.

She looked up at him and he was smiling at her.

'You're not at all what I expected, Jacob Harrington,' Ruby said.

'What were you expecting?' Jacob said.

'Mostly, that we'd sleep together once and I'd never hear from you again.'

'Is that what you wanted?'

Ruby thought about that for a moment. 'Yeah, I've got through the last twelve years with no commitments, no emotional attachments, and it's worked pretty well for me. But you're not at all what I imagined. You're...' she trailed off, not able to find the right word.

'Sexy?' Jacob teased. 'Amazing, the best sex you've ever had?'

She smiled. 'Lovely. You're lovely.'

'Ah god, don't tell anyone that, it'll ruin my reputation.'

'My lips are sealed. I wouldn't want to damage the good name of Phoenix Blade.'

'I wasn't talking about him; I was talking about me.'

She smiled. 'So what kind of persona does Phoenix Blade have? Is he dark, edgy, mysterious? Does he ride into his exhibitions on the back of a motorbike, dressed all in leather?'

'I hadn't really thought about making him into a character. Do you think I could pull off dark and dangerous?'

'I think you could. You have this bad boy look that all the women go for. We won't tell them the truth.'

'That I'm secretly lovely,' Jacob said.

'Yes, we'll keep that between us.'

She looked at the Christmas lights inside the shops and houses, twinkling in the receding light of the day. It looked magical.

'What should I expect from this meeting this afternoon?' Ruby said.

'There'll be mince pies and mulled wine, I expect, maybe some gingerbread men and

other festive treats. Kitty and Ken will introduce you and you will generally be expected
to give a short speech and then everyone will
mingle.'

Ruby looked at him in alarm. 'What? Back
up. A speech? Why didn't you mention this
before?'

'I thought you knew. It's in the welcome
pack.'

'Christ, I haven't read that yet. It was on
my to-do list once I'd finished unpacking.
What do I need to say in my speech?'

'Something about what you will bring to
Happiness. I mean, it's not a big deal. Kitty
and Ken just want people to fill the village but
the whole *free rent for a year* thing is kind of on
the proviso that you can bring something to
the village. Kitty and Ken have already given
you a home and a shop so it's not like this
speech is some kind of test. They just want the
villagers to know who you are.'

Ruby let out a big breath. 'What did you
say in yours? Great sex to all who want it?'

He laughed loudly. 'I said that I offered diversity, that my art was something that could bring visitors to the village and that I was also pretty handy with bits of metal so, if anyone needed anything welding, I was their man. That and the great sex obviously.'

'God, what do I have to offer?' Ruby said.

'How about the joy of Christmas all year round.'

'OK, that's a start.'

Ruby wracked her brains for something else she could add.

'I know,' Jacob said. 'The village came together when Willow gave mystery gifts to everyone in the summer. Christmas is the time of giving. What about some kind of… advent calendar gift thing?'

'It's the eighteenth of December already, I've kind of missed that… But maybe I could do some kind of Secret Santa thing.'

'Yes, that could work.'

She thought for a few moments about how she could do it and then she noticed Willow and Andrew waiting for them outside the pub. They were still quite some way ahead and hadn't yet noticed her and Jacob.

'I might have to drop your hand now,' Ruby said. 'I will never hear the end of it if Willow sees us together like this. She'll be buying a hat for the wedding before the end of the day.'

Jacob immediately let go of her hand. 'No problem. But if you need to, my hand is here to hold anytime.'

She smiled. 'Thank you.'

Willow moved to give her a hug as they drew close but stopped short.

'Have you been crying?'

Damn it. Ruby had washed her face and put on a tiny bit of make up to cover the red blotchiness, but of course Willow would spot it.

'A little. It's nothing.'

'Of course it's not nothing,' Willow said. 'What happened?'

'I found my wedding album amongst all

my stuff as I was unpacking. I haven't looked at that for years.'

'Oh no, I hate the thought of you looking at that on your own.'

'I wasn't alone, Jacob was with me,' Ruby said.

Sure enough, Willow's eyes lit up at the idea of Jacob comforting her. But before Ruby could start to deny anything had happened, Jacob smoothly stepped forward.

'Welcome home by the way. I hear we're going to be family now, congratulations,' he said, hugging his future sister-in-law.

Willow's face erupted into a huge smile as she hugged him. 'I know, I can't believe it.'

'Yes, congratulations, Andrew.' Ruby hugged him. 'I'm sure you two are going to be very happy together.'

'Thank you,' Andrew said. It was clear to see he was as happy as Willow was.

Jacob clapped Andrew on the back. 'Good job little brother, I think you picked one of the good ones here.'

'She's the best,' Andrew said, fondly, kissing Willow on the head.

Ruby smiled. The two of them really were perfect for each other.

'Come on, let's get inside,' Jacob said. 'It's freezing and there's a mince pie in here with my name on it.'

He ushered them all inside the pub and Ruby gave him a grateful smile that he had managed to distract her friend from the fact that she had been crying and that he had comforted her. Although she didn't think for one minute that that would be the last she would hear of it from Willow.

The pub was rammed, young families, couples of varying ages and some of the older folk that had been the backbone of the village when she'd first visited in the summer. There was such a difference from how it had been a few months before. At that time the village had been largely in ruin and they had been having trouble attracting people to want to live there. Now it was a happy, buzzing, thriving place, and Ruby couldn't help but smile. There was a huge twinkling Christmas tree in one corner and a wonderful holly berry garland over the fireplace that had a welcoming fire roaring away underneath. It looked cosy and festive.

Willow led her over to Kitty and Ken, who she'd met briefly before when she'd been there in the summer. Kitty looked effortlessly glamorous with her platinum-blonde hair in gentle waves. Ken, with his white, walrus moustache, looked like he had come from the circus, and the bright red waistcoat adorned with satin green holly leaves he was wearing completed the look.

Kitty smiled when she saw her and gave her a big hug.

'Ruby, it's so lovely to see you again. I'm so sorry about your shop, we should have it fixed and cleaned out straight after Christmas.'

'It's no problem at all. Jacob has been very welcoming,' Ruby said.

Jacob smiled at her in a way that suggested

he'd wanted to welcome her in much more interesting ways.

Kitty eyed the two of them and her face lit up. 'Well that's wonderful. If you want you can always stay in that shop.'

'No, no, I wouldn't want to intrude on Jacob's creativity longer than I have to and it would be nice to have my own space too.'

Jacob shrugged. 'I'm happy either way.'

Ruby couldn't imagine what it would be like to work alongside Jacob every day and still hold onto her willpower to not sleep with him. The next few weeks were going to be hard enough, especially as he was being so bloody lovely. She kind of would have preferred him to be a complete ass about it as then her decision to not let anything more happen between them would have been a hell of a lot easier.

'Well, I'm glad it's all working out,' Kitty said. 'I knew Jacob would be the perfect person to put you with.'

Ruby narrowed her eyes slightly. 'Oh, I did

wonder about that. Why didn't you tell me I was sharing with Jacob instead of Phoenix Blade?'

Kitty blushed. 'Oh, erm… I wasn't sure if I was allowed to divulge his real name.'

'But I know Jacob.'

'Oh, yes, of course you do. I must go and say hello to Shannon and Pete. I haven't met their new baby yet.'

Kitty hurried off to the other side of the room where a collection of elderly ladies were all cooing over a new baby.

Ruby smirked. Not telling her she was going to be sharing with Jacob had definitely been deliberate. She wondered if the flood in the shop had even happened at all.

'Are you ready to do your speech, dear?' Ken said, interrupting her thoughts.

'Umm, sort of,' Ruby said.

'It's nothing to worry about, just say a few words about who you are, where you're from and what you will bring to the village.'

Ruby smiled. No big deal at all.

'Well, we're very glad you're here,' Ken said. 'I'm sure you will bring a lot to the village. One of the reasons we wanted you to come here was because of your love of Christmas and we wanted you to bring that magic to the village itself. We have put a lot of time and effort into organising the Christmas ball but we haven't really done a lot else to celebrate Christmas. If you could think of something else to help us mark the big day, that would be great. I know we only have a week until Christmas so nothing big, but maybe you could have a think about some little ideas that we can all take part in.'

Kitty flapped her hands at him as she rejoined them. 'Ken, the girl has only just got here. Maybe we should let her unpack first before we push her head first into village life.'

'Well, I did have one idea I was going to suggest in my speech. I'm not sure what the villagers will think of it, but it's something everyone can get involved with if they are willing,' Ruby said.

'I think people will,' Kitty said. 'The village has changed so much since we first came here. Everyone was so removed from the community but now everyone actively embraces it. They all want to be a part of it, help each other out, give something back. I think you'll fit in here just perfectly.'

Ruby smiled.

'Well, let's get the show on the road,' Kitty said. 'And then we can tuck into these glorious goodies that the villagers have made for us.'

Ruby looked over at the table that was almost bowing under the weight of mince pies, mini Christmas cakes, gingerbread men, fudge, chocolates, cookies and other snacks.

Kitty banged on the side of the cup with her spoon and the whole pub fell silent and looked over at her expectantly.

'Everyone, our little village has now been filled, every house, every shop has now been taken. And the last person to move in is our lovely Ruby here.'

Everyone cheered and clapped and Ruby gave a little wave.

'Ruby, do you want to say a few words?' Ken said.

Ruby cleared her throat.

'Hello everyone, my name is Ruby Marlowe. I'm from St Octavia which is... very far from here. I'm friends with Willow and Andrew.'

Jacob coughed theatrically and she smiled.

'And Jacob.' She couldn't help noticing Kitty and Ken exchanging smiles at that. 'My shop in the village is going to be called The Happy Little Christmas Shop which, as you might have guessed, sells Christmas decorations. I love Christmas, it's my favourite time of the year, and I will be bringing the joy of Christmas to the village all year round. And on that note, I wonder if some of you might be willing to take part in a Secret Santa? I know the gift-giving that Willow started in the summer was a huge success but Christmas is the perfect time to give a secret gift. Of course we can't all give gifts to everyone in the village, but maybe we can give just one. It doesn't have to be a present you will buy, but maybe you could make one instead.'

There were nods and murmurs of agreement around the villagers. She looked at Kitty and Ken and they were nodding their approval.

'Do we have any paper and pens?' Ruby asked them quietly.

Ken waved his notepad in the air and gestured to his pencil case. Clearly he came prepared to these meetings.

Ruby turned back to the villagers. 'If those that want to take part can please come forward and write their name on a piece of paper. We'll put all the names in a hat and then you can all pick a name out and that is who you have to give a present to. On Christmas Eve we can put all our wrapped presents under the tree here with a gift tag to say who they are to, but not who they are from, and then we can open all of our presents together. Just one rule, you can't tell the person you're giving the gift to that the present is from you. It has to remain a secret. How does that sound?'

There were more nods around the room and people started coming forward to write their names on a piece of paper.

'Fab idea, Ruby Marlowe,' Jacob said. 'But only one small problem.'

'What's that?'

'We don't have a hat.'

She laughed.

'I'll go and ask Tabitha if we can borrow a bowl from the kitchen,' Jacob said and disappeared through the crowd.

Ruby watched as everyone wrote their names on a bit of paper which Ken was temporarily storing in his empty mug. Everyone wanted to be a part of this and she liked that she had done something small for the village already.

Jacob came back with a bowl and slowly it started filling up with little bits of paper.

After it was clear that everyone had put

their name into the bowl, Kitty banged her spoon on the side of the cup again to quieten everyone down.

'Has everyone who wants to take part put their name in the bowl?' Kitty asked and everyone nodded. 'Then can you all come forward to draw the name of the person you will be giving the gift to, but remember to keep it a secret.'

Ken mixed all the names up and slowly everyone came forward and took a name from the bowl. There were chuckles and gasps as people found out who they were giving gifts to. As the last few people came forward to collect their name, Ruby stepped forward and took a name from the bowl. She stepped away to see who she had to give a gift to. She didn't know most of the people in the village so it could be tricky. She unwrapped the ball of paper to read the name and smiled when she saw it.

Jacob Harrington.

She shook her head. Of course it was.

CHAPTER 5

RUBY WENT OVER TO THE TABLE WHERE THE mulled wine was and poured herself another glass. This stuff was good and, coupled with the Christmas cake and gingerbread men, it felt like Christmas had definitely arrived.

A woman a few years younger than Ruby approached, carrying the new-born that everyone had been gathering around for the last hour. She poured herself a glass too.

'Hi, I'm Megan,' she said.

'Ruby, nice to meet you. And who's this handsome chap?'

'This is Toby, my sister Shannon's son.' Megan indicated the blonde in the corner, who was obviously retelling the dramatic events of the birth. Shannon looked altogether too neat and awake for someone who had given birth only a few days before.

'Toby's her third, so she's done this before,' Megan said, as if reading her mind.

Ruby nodded. 'I think I'd be on my knees sobbing from exhaustion if I'd just given birth.'

'I know, the amount of crying this one does, kind of puts me off having children for life,' Megan said.

Ruby looked at Toby who was fast asleep, his head resting on Megan's shoulder. He looked like butter wouldn't melt in his mouth.

She felt a pang of something inside her. She had wanted children; she and Harry had talked about having a big family. They'd even started trying for a baby. When he'd died, not only had he taken her dream of her happy ever after with the man she loved, he'd taken her hopes of having children too.

'So I hear you're sharing a shop with Jacob,' Megan said, interrupting her thoughts. Ruby pushed down the pain in her heart and focussed on Megan who was watching her with wide eyes, visibly hoping for some gossip. She wasn't the first person to bring up her new neighbour. The fact that Ruby was adamant that nothing was going to happen between them didn't stop the idle speculation of when and how she and Jacob might get together. 'It's set the cat amongst the pigeons, let me tell you.'

'I know, everyone wants us to get together,' Ruby said, wearily.

'Not everyone wants that, believe me,' Megan said, bouncing Toby gently in her arms.

Ruby looked at her. She was very pretty in that lovely soft, gentle way, caramel-blonde hair in waves, a fluffy red jumper, large blue eyes. She wondered if Megan would be Jacob's type. She was surprised by the jolt of jealousy that hit her at that thought.

'Oh, not me,' Megan said, she gave a little

laugh. 'I've been single for about a year now and if he asked me out I think I'd probably die of shock. I mean, he's gorgeous and of course I'd say yes, but he's not really my type, at all. I think I'd be terrified if it got as far as the bedroom. I'd probably just sit in the bathroom and hyperventilate into a paper bag; I mean, look at him.'

Ruby looked over at Jacob and felt another surge of jealousy to see that a woman with sleek brunette hair and a very short dress was talking to him, tossing her hair around like a frisky pony. While Jacob didn't seem that keen, Ruby couldn't say that he wasn't interested. He was laughing at something the woman was saying. Jacob was ridiculously good-looking, he had those big arms that a lot of women went for, and with his dark hair, denim-blue eyes and that beautiful face, he could easily be a model. He had that rough edge to him as well, like he was dark and dangerous. She was sure that was an attractive feature.

'And look at me,' Megan went on, giving a little self-deprecating laugh.

Ruby looked at her. 'Megan, you're lovely, what man wouldn't want to go out with you?'

Megan looked briefly across the room at another man standing near Shannon and her husband, Pete. He was wearing a bright green knitted Christmas jumper with what looked like the Batman symbol in the middle and snowflakes around the top. Ruby smiled when he glanced over in Megan's direction and Megan quickly looked away.

'Anyway, I wasn't talking about me,' Megan said, nodding her head over to a gaggle of gorgeous women. Ruby hadn't had the courage to go over to them yet. She had over-heard a few snide comments from them and, although she didn't think they were directed at her, it made her think they weren't the nicest of people. They were all staring at the brunette talking to Jacob with daggers. 'They all fancy their chances with Jacob. Lucy, the one with the pink top, knows him from when they both lived in Penzance. Apparently he had a different woman every week and he's some kind of god between the sheets.'

'Lucy knows that personally, does she?' Ruby asked.

Megan shrugged. 'I think so from the way she crows about it but I don't know for sure. I just listen to them talking when they're in the pub. I don't hang out with them.'

Ruby smiled. 'Not your type.'

Megan laughed. 'Exactly.'

Ruby looked back over to the pack of women. Lucy was undeniably beautiful. Ruby could imagine she would be exactly the type Jacob would go for. Of course she knew Jacob had been with lots of women so why did the thought of him with Lucy or any of her friends suddenly hurt so much?

'Apparently he's going through a dry patch,' Megan said.

'He is?' Ruby said, in surprise.

'He's been here three or four months, he moved here not long after I did. Well, he hasn't been with anyone from the village since he arrived.'

For some unknown reason, that made Ruby feel suddenly a bit happier.

'They all think they can be the one to bring him out of it.'

Ruby thought about this. Jacob was not the shy retiring type. If he was interested in any of these women, he would have made a move by now.

'Maybe he just doesn't want the awkwardness of sleeping with someone he has to see every day,' Ruby said.

'Maybe,' Megan agreed. 'He could totally be screwing around with every woman in the next village for all I know.'

Ruby's little bubble of hope popped.

'Yeah, I bet he is,' she said. She shrugged. She didn't care. She really really didn't care at all. She took a large swig of her mulled wine as she watched him across the room. She wasn't bothered in the slightest.

Just then the man in the green Batman

Christmas jumper came over to them and Ruby smiled as Megan blushed. 'Meg, Shannon and Pete are going now, it's Toby's bath time.'

'OK. Ruby, this is Lucas, Pete's brother and Toby's uncle.'

Lucas smiled.

'Hi Lucas,' Ruby said.

'Hi, good to meet you.'

'You're Andrew's assistant, aren't you? I've been hearing all about how brilliant you are,' Ruby said.

Lucas blushed. 'Well, I, erm, that's very nice.'

Megan gave her a little wave as they both walked back across the room. Ruby diverted her attention back to Jacob who had managed to separate himself from the brunette and was now talking to Dorothy. He glanced over and saw her watching him and broke into a huge smile. He gave her a little wink which stupidly caused her heart to leap.

This man. He was infuriatingly likeable.

JACOB TOOK a bite of his mince pie, savouring the potent fruits and spices mixed with rum or brandy or something else equally heady. Liz's pies were always amazing, it would be a shame when Christmas was over and he wouldn't get to have them anymore. He might have to get her to make him a batch that he could freeze and thaw out whenever the craving got too much.

He watched as Ruby made her way around the room, chatting and laughing with everyone who came up to her. She was definitely not the wallflower type, she was doing a really good job of mingling and introducing herself to everyone.

Julia Dalton, the postmistress, came up to him and took a piece of fudge from the buffet table.

'Mmm rum and raisin, my favourite.'

Jacob took a piece and popped it into his

mouth. 'Mmm, this is good fudge, who makes it?'

'I do.'

Jacob laughed at the lack of modesty.

'I make lots of different flavours, but some of them are not so good,' Julia said honestly. 'I put them in different containers but I don't always label them up correctly so sometimes it's a bit of a surprise when I open them. It seems Ruby got the good stuff today.'

Julia leaned against the table next to him.

'I'm going to make your fan club jealous by talking to you,' she said, gesturing to Lucy, Saffy, Pippa and their friends.

He knew there was a bet between them on who could get him into bed first. He wasn't sure whether to be flattered or appalled by that. The old Jacob probably would have slept with all of them but the thought just didn't appeal to him anymore.

'We should kiss, that would really upset them,' Julia said.

Jacob laughed. 'Is that your game, you wily minx?'

'I don't mind you using me to make them jealous,' Julia said and he laughed again. 'I just overheard them talking, Lucy is going to ask you to the ball.'

'Thanks for the heads up.'

'Do you have a date?'

'Are you asking me out?' Jacob gave her a nudge.

'No, I'm just thinking if you needed an excuse not to go with Lucy, maybe you should ask someone else.' Julia tilted her head over in Ruby's direction. He looked over at her and watched Ruby as she laughed loudly at something someone said to her. He smiled at the not-so-subtle matchmaking.

'I like her,' Julia said.

'I do too.'

'This idea of Secret Santa is a good one, who did you get?'

Jacob smiled. 'Isn't that supposed to be a secret?'

'You can trust me, dear. The different parcels that come into the post office for the villagers,' Julia said with wide eyes. 'I could tell you a story or two, but I don't. That's confidential. Just because I know everything going on in the village doesn't mean that I tell anyone about it.'

Jacob wasn't sure he totally believed that. She might keep the post confidential but the village gossip was definitely a free-for-all.

'Who do you have?' he asked.

'I have Ruby. I thought you might want to swap.'

Jacob frowned in confusion. 'Why would I want to swap?'

'Because you haven't taken your eyes off her since you both walked into the pub over an hour ago.'

Jacob chuckled, running his hand through his hair. Was he really that obvious?

'I'm just…'

'It's OK, you don't need to explain yourself

to me. I know what happened between the two of you in the summer.'

He shook his head incredulously. How could she possibly know that?

'And I know what's happening now,' Julia said.

'Nothing is happening now.'

'Really?' Julia leaned in a bit closer. 'You were in her house for an awfully long time this afternoon.'

Jacob couldn't help but laugh. Because he wasn't going to tell the truth about looking at Ruby's wedding album with her, he decided to tease Julia. 'Well I'll leave that to your imagination what we were up to.'

Her eyes widened excitedly and he regretted it instantly.

'So you were...' she gave a rude gesture and he laughed loudly.

'No, we weren't, I was just messing with you. Nothing is going on between us. What happened in the summer is in the past now. As we're both living here, we've decided to put it behind us and just be friends. We don't want things to be awkward between us.'

'It might be over for her, but I don't think this thing is over for you,' Julia said.

He shrugged. 'It is what it is. She doesn't want anything to happen and I respect that.'

'You're a good lad. So do you want her for the Secret Santa or not?' Julia held out the piece of paper with Ruby's name on it.

He stared at it. Ruby was definitely going to be easier to get a present for than Elsie, who he'd probably only said hello to a handful of times since he'd moved in. Besides, Ruby was his friend, he could do something nice for his friend.

'OK, sure.'

He took the name and swapped it for the piece of paper with Elsie's name on it. He smiled as he held Ruby's name in his hand. This was going to be fun.

AFTER RUBY HAD FINISHED TALKING to Kitty and Ken, she turned round to see that Julia, Dorothy, Liz and her brother Roger were seemingly waiting for her to join them. She knew they would want to talk to her about Jacob and there wouldn't be any escape from their matchmaking and thirst for gossip, so she decided to change the subject before it even started. She took a few steps to join the throng and then lowered her voice conspiratorially.

'So what's the deal between Megan and Lucas?' Ruby asked, nodding over to where the two of them were seated in a booth, chatting away happily. She felt bad about using them to deflect the attention away from herself and Jacob, but even though she didn't want romance in her life she wasn't opposed to a bit of matchmaking for others and maybe the villagers could help her.

'Oh I know. Look at the two of them, they're perfect together, but neither of them are prepared to do anything about it,' Julia said, with exasperation.

'He's crazy about her,' Dorothy said. 'You can see that from the way he looks at her.'

'So why hasn't he asked her out?' Ruby said.

'I suppose it's a bit weird now, they're family,' Roger said.

'Only by marriage. Lucas is her sister's brother-in-law, not hers,' Ruby said.

'Does that make him her brother-in-law-in-law?' Liz asked.

Dorothy shook her head. 'There's no such thing. Lucas is related to Shannon by marriage, not Megan. Anyway, I don't think that's what's holding them back. He's just too shy to ask her and she was hurt in her last relationship and is too scared to put herself out there again.'

Ruby took a sip of her mulled wine. She knew that feeling all too well.

'Is that what happened to you, dear?' Julia asked.

Ruby let out a breath. Bloody hell. Was Julia some kind of mind reader as well as post office mistress and emporium owner extraordinaire? And how had the subject turned back to Ruby so quickly?

'How are you settling in with young Jacob?' Liz asked, despite the fact that it had only been a few hours since she'd seen them all in the post office that morning.

'What she means is, have you used those condoms yet?' Dorothy asked bluntly.

'I didn't mean that at all,' Liz said. 'Well, OK, I did.'

'We know that Jacob was helping you unload the removal van and that he stayed in your house with you long after they'd gone,' Julia said. 'And then you came out holding hands, so we just wondered if...'

'He'd parked his car in your garage,' Roger said, eyebrows wiggling mischievously.

'What?' Ruby laughed.

'Had a bit of rumpy-pumpy,' Liz supplied helpfully, although Ruby didn't need the translation.

'Making whoopee,' Julia said.

'Had hot sex,' Dorothy said, getting straight to the point.

'I've not even been here a day,' Ruby protested.

'Well that didn't stop you last time,' Dorothy said.

Ruby blushed.

'Ah, there's nothing to be embarrassed about,' Roger said. 'We've all been there, those passionate, clothes-being-torn-off, having-sex-on-the-nearest-hard-surface kind of moments. And a man as fine as that Jacob Harrington wangling it in your face, well how could you say no.'

Ruby burst out laughing. 'There's been no wangling in my face, I can assure you. As I said to Julia earlier, we're friends and nothing is going to happen between us.'

'Maybe not yet,' Liz said.

'I'll give it to Christmas Eve,' Julia said.

'I agree with Ruby's approach,' Dorothy said. '*Treat them mean, keep them keen.*'

'That's not what I'm doing,' Ruby said, getting a bit frustrated now. 'I'm not playing a game with him. We just decided we were better off as friends. I know we have history but that's exactly what it is, it's in the past.'

They were all quiet for a moment.

'Sounds like she's trying to convince herself more than she's trying to convince us,' Roger muttered.

Ruby rolled her eyes but she knew Roger was right. Being just friends with Jacob was going to be very hard work indeed.

CHAPTER 6

RUBY WAS DANCING AROUND HER SHOP, Christmas tunes playing on the little CD player she'd brought with her as she unpacked her Christmas decorations and paraphernalia and started making the shop come to life. She'd already decorated two big trees that stood sentry either side of the door and she'd set up her collection of baubles in little boxes on the main table in the middle of the shop. Now she just had to work on the window display.

She was used to having a little market

stand in a big hall filled with other stands selling everything under the sun. She'd put out different things each day on her table but it wasn't exactly a display. She did a better trade online but she got quite a bit of attention each day when she sat and handmade the different pieces. Her most popular items were her baubles, which were made in lots of ways; she had fabric ones, papier-mâché ones and plain glass baubles she'd bought and then hand-painted using a variety of different ways.

This was the first time she'd had a proper shop and she couldn't wait to Christmassify the whole place.

She peered through to Jacob's shop. It was very minimalist. There was a large peacock made entirely from spoons standing centre stage illuminated with spotlights that gleamed off the steel. There was a lizard made from bike chains crawling across the wall and in the window were a few smaller birds, frogs and dragonflies. There was nothing Christmassy in there at all.

Jacob had been working away on some piece at the back of the shop but he had disappeared upstairs to his flat a while before. She wasn't sure if he was coming back down or if he was done for the day. It was already gone seven o'clock and outside the road was dark, lit only by the streetlights and the twinkling Christmas lights that flashed and danced above them.

Still singing along to the Christmas tunes, this one 'The Fairytale of New York' by The Pogues, she grabbed a few bits and danced into his side of the shop. She draped a piece of blue tinsel round the neck of the peacock like a very dashing scarf, then moved over to the lizard and hung an emerald-green bauble from his tail. She hung some tiny fairy lights over the window display and plugged them in so they sparkled against the metal.

Suddenly she heard footsteps on the stairs and she quickly scampered back into her own shop, giggling to herself.

To her surprise, Jacob appeared in her shop with two plates of food.

'I made chicken stir-fry, I thought you might be hungry,' he said.

Ah, now she felt guilty. While he'd been upstairs doing something nice for her, she'd been down here causing mischief in his shop.

'That's really nice of you, thank you.'

He shrugged and handed her a plate and then pulled out some knives and forks from his pocket. She watched him drop down onto the floor, placing his plate in front of him, and then start eating. His back was to his own shop so he hadn't noticed her *improvements*.

She sat down on the floor too, tucking in. She really was very hungry.

'This is wonderful, thank you.'

'No problem at all, it's been a busy day for you.'

And he had helped her through all of it.

'So any more events coming up on the village forum that I need to be aware of? I've still not had a chance to look at it,' Ruby asked.

Jacob nodded as he chewed and dug his phone out of his pocket. He pressed a few buttons and swallowed his food.

'There's not a lot going on actually. We have carols on Wednesday the twenty-second at the big Christmas tree on the green by the castle and then we have the ball on Christmas Eve.'

'Oh, a Christmas ball, how wonderful. Kitty and Ken mentioned it earlier but I was too focussed on my speech to pay too much attention. Are they having it up at the castle?'

'Yes.'

'But I thought the castle was in ruins?'

'It is, but the great hall is still intact enough to hold a do in there, and they've hired outdoor heaters to keep the place warm and caterers and a band. It's going to be quite the night. I think Kitty and Ken's focus has all been about that so they haven't organised any other Christmas events'

'Well, I bet that will be lovely.'

'Want to be my date?' Jacob said. 'I promise, no kissing, no sex, I won't even squeeze your bum.'

'There definitely won't be any sex, I can assure you of that.'

'But you don't mind the other two? That's fine as long as I know where the boundaries are,' he teased.

She shook her head fondly. 'You're incorrigible.'

He smiled as he ate. 'I'll be on my very best behaviour.'

'A handsome man like you doesn't have a date for the ball already?'

'Believe me, I've had to fight all those women off with a stick. Liz, Julia, Mary, Ginny, they all wanted a piece of me,' Jacob said, listing all the women in the village over the age of seventy.

Ruby laughed, playing for time for a few moments as she continued to eat. She knew she wanted to go with Jacob. He was lovely and made her laugh, but that would be sending him and the rest of the village some very mixed messages.

'I… I'll think about it.'

'Well, don't think too long or some octogenarian will have snapped me up.'

'I'm sure they will.'

She watched him eat for a while as she enjoyed her stir-fry too. She was actually surprised he didn't have a date. There must be several single women in the village or the surrounding areas who would jump at the chance to have a date with him; Lucy, and her gang, the pretty brunette, even Megan. He was sweet, funny, artistic, kind and sexy as hell. In fact he was exactly the sort of man that should have been snapped up and married years ago. When she had first met him she got the impression that he was a bit of a lad and liked playing the field, which had suited her just fine. But now, to hear him talk about one day settling down, she had to wonder why he hadn't chosen that life for himself before now.

'So why don't you have a date?' Ruby said.

'Ah, I'm a free spirit,' Jacob shrugged.

Ruby frowned as she finished off her stir-fry. There was something he wasn't saying here.

'So no stories of broken hearts?'

His eyebrows slashed down. 'I hope to god I haven't broken anyone's heart. Women know what they get with me, I never give them any false promises or pretend it's anything more than it is.'

She watched him and she got the feeling she had touched on a nerve. She waited to see if there was any more. He glanced up and saw her looking at him.

His face softened. 'I think, as you shared your demons with me earlier, maybe I should share some of mine. My dad walked out on us when we were kids. Lottie and Andrew were still so young when he left but I was old enough to see how much it broke my mum's heart. It utterly destroyed her. He'd had an affair, multiple affairs actually, and I think that was a lot worse than him just leaving. It made my mum feel she wasn't good enough if he had to go elsewhere for sex. Even as a boy, I could see the ramifications of another person's actions, how one person could ruin another person's life. I vowed then that I would never be that person. As I grew up, all the family and my parents' friends used to tell me how much like my dad I was, how similar I looked, acted, we were into all the same things, had the same mannerisms, told the same stupid jokes. And, to be honest, I was scared that maybe I'd be too similar. I've always enjoyed women's company, just like my dad. When I was a teen I had more girlfriends than I could count. I was worried that maybe one day I'd have a relationship with a woman and break her heart just like my dad. What if I couldn't remain faithful? I don't want to be like my dad and I don't want any woman to cry herself to sleep night after night because of me. So keeping my relationships with women casual seemed like the best thing. Then no one can get hurt.'

Ruby stared at him. That was very selfless.

He cared more about the women than himself. 'So there's never been anyone that made you want to rethink that philosophy?'

'Not really. I've never been with a woman long enough to develop feelings for them. There was one woman who made me think that things could turn into something more but she didn't want that so nothing happened.'

'She broke your heart?'

'God no, it didn't get that far. My heart is completely intact,' Jacob said, quickly. Possibly too quickly and she got the feeling he wasn't being entirely truthful about that.

'But now you're here in Happiness, thinking about settling down,' Ruby said.

'No, I'm not thinking about that.'

'You said you wanted to raise a family one day.'

'I suppose I will one day, but not now,' Jacob said, seemingly backpedalling away from that lifestyle.

'OK, but how can you do that if you only want something casual?' Ruby asked.

'I came to realise something. When the right woman walks into my life, when I fall in love, I'll never need anyone else. When I love someone as much as Andrew loves Willow, I could never be unfaithful to them, I could never do anything to hurt them.'

Ruby nodded. 'You're in control of the kind of person you are, not genetics or your history. You can't let what happened in your past define your future. I think you'd make someone a wonderful husband one day.'

He smiled at her. 'I'm not scared of love anymore, Ruby. But I think the whole *don't let your past define your future* thing is *very* good advice.'

He fixed her with a look and she rolled her eyes with a smile. She'd walked straight into that trap.

'Marriage isn't for me, I tried it once, never again. But I'd be very happy to come to your wedding. I'll even wear a big hat.'

The thought of watching him getting married to someone else did something inside her she didn't like. She decided to change the subject.

'So are you going to the carol concert?' she asked.

'Of course, are you?'

'I can't sing.'

'Neither can I, but I think everyone in the village is going. Standing around that big tree. I think it will be quite special,' Jacob said.

'I need to go and see this tree; I only saw it briefly last night.'

'When you were stealing Jesus from the nativity.'

Ruby laughed. 'That wasn't me.'

'I found him hidden at the back of my shop. I nearly called the police but I thought harbouring a fugitive was much more fun.'

She laughed again. 'If we go down, we'll go down together.'

'Exactly.'

'I only did it to wind Willow up. I know she's responsible for the decorations, but now Julia has put up all those posters and it just makes me want to keep him a bit longer and wind her up even more.'

'Willow didn't do the nativity, Julia did,' Jacob said.

'Oh. Well, that explains it then. Do you think I should return him?'

He shook his head without hesitation. 'No, I think we could have some fun here.'

'Are you joining forces with a known criminal?'

'It looks like I am.'

She grinned.

'Oh, talking of the other decorations. Am I the only one who thinks they look like…'

'Penises and pants? Yeah, I thought that too. Although almost everyone else thinks it all looks wonderful.'

'What was Willow thinking?'

'I think she was given a really tiny budget and got the lights second-hand and really cheap, for obvious reasons. She was mortified when she saw them once they were up but no one else seems to have noticed.'

'I must go out and see them again, best laugh I've had in a very long time.'

'We can go and see them now if you want, pop down and see the tree too.'

Ruby looked around the shop. There was still much to be done but she figured she was probably finished for the night.

'OK, sounds good.'

'Great, I'll just grab my coat.' Jacob picked up the two empty plates and ran upstairs.

She stood up and pulled her coat on, found her hat in her pocket and put that and her gloves on too. Jacob reappeared with his long grey coat, a bright red scarf and a grey beanie hat covering his dark curly hair. He looked like he'd just stepped out of a Christmas movie in the role of the gorgeous hero. And to top it all off as they stepped outside, tiny snowflakes were dancing in the air.

'It's snowing,' Ruby said in surprise as Jacob locked the door behind him.

He turned round to watch the tiny flakes swirl around them. 'Oh, well that is romantic.'

'There's nothing romantic about snow at all.'

Jacob shoved his hands in his pockets as he fell in at her side. It seemed they wouldn't be holding hands this time and she didn't know whether to be pleased or disappointed by that.

'For someone who is so in love with Christmas, you're a bit anti-snow,' Jacob said.

'I'm not. I love snow, but I don't think it's romantic. It's just... fluffy rain and no one thinks rain is romantic,' Ruby said, feeling like she was trying to backpedal away from him and doing a terrible job.

'I happen to think kissing someone in the rain is very romantic. So walks in the snow is also one of the things to avoid, along with tree decorating. I'll add it to my anti-romance list.'

She rolled her eyes. 'Will you stop with all the romance talk. I much preferred it when you were talking about no-strings-attached sex.'

'Well, we can definitely talk about that.'

She smiled and they walked on in silence

for a bit. The street was deserted, everyone tucked up in their houses or sitting in the pub in front of that roaring fire. The Christmas lights danced and twinkled above them and she couldn't help but giggle again as she looked at them. They were utterly ridiculous and how people hadn't spotted what she had seen was beyond her.

She looked at Jacob as he walked next to her. In her heart she knew she was fighting a losing battle by keeping him at arm's length. Avoiding romantic situations was not going to help. There was no doubt in her mind that she was going to end up in bed with him again and he probably knew that too. The connection between them was too strong to try sweeping it under the carpet. And while that prospect was completely thrilling, she was more worried about the feelings she'd be trying to suppress if she was to sleep with him again. In reality that had been the reason she had blanked all of his calls and texts. Because she *had* felt something for him in the summer, it *had* been more than just sex. She really didn't want any of those feelings and she was going to do everything she could to keep them under lock and key.

They reached the end of the high street and there, in the middle of the green on the slopes leading up to the castle, was a towering Christmas tree glittering under the weight of the decorations. There were baubles of every colour the size of her head, interspersed with smaller ones. There were silvery ribbons blowing gently in the breeze and thousands of fairy lights that twinkled in the darkness.

'Oh, it's beautiful,' Ruby said softly. 'So many people just go for one colour when they have a big tree so it doesn't look too messy, but I think lots of different colours like this is a celebration of everything Christmassy.'

'I agree, the more colours the better,' Jacob said.

Ruby grabbed her phone from her pocket and took a picture for her Instagram.

She walked up to it and smiled when she

could see her reflection in one of the huge glass baubles. She reached out and touched the branches, giving a small sigh of relief when she realised the tree was real.

'If there was a list for the perfect Christmas, having a real tree would be on it. I know I have artificial ones in my shop, they are easier and more cost-effective to display my things on, but in my own home it has to be real.'

She looked up at the very top and was suddenly hit with a memory.

'Harry took me to New York for our honeymoon, specifically so I could see the Rockefeller tree, one of the biggest Christmas trees in the world. New York really is spectacular at Christmas. He promised me we would travel the world to see all the big trees, the ones in Vienna, and the German markets. There is one in Italy that is a giant tree made of lights displayed on the side of Mount Ingino, it's over two thousand feet high. Obviously we never got to see them.'

'You know, I learned when I was young

how fragile life is and you have to live it while you have it because it can end just like that.' Jacob snapped his fingers. 'And you know that too with what happened to Harry. To have these dreams of what you want to achieve in your life but never ticking them off because of what life has thrown at you is a little bit sad. If you want to see these things, if you want to go to Mount Ingino to see the world's biggest Christmas tree, then you should do it. I know it won't be the same without Harry, but Harry would never have wanted your life to stand still because of him, for you to miss out on the things you really want just because you can't do it with him.'

She stared at him. In her heart she knew he was right. The plan to see the Christmas trees was always something she and Harry were going to do together but in reality she had known he was doing it all for her. Would it be really wrong to go and see these things on her own?

'And I know it's scary, the thought of

having another relationship again,' Jacob went on. 'But Harry wouldn't have wanted you to spend the rest of your life alone either. Sometimes you have to do the thing that scares you the most because the rewards far outweigh the risk. And I'm not talking about having a relationship with me, just that maybe one day you might be open to having that with someone again.'

She stepped back from the tree a bit to look at Jacob. He was watching her carefully. She didn't want to talk about this, mainly because she didn't want to admit that he was right.

'Let's change the subject, I don't want to burden you with all this. I never speak about him and now you've opened up a massive can of worms with finding that photo album earlier today. I promise I'm not going to cry again.'

'It's OK, I don't mind you talking about him.'

She pulled a face.

'Isn't it a bit weird, me talking about my ex-husband with my current…' She trailed off, not sure how she could define her relationship with Jacob.

'With your friend,' Jacob said, firmly. 'We're friends and we're supposed to talk about stuff like this with our friends. And even if we were more than friends, I still wouldn't mind you talking about him. So no, it's definitely not weird. What's weird actually is that you don't normally talk about him. He was a huge part of your life, you were married. You shouldn't just try to forget about that time, slam the lid shut on those memories. You should bring them out to look at now and again. Remember the good times you had with him. If he was as wonderful as he sounds, he deserves that.'

She stared at him, the tiny flakes of snow swirling around him, and she knew he was right. She had been trying to forget Harry and he was worth so much more than that. It was hard to know what she felt about him now. He had been gone for over twelve years so she couldn't say she was still in love with him, but she knew there would always be a tiny bit of her heart that belonged to him. She touched the snowflake necklace again.

'It was always easier to try to forget those memories. At first it was too painful and later, when I did try to talk about him, his family and friends didn't like it. It was always awkward talking to the grieving widow about her husband, I could see how uncomfortable they all were. Death is such a funny subject, it affects us all, but no one wants to talk about it. I suppose it became the norm to not talk about him at all. I talk about it with Willow sometimes – she never knew me when I was married to Harry so maybe it's easier for both of us.'

She reached out and touched one of the silver stars on the tree.

'When he died, I wanted to do something to honour his memory. His parents got a bench with his name on it in the park where he used to play as a kid. I don't know, it just felt so... wrong. A wooden bench didn't sum up Harry.

He was so… active, so alive, so mischievous. He used to do so much for charity, sponsored fun runs, abseiling, parachute jumps. I had no idea what kind of memorial I could do for him that would honour him in the right way. So in the end I did nothing and I always regret that.'

'It's not too late,' Jacob said.

'It's been over twelve years.'

'So?'

'What could I do?'

Jacob turned his attention to the tree for a moment as he thought.

'You could do something for charity, just like he would have done. Organise an event in his memory. Raise money for the British Heart Foundation. A memorial doesn't have to be a static thing, a place to visit. You keep your memories of him in your heart, but if you want to honour him, then this might be a good way to do it.'

She looked up at the snow dancing in the inky darkness above them, feeling the tiny flakes pepper her cheeks.

'I think that is a wonderful idea.'

But what could she do? Whatever it was, it needed to be done before Christmas. Harry had loved Christmas almost as much as she did. She suddenly wanted to get back home and come up with some ideas.

'Come on, let's go,' Ruby said.

Jacob fell in at her side as they walked down the slopes of the green and she slipped her arm through his.

'Thank you.'

He looked down at her. 'For what?'

'For listening, and for just being so bloody lovely.'

'Ah god, there's that word again.'

'It's your own fault, Jacob Harrington. You're a man who's very hard not to like. It's quite annoying really.'

'Sorry about that.'

'Can you try harder to be horrible? It would make my "nothing is going to happen between us" edict a lot easier to stick to if you were.'

He smiled. 'I'm not sure that is great motivation but I'll do my best.'

'Thank you.'

They walked on in silence for a while, but it wasn't awkward, it was easy between them. Everything was easy with Jacob, including talking about her past. The only thing that wasn't easy was trying to ignore that incredible connection.

'So what else would be on your list for a perfect Christmas?' Jacob asked.

'Oh, I love Christmas food, mince pies, Christmas cake with that hard white icing on the top, gingerbread men. And hot chocolates with lashings of squirty cream and marshmallows melting in a goo on the top. There'd be lots of snow,' Ruby gestured to the sky. 'A lot more than this. I'd want a Dickensian kind of Christmas, with all the roofs and roads covered in at least a foot of the stuff. And then I'd make a big snowman outside my house, the traditional kind with a top hat, a red scarf, lumps of coal for the eyes and of course a carrot for the nose. Christmas Day would be with all the people I care about, we'd eat too much, play games and watch cheesy Christmas movies.'

'What's your favourite Christmas movie?'

'Ah, that's like asking me who is my favourite child. I love *Santa Clause: The Movie* and *Miracle on 34th Street* – the most recent one. I love *The Holiday* and *Elf*, but I also love the classics like *White Christmas* too. Do you have a favourite movie?'

'I like *Elf* as well; Poppy loves it so I've watched it several hundred times with her. It never gets old.'

'What about your perfect Christmas?' Ruby asked. 'What would be on your list?'

'Oh, I don't know. I suppose food, family, the usual.'

'Is that it?'

He grinned. 'I love Christmas, but I'm not in *love* with it like you are.'

'That's because you've obviously never had a *perfect* Christmas before so you don't know what to look for. Maybe we can change that for you this year.'

'I'll let you know when I find it.'

They reached his shop.

'Are you coming back in? We can have a drink, maybe toss some ideas around,' Jacob said.

'Not tonight,' Ruby said.

'OK, I'll walk you home.'

'There's no need.'

'Trust me, there's some pretty unsavoury types in the village.'

Ruby laughed as they carried on walking down the hill, knowing that was very unlikely. The snow was starting to settle now, dusting the tops of the roofs ahead of them and gathering at the edges of the road. It really was starting to look romantic.

She looked up at Jacob. She really liked this man and she knew it was more than just the romance of the snow.

They arrived back at her cottage and she

opened the door and stepped inside, turning back to face him.

It was on the tip of her tongue to invite him in but she knew that was a terrible idea. Even still, there was a huge part of her that didn't want him to go. In the end he made the decision for her.

He leaned down and placed a kiss on her cheek. 'Goodnight Ruby Marlowe.'

She closed her eyes at the softness of his lips against her skin, her heart thundering against her chest at that simple tiny gesture.

He stepped back, gave her a smile and then turned and walked away.

She watched him go, wondering if he would look back. Just as she was about to go inside, he looked over his shoulder and saw her watching him. He gave her a wave before he disappeared into the snow-studded night.

She closed the door and leaned against it with a smile. It was going to be really hard to not fall in love with Jacob Harrington. But she knew things would be even harder if she did.

CHAPTER 7

RUBY WAS JUST GETTING READY FOR BED WHEN her phone rang. She smiled as she knew who it was. Only Cal, her brother, would be ringing her at this time of night as he was currently touring the US, so it wasn't late for him.

'Rubes, how's it going?' Cal said. It sounded like he was walking or maybe even running, he never stood still.

'It's going well,' Ruby said.

'Are you finally in Happiness?'

'Yes, I got here late last night.'

'I can't believe all that stress with selling

your place meant it took all that time. Well, you're there now, that's what matters,' Cal said. 'So tell me everything, what are the neighbours like?'

Ruby climbed into bed. 'Lovely. Nosy, meddling, interfering, gossipy but lovely.'

Cal laughed.

'Willow's engaged.'

'Ah, that's fantastic, pass on my congratulations.'

'I will,' Ruby paused. 'Jacob's here too.'

There was silence from Cal for a moment and Ruby wondered if he remembered her mentioning him. When she had returned from Happiness in the summer, Cal had been staying at her house for a few days, and Ruby had been stupidly giddy about the time she had spent in the little village and her excitement about moving there, and of course Jacob had been mentioned. He had been a big part of why she had enjoyed her time in the village. When she had shared a bottle of wine with her brother, Jacob's name had come up on many occasions. It was possible she might have gushed about him. Cal had grilled her about him and over the next few days he had pushed her to take a chance with Jacob, to return his calls and texts, but Ruby had refused to even consider it. Cal had eventually given up pursuing it.

'Jacob Harrington?' Cal said.

Yes, he definitely remembered.

'Yeah, it's no big deal though. We're just friends. Nothing is going to happen.' How many times had she said that in the last twenty-four hours?

'Right, sure. Out of all the men you've been with over the years, Jacob is the only one you've told me about. What Jacob did, what he said. I feel like I already know him and we've never met.'

'He's a nice guy, he just came up in conversation,' Ruby said, knowing it was a lot more than that.

'So you're both living there now?' Cal asked.

'Yes. We're working together in the same shop.'

'And nothing is going to happen between you?'

'No.'

'You have no feelings for him at all?'

'Look, the man is sexy, there's no denying that and, yes, if I'm honest, I wouldn't mind a repeat of what we had in the summer. But what I feel for him is lust, there's nothing more to it than that. He makes me laugh and he's good to talk to. He's been really nice actually. We talked about Harry and he's been really supportive. But I don't *like* him, not in that way.'

'You told him about Harry? You never talk about him with anyone. Don't you think that's something significant?'

'He found out,' Ruby said. 'You don't need to make this into something when it's not. I've had enough meddling from the villagers without having that from you too.'

'That's because they can all see what you

refuse to see. You like this man but you cling to your memory of Harry like a safety net and you won't let anyone in. Do you think Harry would have wanted this life for you where you spend the rest of it alone for fear of having your heart broken again?'

Only Cal could get away with pushing her like this. She thought about what Jacob had said about not giving up on her dreams, of living her life now because it could be gone in an instant. They were both right, but it didn't mean she could just forget the pain Harry's death had caused, she couldn't let go of that fear of it happening all over again.

'Tell me about your tour,' Ruby said, changing the subject because her heart and her head were at an impasse.

'Is that you closing the subject?'

'Yes, how's America?'

Cal sighed. 'I'm letting this go, for now, but we are going to talk about this again.'

'I know,' Ruby said, quietly because Cal was a determined, tenacious little bugger.

Cal started talking about his tour. As a Paralympian, when he wasn't in training for the next Paralympics or other sporting events, he toured around the world giving talks and inspiring hundreds and thousands of people. He had lost his leg in a car accident when he was a kid and it would have been so easy for him to give up on life there and then, put in the bare minimum. He couldn't play with his friends anymore, his dream of becoming a professional footballer gone in the blink of an eye, he'd been contained to a wheelchair for the first year or so after his accident, which he'd found beyond frustrating. But he was a poster boy for how to overcome adversity, for not letting the bad things in life define him. He had gone on to be one of the greatest Paralympian athletes, winning gold on multiple occasions in countries across the world. Maybe she needed to draw inspiration from him too.

JACOB WAS busy welding together bits of metal and cutlery the next day, in an attempt to make a large Christmas tree. He was more used to making animals than anything else, but he had been inspired to do something Christmassy by his lovely neighbour. He had come down to his shop that morning to find the Christmas additions that Ruby had left for him on his art-work the night before and had decided to try his own piece of festive art. He wasn't sure he was totally pleased with the way it had turned out, but he was sure Ruby would appreciate his efforts to get into the Christmas mood.

He hadn't been able to stop thinking about her all night. To lose her husband, the love of her life, at such a young age... he wasn't sure she could ever really get over that. At that age she would have been so idealistic, all those hopes and dreams of a happy ever after gone in an instant. Part of him understood her wanting to keep men at arm's length. She didn't want to fall in love and then have her heart broken again in the same way. But part of him wanted her to take that risk again because being in love had to be worth it. He had no idea what would happen between them and he was more than happy to just be her friend right now, but he hoped he could eventually get her to open her heart to a proper relationship, even if that relationship wasn't with him. Part of doing that was getting her to remember Harry properly, not locking that box of memories away never to be seen. Only when she had dealt with that loss could she really move on.

Just as he was attempting to create a star for the top of the Christmas tree out of several old forks, the woman herself arrived in his shop, shaking the snow that had been falling steadily all morning out from her hair. He lifted his face mask temporarily so he could say hello to her but realised straight away that she was bursting to talk to him. He switched off his welding torch and took off his mask.

'Good morning, beautiful,' Jacob said and she clearly stalled in what she was about to say.

'You promised that you were going to stop being charming,' Ruby said, taking off her coat and unwinding her scarf.

He grinned. 'I can't help it, charming is just the way I am. You'll just have to get used to it.'

'Smooth more like. You're just trying to get into my knickers.'

He laughed. 'No, just telling the truth. How was your night?'

'I've been thinking about what you said, and I've had some ideas. I think a charity event is a really good idea to celebrate Harry's life. I realise that most of the people round here are elderly and probably don't have that much money, and the young families probably won't either. But maybe we can come up with a few events that might charge a small entrance fee rather than asking for sponsorship. And maybe this can be something I can give to the village. You said yourself that there wasn't a lot going on for Christmas, and I know Kitty and Ken are hopeful that I might be able to do something. Maybe I can spread the joy of

Christmas now. This time of year, families are always looking for ways to keep the children occupied. I don't imagine we would raise a lot, but a few hundred pounds would be nice. I'd like to do something this side of Christmas which, with only six days until the big day, doesn't give us a lot of time to organise.'

'Don't forget we have the carolling on Wednesday night.'

'Yes, I think we could do something in the day too. And some of these things could be spread over a number of days.'

'What do you have in mind?'

She smiled. 'I have quite a few ideas actually. But you were the inspiration for this first idea. I thought that we could have an Angel Festival and people can make angel sculptures out of anything they wish. It could be papier-mâché or old bits of wood or metal, maybe even last week's recycling. It doesn't have to be big or grand, it could just be something that families might enjoy doing together in the comfort of their own homes. We charge them a pound to enter the competition and then on the day people can position their sculptures around the village and choose their favourite by putting money in the jar next to the sculpture.'

'Well, I think that sounds like a wonderful idea and it's something that the villagers could easily do.'

'I also thought that we could have a Christmas Cookie competition and people can pay to enter. We'll get some plain biscuits and some icing and sweets and give them fifteen minutes or half an hour to decorate the biscuits as they see fit. Again we can choose a winner with the money in the jar, just a few pennies.'

'Again that's not a bad idea, it's something that anybody could easily do.'

'I'm going to offer a Christmas wrapping service too so people can bring along their presents and I will wrap them for a small fee.'

'I think you might be inundated with people wanting you to do that. I love buying presents for people but I hate wrapping them. I imagine lots of people feel the same way.'

She smiled. 'You've been very supportive but I don't think that you're going to be as encouraging about my next suggestion.'

He narrowed his eyes suspiciously. 'What's the idea?'

'How about a Polar Bear Plunge?'

His heart sank into his stomach. He couldn't think of anything worse.

'I have to say, I'm not liking the sound of that already. I hate the cold.' It was something much more than that but he wasn't going to tell Ruby that.

'You were the one who said the snow was romantic,' Ruby said.

'Yes, when I'm bundled up inside a hat and coat or watching it from inside. But swimming in minus temperatures is definitely not for me.'

'It's not minus temperatures, it's probably about ten degrees, that's practically tropical.'

'You're not going to convince me.'

'I thought it might be fun. We can all wear

fancy dress and run into the sea. We don't have to be in there long. People can pay to enter and we can sell hot chocolate after to warm everybody up,' Ruby said.

'You do realise that a large proportion of people in the village are over the age of eighty? I would be worried about dodgy hearts giving out in the freezing cold water.'

She frowned and he felt suddenly sick. What a crappy thing to say when her husband had died from a heart attack.

'Shit. I'm so sorry,' Jacob said.

'It's fine, don't worry.'

'No, that was a really thoughtless thing to say.'

She smiled. 'There is not one single part of you that could ever be considered thoughtless. And you're probably right that a Polar Bear Plunge might not be suitable for a lot of people in the village.'

He shrugged. 'Maybe you give people the choice, let them make up their own minds.'

'Maybe we do a Polar Bear Paddle instead.'

He laughed at the compromise.

'Why don't you go on the village forum and write a post about all of your ideas? Tell them it's to raise money for charity and ask people to vote for what they are interested in doing. People can comment too and they might have some ideas of their own.'

'Great idea but will everyone have access to the forum? I imagine some of the older folk might not even have a computer.'

'You'd be surprised. It was Julia that set it up and she celebrated her seventy-fifth birthday last month. Everyone is on there as they can access it on their phones. They're all pretty active on it too.'

'OK, I might need you to show me how to log on to this thing.'

'Come on.'

She followed him to the computer. He spent a few minutes setting up her profile and then showing her how to add a post on the forum and then left her to it.

He was glad that she was doing this. She

needed to remember her husband in the right way, not forget he ever existed. And hopefully this would help her to celebrate his life and to be more open about talking about him.

After a while she stood up.

'OK, that's all done. Now we'll just have to wait to see if people are up for it. Right, I must get on with some work in the shop. I'd like to open up tomorrow.' She made a move to walk through the archway but suddenly seemed to notice the Christmas tree he was making.

'Oh my god, that's amazing.' She hurried over to take a look, fishing out her phone to take a picture.

'It's nowhere near finished yet but I was inspired to be Christmassy by your lovely additions to my shop.'

She looked around. 'You didn't take them down.'

'Of course I didn't.'

'I thought you'd think it wasn't really in keeping with the minimalist arty atmosphere.'

'It looks great,' Jacob said, honestly. 'In fact, feel free to add some more.'

She smiled. 'You're going to regret saying that.'

He watched her disappear through the archway. Having her next door was going to be fun.

CHAPTER 8

Ruby was busy decorating one of her trees with hand-painted glass baubles. The tree was nearly finished but she had so much stuff to do in the shop. She had promised Andrew she would pop up to her other shop later so she could see the damage and talk about plans for redecoration, then she was meeting Willow for lunch. There didn't seem like there was a lot of time left now and with less than a week until Christmas, she really wanted to open up tomorrow.

At a noise behind her, she turned to see

Jacob walking in with two hot chocolates, topped with squirty cream and marshmallows.

She smiled as she took her mug. He had obviously been listening the night before when she had talked about her perfect Christmas. It had been small little gestures like this that she had really loved about Harry. She frowned and pushed away the comparison. Harry had been the love of her life. Jacob was a great friend who she'd had amazing sex with. There was a big difference. She did not have feelings for Jacob just because he had bought her a hot chocolate. That would be ridiculous.

She stared at the hot chocolate for a moment. The marshmallows were already melting into little lumps of goo in the heat of the drink. It really was the perfect cup of hot chocolate.

'Thank you,' Ruby said.

'My pleasure.' Jacob took a sip, leaving a blob of cream on his lip. She had a sudden overwhelming desire to kiss it off. God, that wasn't good.

His phone pinged in his pocket and he frowned. 'My phone has been beeping with notifications from the village forum ever since you went on there this morning. I'm guessing people are commenting on your ideas for Christmas.'

'Do you get notified every time someone comments about something? That could get tiresome.'

'Not normally. Usually I only get notified if I'm being tagged in something or if someone is replying to a post I've made.'

He pulled his phone out of his pocket as Ruby moved to the computer to see all the comments for herself. She'd asked people to vote if they were interested in taking part in an event. Lots of people were keen to do the Angel Festival and the Christmas Cookie Competition. There was also a lot of interest in Ruby wrapping presents for people.

'Oh god,' Jacob muttered behind her.

'What's that?' Ruby said as she scanned

through the different comments. Everyone was being hugely positive about it all.

She scrolled down to the bit about the Polar Bear Plunge. Not surprisingly, no one had indicated they were willing to do it, but there were a ton of comments about it underneath. She clicked to open the comments and read a few people saying that it was too cold for them but that they were happy to sponsor someone else to do it. Then she saw a comment from Julia.

Julia: *I'll sponsor Jacob £50 if he does it.*

She burst out laughing. 'Have you seen what Julia has put?'

'Yes. Have you seen the other comments?' Jacob said.

She scrolled down a bit more.

Liz: *I'll also sponsor Jacob £50.*
Dorothy: *I'll add £100 to the charity pot if Jacob does it dressed as an elf.*

Kitty: *We'll add another £100 to the pot if Jacob does it.*

Tabitha: *The Welcome Home will also add a £100 for Jacob to do it.*

There were several more comments with people offering ten, twenty or fifty pounds if Jacob did it and Ruby couldn't help but laugh.

'It's OK for you, it's not you that's going to die in the freezing waters,' Jacob said.

She turned round to find him looking very grumpy about the whole thing. 'You don't have to do it. Everyone is just having a laugh. I don't think anyone really expects you to go through with it.'

'Oh, I'm doing it. The pot is currently at over seven hundred pounds. I'm not going to let you down. Of course I'm doing it.'

Ruby smiled, her heart filling for this man. He was making it really bloody difficult not to have feelings for him. She'd thought she'd be safe. Just friends, no sex, and those pesky feelings would just go away. But it hadn't worked out like that. He was too lovely. In fact, spending time with him, talking to him, laughing with him, getting to know him on a deeper level, the feelings she had for him were just getting worse and she didn't know what she could do about it.

RUBY LET herself into The Happy Little Christmas shop as she could see Andrew busy working away inside.

He was on his hands and knees when she walked in and he looked up and grinned at her.

'Hey Ruby.' He stood up and wiped his hands.

'Hey,' Ruby said, noticing Lucas working at the back of the shop. 'Hi Lucas.'

He came forward. 'Hi Ruby.'

She had a sudden idea. Megan might not thank her for it but she was going to follow her gut on this one.

'So are you both looking forward to the ball?'

Andrew nodded and Lucas shrugged.

'I think everyone is in a last-minute panic to get dates for the ball. Do you have a date, Lucas?' Ruby said.

'Oh, I probably won't go.'

'Ah, that's a shame.' She turned to Andrew. 'I think Jacob is going to ask Megan to go with him.'

Andrew looked confused. 'Really?'

'What?' Lucas said, suddenly visibly alarmed.

'Yes,' Ruby nodded. 'I think he likes her. And I was speaking to Megan and she hasn't got a date yet, so I imagine she'll say yes. Unless she gets a better offer before Jacob asks, of course.'

Lucas frowned. 'I need to get some tools for this.'

He hurried out the shop and Ruby giggled to herself as the door closed behind him.

'Jacob's not going to ask Megan out, is he?' Andrew said.

'Not that I know of,' Ruby said. 'But I think she's keen on your new assistant. I just thought I'd give them a little nudge in the right direction.'

'That felt like a bloody big shove rather than a nudge.'

Ruby shrugged. 'If I'm wrong, I'm sure Megan will be brave enough to say no if Lucas actually asks her. If I'm right, well, only good can come of it.'

Andrew shook his head with a smile. 'How are you settling into Happiness anyway?'

'Good, my temporary shop is looking particularly festive. I'll probably be able to open the doors for business tomorrow and everyone has been very welcoming.'

Andrew smirked. 'Did my brother welcome you with open arms?'

Ruby smiled. 'He's been very… helpful.'

'I bet he has.'

'What's going on with him anyway? He's

talking about settling down one day, getting married, having children. We went for a walk last night in the snow and he said how romantic it was. And aside from all of that, he's just been so bloody lovely. The Jacob I knew in the summer was very much a love-them-and-leave-them kind of guy. I never thought we'd have serious heart-to-heart conversations but we have. He's changed.'

'Jacob can do serious if he wants to, he's a good listener. I think he's a complete pain in the arse sometimes but he's loyal and kind. He's always had a lot of time for other people. And I don't know about him settling down and having children, he certainly hasn't mentioned that to me, but I guess it comes with age. He adores our niece Poppy and I've always thought he would make a great dad one day.'

Ruby thought about what Jacob would be like as a dad and knew Andrew was right.

'So he's never had a serious relationship before, never had his heart broken?'

Andrew hesitated before answering. 'In Jacob's case that's two different questions. As far as I know, he's never had a serious relationship.'

'But he has had his heart broken?'

Andrew cocked his head. 'Maybe that's a conversation you should have with Jacob.'

Ruby thought about this for a moment.

'So do you fancy the job of Mrs Harrington?' Andrew said, changing the subject slightly.

'No, thank you. I'm fine staying Miss Marlowe. There's only going to be one Mrs Harrington round here and I think Willow will fill that role perfectly.'

Andrew grinned. 'I cannot wait for her to be my wife.'

Ruby smiled. 'Any thoughts about when the wedding will be?'

'We thought maybe February. It'll be something quite small here in the village or up at the castle.'

'That will be lovely, I can't wait to see the

castle all done up for the Christmas Eve ball, I'm sure you could do something similar for the wedding.'

'Yes, we were going to talk to Kitty and Ken about having it there.'

'I bet they will be all over that idea. The first wedding in the castle.'

'I hope so.'

'So, you don't fancy taking part in the Polar Bear Plunge?' Ruby asked, hoping to gather together more people in the hope that Jacob might feel better about doing it.

'Hell no. I love to swim in the sea, but I'm a fair-weather swimmer. I only go in when the weather is hot.'

'I think Jacob feels the same,' Ruby said.

Andrew shook his head. 'He doesn't swim.'

'He can't swim?'

'Oh no, he can swim, he just never goes in the sea. He's not going to let himself be bullied into doing this Polar Bear Plunge, is he?' Andrew asked in concern.

'He says he's doing it. We're raising money

for charity; he says he doesn't want to let me down.'

'Crap,' Andrew said.

'Why, what's wrong?'

He shook his head. 'There was an incident, several years ago… Look, I don't think it's my place to say.'

This sounded really serious.

'OK, you're going to have to tell me what happened so I know what I'm dealing with here.'

Andrew didn't say anything for a while but eventually he spoke. 'We grew up in Newquay, which is well known for its big waves and great surfing. Jacob loved to surf. One morning, when he was fourteen, he took his surfboard and went down to the beach. It was very early, before anyone else was up. The beach was deserted but it was a place he had surfed hundreds of times before and I suppose he felt safe.'

'Why do I get the feeling that this story doesn't end well.'

'Well it doesn't. Not really. He got caught in an undertow, he was dragged under the water and carried out to sea. I mean, I suppose he was lucky, he managed to get back to the surface, but he did get pulled out to sea quite far. He'd lost his surfboard so he had nothing to hold onto. He had already been surfing for an hour and he was knackered and he tried to fight against the rip tide which made him more exhausted. He didn't have the energy to swim back to shore and the tide carried him further and further away. No one knew he'd gone surfing so no one raised the alarm when he didn't come home. Mum just thought he'd gone out with his mates. No one saw him get swept away. He was finally found by some fishermen about eight hours after he'd been swept out. He was exhausted, he had hypothermia, he was in hospital for a few days. There was no lasting damage but... well, he hasn't been back in the sea since.'

'Are you kidding me?' Ruby said, incredulously.

Andrew shook his head. 'No, he had terrible nightmares about it for years after. We've been to the beach with Poppy but he won't go anywhere near the sea. You can see it completely freaks him out whenever he goes within sniffing distance.'

'Oh my god, why the hell is he going through with this?'

'Because he's a determined, stubborn sod,' Andrew said.

'I'll call it off,' Ruby said. 'It was a silly idea anyway.'

'You can't do that! Then he'll know I told you and he should be the one to tell you this. I thought you should know because if he freaks out and pulls out at the last minute, at least you'll understand why and won't give him any grief about it.'

'Of course I won't.' She sighed. 'What a mess.'

Andrew was silent for a while. 'Maybe it'll be good for him, help him get over that fear once and for all. But let him make that decision himself whether he goes ahead with it or not.'

She let out a heavy breath, hating that she had inadvertently put Jacob in this position. She had to find a way to talk to him about this without letting on that she knew.

'So, shall I show you the damage?' Andrew said. He was clearly trying to change the subject after having outed Jacob in that way, though Ruby knew he'd done it for the right reasons.

She nodded, her mind still on Jacob.

'Well, it's quite bad back here.' Andrew walked to the back of the shop and when she followed him she was shocked to see that there was a gaping hole in the ceiling. 'The water tank up in the loft had evidently been leaking for a while and the ceiling eventually gave way. Water has poured through and completely ruined the carpet. We have a new tank on order but I don't think it will be delivered now until after Christmas. In the meantime we are going to repair the ceiling, replace the carpet and redecorate where it's needed. So if there's anything you particularly want in here, or anything you want changing, now would be a good time to do it.'

Ruby looked around. It was smaller than the shop she shared with Jacob, narrower and let in less light. Location wise, this shop was in a much better position in the village but in the short time she had spent in her temporary shop, she had enjoyed having someone to talk to next door. In the market hall in St Octavia where she'd had her little Christmas stand, she had loved talking to the other vendors. They'd get each other cakes, sandwiches and hot drinks and watch their stands for each other if they needed to nip to the loo. Being in here felt quite isolated in comparison to what she was used to. And she liked the layout in the temporary shop with its little shelves and nooks to display her pieces in. It had character and this really didn't. She imagined sharing cups of tea with Jacob, chatting about village life, and she liked the idea of always having someone there.

She shook her head as she caught herself. That was the last thing she wanted. She didn't want to get cosy with Jacob, laugh with him, talk with him, because that would lead her to a road she didn't want to go down.

'What are you thinking?' Andrew said.

There was no way in hell she was going to tell him that she had been thinking about staying in the temporary shop with Jacob.

'Nothing, just... where I would put everything.'

'Well I can put some shelves up if that's helpful?'

'Yes, that would be great. Maybe a big low shelf in the window so I can have a proper window display and then some large low shelves or tables here and over there so I can show off my baubles. And a large table in the middle so I can make my decorations.'

'OK, no problem. Any particular colour you want the walls painted?'

'Oh, I'm not sure. I've never had walls to contend with before. I guess just something neutral like white or cream and then it won't clash with my brightly coloured decorations.'

He smiled. 'I didn't take you for a neutral kind of person. What about silver or gold instead? Those are pretty neutral.'

Ruby thought about it for a moment. 'Gold would be wonderful, thank you.'

'Gold it is.'

Gold was definitely one up on the shop she shared with Jacob and she got to redesign this one to however she wanted. This was definitely the better option. Definitely.

She'd have to keep telling herself that.

RUBY WALKED into the pub and looked around for Willow. It was quieter now than it had been the day before at her welcome drinks but it was still a lot busier than she'd seen it in the summer.

Willow waved to her from a table in the corner and she made her way over. Megan was at the next table, eating her lunch and deeply engrossed in her book.

Ruby gave Willow a hug and sat down opposite her.

'I ordered fish and chips for us both, I hope that's OK,' Willow said. 'Connor does great fish here; it's grilled rather than battered and always comes in this delicious sauce.'

'That sounds great, I'm starving.'

'I bet you are. I was walking past your new shop earlier; it looks amazing in there.'

'There's still a ton to do, but it will be ready for the grand opening tomorrow,' Ruby said.

'And how's the old shop? Andrew says the damage is pretty bad?'

'It is, but Andrew and Lucas are on the case.'

Ruby noticed Megan glance over at the mention of Lucas's name and smiled to herself. There was definitely something between those two. Hopefully her little bit of meddling would help to get them together.

Willow leaned in closer. 'Now, Ruby Marlowe, would you have anything to do with Jesus going missing from the nativity? Because that kind of thing has your name all over it.'

Ruby laughed. 'I only did it to wind you up because I thought you were responsible for the nativity. I didn't realise there were going to be wanted posters and a reward.'

Willow laughed. 'Are you going to give him back?'

'Not yet. Me and Jacob are going to have some fun with him.'

Willow grinned. 'I'm glad you have Jacob to… distract you.'

Ruby smiled; she knew exactly what Willow meant. She and Willow had been carrying out practical jokes on each other every December for years and Ruby knew it was her friend's way of distracting her from focussing on her wedding anniversary on the twenty-third. Ruby appreciated the sentiment and she did enjoy the jokes, but that day was always going to be hard, the day when she was meant to start her happy ever after.

'I have a gift for you,' Willow said, placing the box on the table between them.

Ruby eyed it suspiciously. 'Is this going to contain cockroaches or a poisonous snake perhaps?'

Willow pretended to be hurt. 'No, of course not, it's just a little welcome to the village present.'

Years of knowing her meant she didn't trust her as far as she could throw her, but Ruby carefully removed the lid anyway.

There was a small pop and Ruby saw stars, literally, as a cloud of glitter and sequins exploded out of the box, covering her and the table in a matter of seconds.

Ruby laughed as she shook her hair and her clothes and she could see Megan at the next table giggling quietly into her book.

'Well played,' Ruby said as Willow was almost hysterical with laughter.

Connor came over with the food. 'I hope you're going to clear that up,' he said, grumpily.

Ruby smirked. He hadn't changed, even if the rest of the village had.

'I actually brought a dustpan and brush with me,' Willow said, ever efficient.

Connor grunted and walked away.

Ruby shook her head. 'You know how to make a statement, Willow McKay. Oh, talking of which, what is going on with those street decorations?'

Willow blushed as she ate her food. 'Sshhh. Keep your voice down.'

Ruby laughed. 'It's not exactly a secret, it's out there for everyone to see.'

'But no one has spotted it yet, well apart from Jacob and Andrew who have ribbed me about it constantly. Everyone else thinks they are just really nice decorations.'

'You have penis candles and Y-fronts hanging over the main high street. How has no one else realised?'

'I don't know, maybe because their minds are innocent and pure, unlike yours.'

Ruby laughed, not the least bit offended by

that. 'Where did you get them from anyway, Ann Summers?'

Willow laughed. 'One of the nearby towns was selling them cheap, said they were up-grading their lights to some new ones and just wanted to get rid of them.'

'Did you not think to ask what they were before you bought them?'

'Why would I? Why would I even think that I was getting something other than just normal run-of-the-mill Christmas lights?'

Ruby laughed again and tucked into her food.

'What's going on with this Polar Bear Plunge anyway?' Willow asked.

'Well at the moment, it's just Jacob doing it,' Ruby said, her heart sinking again as she thought about him doing something he really didn't want to do.

'I don't think it's a good idea,' Willow said, diplomatically.

Ruby watched her for a moment. 'Andrew told you too, didn't he?'

Willow nodded. 'We were talking about our wedding and I suggested we could do it on the beach. Andrew said he would prefer his best man not to be standing there freaking out the whole time and then he told me.'

Ruby sighed. 'It's so awful for him. It must have been so scary. But imagine having that fear all your life, and never being able to get past that.'

Willow stared at her.

'I know,' Willow said, deliberately. 'Imagine what it would be like to have a traumatic incident in your past and never moving on from it.'

Ruby scowled and focussed on her food. 'It's not the same.'

Just then Lucas walked into the pub. He saw Megan and marched over. Ooh, maybe he was going to be brave enough to ask her to the ball.

'Megan, I'm glad I found you,' Lucas said and Megan put her book down to look at him.

'Lucas, hi,' Megan said, her cheeks colouring slightly.

'I just wanted to give you a warning.'

Well, that wasn't the romantic start to the conversation that Ruby had been hoping for.

'Jacob Harrington is planning to ask you to the ball,' Lucas said, seriously.

Megan's eyes widened. 'He is?'

'Yes, apparently. I just thought I should warn you so you can say no.'

Megan blinked. 'Why would I say no?'

Lucas clearly hadn't been expecting that. 'A man like Jacob Harrington is no good for you.'

'What does that mean?' Megan said.

'Oh, he's a nice enough bloke, but I know him of old. He's a complete womaniser. Had more girlfriends than you've had hot dinners. He'll break your heart.'

'He can only break my heart if I give it to him and I have no intention of doing that. But going to the ball with him could be fun.'

'Fun?'

'Lucas, I haven't been out on a date for

over a year. If Jacob asks me to the ball, I can do my hair and make-up, wear a pretty dress, dance with a handsome man and maybe have a bit of fun afterwards. Why would I say no to that?'

This wasn't going according to plan at all. Ruby exchanged worried glances with Willow.

Lucas scowled. 'I didn't take you for that sort of girl.'

Megan stood up and shoved her book in her bag. 'What sort of girl is that? The sort that likes to wear a pretty dress occasionally, or the sort that would be more than happy to jump into bed with Jacob Harrington if he asked me to? It's been a year, Lucas, and no one else is asking me out or asking me to the ball.'

'I don't like it.'

Megan slung her bag over her shoulder. 'Well you know what to do about it then, don't you?'

She stormed out and Lucas was left standing there looking very confused.

Ruby wanted to go over and shake him for

completely missing the point but she'd inter-fered enough for one day.

She turned back to Willow. 'Love is a com-plicated thing, isn't it?'

'Yes, but I promise you, it's definitely worth it.'

Ruby turned her attention back to her food. She wasn't convinced.

RUBY WALKED BACK into her shop a while later and called out to Jacob to let him know she was there.

'Hi honey, I'm home.'

She heard the bark of laughter and smiled to herself. She looked around the shop – there was still quite a bit that needed doing before she could open the next day. She frowned. One of her Christmas trees that she hadn't got round to dressing yet had decorations on. And by the looks of them, not any she had seen before.

She moved closer and then laughed out loud when she realised there were spoons of different colours and sizes hanging from the tree. It actually looked really effective.

She looked around to see if Jacob had made any more additions and giggled to see there was a garland of bike chains hung from a shelf and two small colanders had replaced the stars at the top of her trees near the door. Her collection of baubles, which she had displayed artfully in a small pyramid, had been changed to a pyramid of metal serving spoons and spatulas balanced precariously against each other.

She marched over to the archway and stood with her hands on her hips. 'Jacob Harrington!'

He looked up from the Christmas tree he was still working on, which now had various decorations hanging from the boughs, all made from different bits of coloured metal.

'What?' he asked innocently, though it was very clear he knew full well what she was protesting about.

She gestured theatrically to her shop and he grinned.

'I was just making some improvements.'

She laughed. 'I'll give you *improvements*.' She looked back into her shop. In all honesty it looked great and was a wonderful link with Jacob's shop.

'An eye for an eye,' Jacob said, gesturing to the peacock who was still proudly displaying his blue tinsel scarf.

'Oh, it's going to be like that, is it?'

He grinned at the challenge in her voice. 'I guess it is.'

'Listen, I've been thinking about Jesus and what we could do with him,' Ruby said. 'I think we should take photos of him around the village and post them on the village forum. Could we create an anonymous account so the villagers wouldn't know it was us doing it?'

'I love that idea and, yes, I'm sure we could. I created your account in the forum, it would be easy to create an account under the name of Jesus.'

Ruby laughed. 'Let's do it.'

Jacob walked over to the computer and started creating a profile on the forum. 'You know, I was thinking about you stealing him. Did you know there was a webcam on the nativity?'

Ruby's stomach leapt as she remembered manhandling the sheep. God, she didn't want the villagers seeing that.

'Are you serious?'

'Yes, it was put there mainly so the children could watch the animals anytime they wanted, but also so that Julia and Lucas could keep an eye on the animals and make sure they were OK. The animals have come from Lucas's home so I think he likes to keep an eye on them throughout the day, even if he's working.'

'Oh god.'

'I shouldn't worry. It's a live webcam. So unless someone was watching at two in the morning, no one would have seen it.'

'I'm not remotely techy, so if it's live, it

couldn't record footage as well?'

'I don't know, I don't think so. But I wouldn't worry. If someone had seen the footage, you would know about it by now.'

That was certainly true. She would probably have been chased out of the village for being an animal abuser... or worse. What would anyone have thought if they'd seen her trying to give a Heimlich manoeuvre to a sheep? Would they even have believed her if she told them the sheep was choking? OK, there was no point worrying about it. Like Jacob said, if someone had seen the webcam footage they would have been banging on her door by now.

'Right, that's done, we've now created a profile on the forum called "Jesus". This is going to be fun.'

'OK, before you log out I need to put out a timetable of events for the coming week.' Jacob stood up and Ruby slid into his seat and started adding a list of all the events. 'I intend to open tomorrow so I'll be busy with that but the day after, Tuesday twenty-first, we could do the Christmas Cookie Competition. Wednesday twenty-second we could do the Angel Festival and we have the Christmas carols that night around the tree. And then we could have the Polar Bear Plunge on Christmas Eve morning, the Secret Santa thing in the afternoon and the Christmas Eve ball on Friday night.'

He nodded and she inwardly winced when she watched the smile fall off his face at the mention of the Polar Bear Plunge.

She wanted to talk about it but she had no idea how to dissuade him from doing it without bringing up what had happened in his past. But maybe she didn't need to get him to change his mind. Maybe she just needed to support him with whatever he decided.

'And I've been thinking about the Polar Bear Plunge,' Ruby said. 'I'm going to do it with you.'

He shook his head. 'God no, I don't want anything to happen to you.'

Her heart swelled a little at that protective statement. 'Nothing is going to happen to me, it's just a little dip in the sea.'

He brushed his hair from his face. 'Yes, I know.'

'This was my bright idea that got you stuck doing something you don't want to do so we'll do it together,' Ruby insisted.

A small smile appeared on his face. 'Like a date? Because I could think of far more romantic settings for our first date.'

'Not a date,' she said firmly. 'But I'll hold your hand if you like.'

He smiled. 'I'll hold you to that.'

CHAPTER 9

JACOB HUNG THE BAUBLES HE'D MADE FROM spoons onto the branches of the Christmas tree sculpture. Ruby was next door, dancing along to the Christmas songs as she finished off setting out her shop. It had been completely transformed in there since her arrival. It looked festive and inviting, rather than the cold empty room he'd used for storage for the last few months. He smiled as he watched her dance. It really was good having her next door.

He looked outside as fat snowflakes

swirled in the air. It was coming down heavily out there. If it lasted another week, Ruby might get her wish of a white Christmas after all. The weather was certainly cold enough to keep snowing and, according to weather reports, it was only going to get colder. He shivered at the thought.

This Polar Bear Plunge was bothering him a lot more than it should. After what had happened years before, he hadn't been back in the sea since. He'd told himself he just wasn't bothered about going in but he knew there was a lot more to it than that. And this time of year was hardly the right time to dive back into the icy waves for the first time in twenty years. But he couldn't let the bad weather or his fears stop him. He wanted to support Ruby in honouring her husband and help her to raise some money. If the villagers had decided to part with their hard-earned cash in return for seeing him swim in the sea for a few seconds then he was damned well going to do it.

He ignored the sick feeling of unease in his stomach.

The door of his shop opened and Lucy strode in. She was relatively new to the village as well, having been there probably only a month. He'd met her the year before in Penzance, or so she said, when he had slept with her best friend, Amy. He was sorry to say he had no memory of Lucy at all, which made him feel completely crap as she had vivid memories of him – or, more to the point, of what Amy had told her about their night together. And now it seemed that Lucy had set her sights on him too.

'Hi Jacob,' Lucy said, moving into the shop and looking around.

'Hello Lucy.'

'I just came to say hello to our new resident. I didn't get a chance to talk to her yesterday at the welcome drinks so I thought I'd come and introduce myself now.'

'Ah, I see,' Jacob said, wondering why she

hadn't gone straight into Ruby's side of the shop rather than into his. 'Well, she's next door.'

'Oh yes.' Lucy looked over and he saw the tiny wrinkle of her nose as she took in all the glitz and over-the-top glamour of the grotto next door. 'How very festive.'

'It definitely is that.'

Lucy turned her attention away from Ruby's shop and moved closer to him.

'I bet having that next door has been a complete headache,' she whispered, conspiratorially. 'It's hardly the quiet, inspirational environment an artist like yourself needs to work.'

'Having Ruby next door has actually been very inspiring,' he gestured to the Christmas tree.

'Well, that's very classy, almost elegant. But that,' she nodded towards Ruby's shop and giggled, 'most definitely isn't.'

He glanced over at Ruby, who happened to look up from the tree and see them watching her. She blushed and gave a little wave. Thankfully the music in her shop was too loud for her to hear what Lucy was saying.

'It's actually been a breath of fresh air.'

'Really?' Lucy said in surprise. She looked around his shop again. 'I've always thought this place was cool, sexy, unique, it had an edge. The perfect place for the great Phoenix Blade. It would be such a shame to lose that to...' she picked up the end of the blue tinsel scarf the peacock was wearing and let it drop '...commercialism.'

He glanced over at Ruby again, who was subtly watching them as she continued to decorate her tree. It occurred to him that the old Jacob might have flirted with Lucy to make Ruby jealous but he didn't need to do that with Ruby. He had no intention of doing anything to hurt her and he wasn't going to play games with her like that.

'Still, it's only temporary,' Lucy was saying. 'She'll be gone soon.'

Time to nip this in the bud.

'Lucy, Ruby and I are very good friends so this line of conversation really isn't sitting well with me. The people in this village have been very welcoming to me and to you, and I would really hope that *everyone* in the village would give the same courtesy to Ruby too.'

Lucy stared at him, her cheeks flushing bright red. Then she laughed nervously. 'Oh Jacob, I'm only joking, you don't need to take me so seriously. I love Christmas as much as the next person. In fact, I came in here intending to buy some more decorations for my tree.'

'Well her shop isn't quite open yet, but I'm sure she'll be very appreciative of that tomorrow.'

'I'll pop by tomorrow then.' Lucy forced a smile onto her face. 'I do love all these Christmas additions to your shop. Do you have anything planned for the big day?'

'My sister Lottie and her daughter Poppy will be coming round. Andrew and Willow will be having dinner here too. It'll be a nice family thing.'

The thought occurred to him that Ruby would probably be on her own. He would have to make a point of inviting her along for dinner.

'And you?' Jacob asked. He could play nice if Lucy was.

'I'll probably go to my mum's. Are you looking forward to the ball on Christmas Eve?' She twisted a strand of hair round her finger.

'I am. It should be fun.'

'Do you have a date?' Lucy asked.

Oh god, what could he say? Julia had warned him Lucy was going to ask him but he hadn't prepared an excuse.

His phone beeped in his pocket and he seized on the distraction.

'Sorry Lucy, I just need to get this, I've been waiting for an email to come in from a client.'

He grabbed his phone and although he knew the beep was just a notification of someone else sponsoring him to do the Polar

Bear Plunge, he scrolled through his phone while he played for time.

He had no interest at all in going to the ball with Lucy. He glanced at her. Why was that? It wasn't that he didn't find Lucy attractive, she was very pretty in that classic kind of way, the kind you might see on a catwalk – tall, thin, long caramel-blonde hair that was so silky straight she must spend the whole morning straightening it before she stepped out of the house. She was always very well dressed too – tailored trousers, fitted tops or jackets, high heels with every outfit, the perfect accessories. She was flawless in every single way.

She was very different from Ruby, who was dancing around her shop next door in red sequinned Converse, leggings with Rudolph on and an oversized jumper that had a large Christmas pudding on the front with googly eyes. Her scarlet hair was wavy and curly and he got the sense that other than giving her hair a quick brush in the mornings she probably did very little to style it. He couldn't help smiling as he watched her dance, very badly, around the tree she was decorating.

He turned his attention back to Lucy. She was exactly the sort of person he would have gone for six months before, someone attractive he could have casual sex with. But he found himself not wanting that life anymore. He had slept with two people since Ruby, which for him was a record low, but casual sex just didn't seem to tick that box for him like it used to. There had been nothing wrong with the two women he'd been with – they'd been attractive, good in bed – but he hadn't felt that connection he'd shared with Ruby and he missed that. He wanted something more than meaningless sex, he wanted someone he could really talk with, someone he could have a laugh with just like he had with Ruby. He wanted sex with someone special. That realisation was like a slap around the face. He looked back at Ruby. She had ruined him for other women.

He realised Lucy was still waiting and put

his phone back in his pocket. 'Sorry about that, Lucy. You were asking if I have a date for the ball?'

She licked her lips. 'Yes, do you?'

He should just say no, go to the ball with Lucy and get over these silly thoughts of wanting a proper relationship once and for all. But he couldn't do it.

He cleared his throat. 'I'm afraid I've already asked Ruby.'

Lucy didn't need to know that Ruby still hadn't given him an answer yet.

'Oh.' Her face fell and then she let out a nervous laugh. 'I wasn't asking you out. I was just... making polite conversation. I have a date, of course I do. His name is Zayn. Lives in the next town. Anyway, I must dash, things to do.'

She edged to the door.

'Didn't you want to meet Ruby?'

'Oh, I don't want to disturb her if she's getting everything ready to open tomorrow. And as I said, I'll pop in at some point to get some more decorations.'

She gave him a little wave and left the shop.

Jacob didn't think Lucy would ever show her face next door.

Ruby leaned against the archway connecting the two shops. 'Friend of yours?'

He shook his head. 'Lucy, she lives in the village.'

'I think she likes you.'

'You might be right. I think she came here to ask me to the ball.'

'Oh… well you should go with her,' Ruby said, her voice suddenly unnaturally high. Was she jealous? Surely not.

'I'm not interested,' Jacob said.

'Why not? She's pretty.'

He stopped himself from saying, 'She's not you.' Frustratingly that was the truth.

'I don't think she likes Christmas,' he said instead.

Ruby gasped theatrically. 'What kind of weirdo doesn't like Christmas?'

'Exactly.'

'Well, I think you made the right decision there.'

She turned and disappeared back into her shop and he watched her go. He had turned down a date with an attractive woman which probably would have ended in casual sex because he wanted something real with a woman who had no interest in him at all. It certainly didn't feel like the right decision.

JACOB WAS JUST PUTTING the finishing touches to the star that would go on top of his Christmas tree when Ruby came into his shop carrying Jesus, who was now dressed as a reindeer in a cute Rudolph onesie, complete with antlers.

He laughed. 'Where did you get that?'

'I actually bought these baby Christmas costumes a few months ago, thought I might sell them in my shop. I bought some outfits for dogs too. Anyway, I dug this out and I thought it would be perfect for us to dress up Jesus.'

'Isn't that a bit of anachronism?'

'Probably and maybe even sacrilege and blasphemous too. Anyway, shall we take Jesus for a walk around the village?'

'OK, but do you have a bag to hide him in? We're going to have to be really discreet about this. If anyone sees us, we'll be in big trouble,' Jacob said, knowing full well that wasn't going to stop them.

'Ah, the risks are always outweighed by the fun,' Ruby said, slipping Jesus into her rucksack and pulling on her coat.

Jacob grabbed his coat as well and they stepped outside. It was still snowing heavily outside and settling nicely on the roads and roofs. The sun was just starting to set, lending a pinky glow to the twinkling carpet. There were a few people on the street but most of the villagers were tucked up in their homes or the pub.

As the last few stragglers disappeared out of view, Ruby propped Jesus up against the frozen fountain. She positioned the doll standing up with one leg sticking out behind him as if he was skating. Jacob laughed as she quickly took a picture.

'Where should we take him next?' Ruby asked and Jacob loved the spark of mischief and amusement in her eyes.

'Should we dare to take a photo of him outside the post office?' he suggested. 'Julia will have a fit if she knows Jesus was that close to her and she had no idea.'

'That's brilliant,' Ruby said.

They walked up the high street and stopped outside the post office, peering through the window at the Christmas display of cookies, sweets and chocolates while they waited patiently for the street to clear. Ruby giggled next to him and he loved the sound of it.

Jacob looked around and saw that for a

brief moment they were completely alone. 'Quick, now.'

Ruby grabbed Jesus from her rucksack and positioned him outside the door in the snow, while Jacob kept a look-out. When she was happy, she stepped back and Jacob took a picture on his phone.

A movement inside the shop caught Jacob's eye and he looked inside. 'Quick, Julia is coming.'

Ruby grabbed Jesus and just about managed to stuff him in her rucksack before Julia opened the door.

'What are you two lovebirds doing out here?' Julia asked, her eyes wide with excitement at seeing them both together.

'Nothing,' Ruby giggled, zipping up her rucksack.

'Just looking at all your chocolates,' Jacob said.

Julia clearly wasn't buying any of this as she looked between them suspiciously. She stepped outside and closed the shop door behind her. She looked around and then spoke in a whisper. 'Are you here to buy more condoms? You don't need to be embarrassed if you are. I've seen it all, believe me.'

Ruby laughed. 'No, it's OK, we don't need condoms.'

'Some of that sexy underwear I was telling you about?' Julia asked. 'Whips, blindfolds. I have a whole catalogue of stuff like that if that's what you're looking for.'

Well this had suddenly taken a rather kinky turn.

'We don't need any of that,' Jacob said, with a wink. 'I have everything covered in that department.'

Julia swatted his arm playfully. 'Oh, I bet you do. Well if you're not here for that, what are you lurking outside here for?'

'We weren't lurking. Jacob was just showing me which chocolates he wanted for Christmas,' Ruby said.

'Yes, the white chocolate snowman,' Jacob said, pointing.

Julia's face fell. 'Well, that's a bit boring. Come on then, let's go get your snowman.'

Ruby tried to stop her with protests that she would come back later but Julia wasn't haven't any of it. A few minutes later, Jacob was walking up the street eating a chocolate snowman that Ruby had been forced to buy for him, chuckling to himself at how that had turned out.

'I don't know what was funnier, Julia trying to sell us the contents of her Ann Summers catalogue or the fact that I ended up with a free snowman.'

'Oh, you can laugh, you weren't the one that was forced to fork out for a snowman I'd had no intention of buying. You owe me a snowman, Mr Harrington.'

'Noted, but I think we got away without her seeing Jesus which is the main thing,' Jacob said.

'Yeah, let's get back and upload it onto the forum. I need to finish the shop ready for the grand opening tomorrow anyway.'

They walked back into the shop and Jacob watched as Ruby logged in to the Jesus profile on the forum. He smiled when he saw what she'd written.

Taking a break from the nativity scene for a while to explore the delights of Happiness village. Went ice skating and stopped at the post office to try Julia's lovely fudge. Had to go in disguise of course, I don't want to be recognised. But don't worry, I'll be back on Christmas Eve.

Jesus x

RUBY STOOD up and grinned at him.

'I love your sense of humour,' Jacob said. There was actually quite a lot of things he liked about Ruby Marlowe.

'Well, you bring out the best in me.'

He liked that.

'Or the worst,' Ruby said. 'Depending on which way you look at it. An upstanding decent member of the community would tell me to take Jesus back, not join in with the antics.'

'But where's the fun in that?'

She smiled. 'I like you, Jacob Harrington.'

Ruby walked back into her shop and he watched her go. He liked her as well, too damned much.

CHAPTER 10

RUBY GAVE ONE LAST LOOK AROUND THE SHOP. Everything was ready for the big opening tomorrow. And now the snow had settled and was continuing to fall outside, she couldn't have asked for a more festive start to her big open day. She switched off the lights and moved to the archway.

Jacob was busy sorting out cutlery into different piles, no doubt for his next project.

'I'm off now, I'll see you tomorrow.'

He looked up and smiled. 'Before you go, I have a present for you.'

She frowned. 'A present?'

He shrugged. 'Let's call it an opening day present.'

He stood up and grabbed a neatly wrapped shoe box from the side and brought it over to her.

'Should I open it tomorrow?'

'No, I think you should open it now. You might want to do something with it tonight.'

She smiled and eagerly lifted the lid. She stared at the contents for a second. A red scarf, some coal and a carrot.

Her heart leapt and she looked up at Jacob as he presented her with a grand-looking top hat.

'It's a snowman-making kit,' he explained.

'Oh my god, I love it.' Ruby threw her arms around him to say thank you and he wrapped his arms around her. She quickly pulled back before she could get too carried away. 'Thank you, this is amazing.'

'Well, you said I owed you a snowman and I thought you might want to make one tonight, outside your shop ready for the opening tomorrow.'

'That's a wonderful idea. Will you help me?'

'I'd love to. Let me just get my coat.'

He raced off upstairs and, as she heard him moving around, it occurred to her that making a snowman together was definitely a very coupley thing to do. But right now, there was no one in the world that she wanted to make a snowman with more.

He came back downstairs and into the shop all bundled up against the cold as Ruby pulled her own coat and hat on.

She grabbed the box and followed Jacob outside. It was still snowing but not quite as heavily as before. The whole street was covered in a thick blanket of white glitter, making it look magical. There was not a soul in sight and it was completely and utterly silent. It felt like they were the only two people in the world.

'It's so beautiful,' Ruby said softly.

'It is. Some might say it was romantic.'

She looked up at him and smiled. 'I think I'll have to give you that.'

He grinned, then looked around. 'OK, you're in charge, what shall we do first?'

'Right, we need a big bottom,' Ruby said, gathering snow together to make a ball and then beginning to roll it across the ground so it gathered more snow. Jacob started helping her, as it was getting heavier as it got fatter. 'God, I haven't made a snowman in so long.'

'Is it like riding a bike?' Jacob asked.

'Yeah, you never forget.'

They finished the bottom and packed snow around the ground to make it more solid and then smoothed off the sides.

'Now I don't know about you but I'm definitely a three-ball snowman kind of person.'

Jacob smiled at her, the snow catching on his beautiful long eyelashes. 'I have no preference either way when it comes to how many balls a snowman should have. Generally two balls are enough in most cases, but I'm happy to go with three on this occasion.'

'Are you being rude, Jacob Harrington?' Ruby laughed.

'No, I wouldn't dream of it.'

'OK, well you can make the middle ball and I'll make the top.'

She watched him for a moment, carefully rolling his ball. He was taking this very seriously.

Soon the three balls were finished and stacked neatly on top of each other, the edges were smoothed down and snow was packed between the layers.

She picked up the box and took out the red scarf, wrapping it around the neck of the snowman and tying it in a knot. Jacob placed the hat on its head and she set about adding the coal for the eyes and buttons. He passed her the carrot so she could add the final finishing touch. She carefully wedged it into the face until it was firmly in place and then stood back to admire their handiwork.

'He does look really rather splendid, doesn't he?' Ruby said, leaning her head against Jacob's shoulder.

He wrapped an arm around her. 'He really does.'

They stood there in silence for a while, admiring their snowman as the snow continued to fall around them in the inky darkness.

'Honestly, this is the nicest thing that anyone has ever done for me.'

'Ah Ruby Marlowe. You set the bar very low, if a carrot and a few lumps of coal can make you this happy.'

She laughed. 'I can't help it, anything Christmas-related and I'm sold. Thank you for doing this.'

'It was my pleasure.'

She looked up at the sign above Jacob's half of the shop. Phoenix Blade. The sign above her shop was currently blank, which looked a bit odd. It was almost as if he was waiting for his other half to be complete. Could she fill that gap? Professionally of course. Or maybe… something more?

She glanced up at him and he stared down at her. Their lips were now only inches apart and she could feel his breath on her cheeks. Her heart started racing, his eyes darkened. God, he was going to kiss her and she wanted that more than anything.

She straightened and stepped away. 'Well I better go; I need to make some gingerbread men for tomorrow and Willow is coming round to help me.'

He shoved his hands in his pockets and kicked the snow with his foot. He nodded and smiled sadly. 'I'll see you tomorrow.'

She gave him a little wave and hurried off into the darkness, not daring to turn around.

What was she doing?

RUBY CAREFULLY PIPED ICING onto the ginger-bread men she had made ready for the grand opening the next day, focussing all her attention on that and not what had nearly happened between her and Jacob.

'I saw your post on the forum from Jesus,' Willow said, with a grin. 'I think if you didn't want to make it into a big thing, you failed spectacularly. No one really cared before apart from Julia, now the whole village has got involved.'

Ruby laughed. The reaction and comments from the villagers about Jesus's holiday had been far better than she ever could have dreamed of. Every single comment had been about how hilarious it was and asking where Jesus was going to show up next. She barely needed any encouragement but she knew she'd have to up her game for the next post.

Ruby looked at all the gingerbread men. Some of them were wrapped, some were drying, others that were waiting to be decorated.

'Do you think I made too much?'

'No, I think they'll be very popular and you can always sell the ones that don't get taken in your shop or at the Cookie Competition the next day.'

'I hope people come tomorrow,' Ruby said as she passed the biscuit to Willow so she could add on the Smarties for the eyes and the buttons.

'They will, of course they will. It's a new shop so people will be curious to see what you're selling. And we are only just under a week away until the big day so everyone is feeling in the festive mood,' Willow said. 'Plus you have Jacob next door and he's very popular with all the ladies.'

And there he was. He was impossible to get away from, even when he wasn't physically in the room. Ruby tried to ignore the pang of jealousy that cut through her at those words.

'I bet he has loads of girlfriends,' Ruby said, trying to carry off an air of nonchalance. She focussed her attention on the gingerbread men so Willow couldn't see how much she was interested in her answer.

'If he has, I've certainly never seen him

with one since he moved here. He might be with women outside of Happiness but he definitely hasn't played hide the sausage with anyone here.'

Ruby laughed loudly at that lovely image.

She carried on icing the gingerbread man. 'What about Lucy?'

'Oh, I don't think you have anything to worry about there,' Willow said, placing her finished man on the baking tray to set.

'She likes him.'

'I think they have history,' Willow said.

Ruby found her head snapping up to look at her. Megan had said the same thing.

'Oh, not like that,' Willow said. 'At least I don't think so. I think he just knew her before he came here.'

'*Knew her*?' She gave a hefty squeeze on the icing bag. As Jacob himself had said he didn't have any female friends, it was unlikely they'd had that kind of relationship. Willow was watching her reaction with interest. Ruby shrugged. 'Oh, I'm not bothered. He can do what he wants, see who he wants, I don't care.'

Willow took the gingerbread man Ruby was icing off her. He had been doused rather heavily with icing as she had been talking. 'It's OK to care.'

Ruby sat down on one of the bar stools in the kitchen and sighed because she did care and she didn't have any right to.

'So it's all going well with Jacob?' Willow asked.

'It's going very well, better than I could have hoped for actually,' Ruby said. 'I didn't think we could really be friends after what happened in the summer. I thought we might be polite to each other but it's been really lovely. I have loved working alongside him over the last few days. He makes me laugh, he is easy to talk to and he's just a wonderful man.' She cringed a little about gushing so much over him. But she could at least be honest with her best friend. 'We nearly kissed tonight.'

'What?' Willow stared at her; the ginger-bread man forgotten.

'I told him yesterday that making a snowman would feature very high on my list of a perfect Christmas and that he had to have a red scarf, coal for eyes and a carrot nose. And tonight, as I was getting ready to leave, he gave me a snowman-making kit with those things in,' Ruby swallowed down the lump in her throat because it was ridiculous to get emotional about a few lumps of coal. 'And we made a snowman together and then... well there was snow and just the two of us and...' she cleared her throat, 'and then I ran away.'

'Oh Ruby.'

'He makes me feel things I don't want to feel.'

'But you can't just run away from that.'

'It worked pretty well tonight.'

'Come on, what are you going to do?'

Ruby grabbed another gingerbread man and iced a sad face onto its head.

'It's not as if sleeping with him would

help to get him out of my system. I already know what that's like and it's bloody spectacular.'

'Well that sounds like something you should definitely pursue,' Willow teased.

If only it was that simple.

Willow frowned. 'You're not thinking of leaving, are you?'

'Why would I leave?'

'So you don't have to be around him.'

'But that didn't work, did it? After I saw him in the summer I didn't see him for four or five months and I come back and those feelings are still as strong as they were then.'

Willow's concern clearly didn't lessen any.

'I'm not leaving, this is my home. This thing between me and him is not serious,' Ruby said with more conviction than she felt. 'I might have feelings for him but I don't love him. And like eating chocolate every day, you can have too much of a good thing. I'm sure I'll soon get bored of him.'

'I don't think I could ever get bored of

chocolate,' Willow said. 'Even if I did eat it every day.'

Ruby sighed because Willow was right. She didn't think she would ever have her fill of Jacob Harrington.

JACOB WAS WATCHING TV when he heard someone letting themselves into the shop and then start walking up the stairs to his flat.

He wondered if it was Ruby and he quickly shot up and started tidying up, taking his dirty cups to the kitchen. Then he realised the foot-steps on the stairs were a lot heavier than someone Ruby's size would produce.

Andrew appeared in the doorway and grinned at Jacob obviously mid-tidy.

'It's OK, I'm not Ruby,' Andrew teased.

'I could tell the difference with you galumphing up the stairs.'

Jacob flopped back down on the sofa and immediately grabbed the TV remote and switched on the subtitles. It was an automatic thing. Although Andrew could hear pretty well with his hearing aids in, it was still easier for him to follow what was happening on TV with subtitles on, even if he had no interest in the programme about the Ancient Greeks Jacob had been vaguely watching.

'So are you really going through with this Polar Bear Plunge?' Andrew said, as he helped himself to a beer from the fridge.

The mention of it gave Jacob a sick feeling in his stomach.

'I think I have to. I've been telling Ruby she has to face her fears. It'd be a bit hypocritical if I couldn't face mine,' Jacob said.

'It's a bit different, you nearly died.'

'I don't know if it's that different. She lost her husband; I cannot even begin to imagine the pain she suffered from that. The courage to face that fear feels... insurmountable in comparison to a twenty-second swim in the sea.' He took a swig of his beer, trying to get rid of the bitter taste in his mouth. 'Although it doesn't mean I'm happy about doing it.'

His brother clearly had more to say on the subject but Jacob cut him off before he could dwell on it any longer. He really didn't want to talk about it anymore.

'What do I owe the *pleasure* of your company tonight anyway?' Jacob said.

'Well, I thought, as the girls are probably occupying themselves with talk about us, we could hang out and talk about them.'

'I'm sure Ruby has better things to talk about than me,' Jacob said.

'Well, she came to her shop today while I was fixing it. You definitely came up in conversation.'

He wasn't going to rise to the bait. He grabbed the remote again and flicked through the channels.

Andrew took a long deliberate swig of beer.

'Do you mean, *you* brought me up in conversation?' Jacob said.

'I can't remember how you came up,' Andrew said vaguely.

Jacob sighed. 'Go on then, I'll bite. What did she say?'

'Well, she's a bit concerned by your plans to get married and settle down.'

'She's concerned because she thinks those plans involve her.'

Andrew stole one of the crisps that were in a bowl on the table. 'And do they?'

'Do I want to marry someone who is terrified of marriage? I don't think so,' Jacob said, knowing he wasn't being entirely truthful with his brother. There was something about Ruby that made him think about forever.

'It's not as simple as that though, is it?' Andrew said. 'She's not terrified of marriage because she has weird commitment issues. She's scared of falling in love again and having that person cruelly taken from her.'

'I know,' Jacob said, softly. It was a lot more complicated than any relationship he'd ever had before, if the casual flings could be called that. He had avoided any baggage or emotional drama quite successfully with the women he'd been with in the past. But, strangely, Ruby's issues hadn't put him off.

Andrew sat down; all humour gone from his face. 'You like her?'

Jacob continued flicking through the channels before he sighed and turned to face his brother. 'I do and for many reasons that don't just involve great sex. She makes me laugh and I can really talk to her. Did you know she's started learning sign language so she can communicate with you and Poppy?'

'Well, that's really nice. A lot of people wouldn't bother to do that.'

Jacob nodded. 'I think I fell a little bit in love with her because of that.'

Andrew let out a heavy breath. 'I didn't realise… I just thought you two would pick up the casual arrangement you had in the summer; sex, no commitments, no attachments.'

'You know, I realised something today. I don't want that life anymore. I look at what you have with Willow and I want that. I think I've reached a point in my life where I don't want lots of meaningless women to keep me company, I want someone special to spend the rest of my life with.'

He waited for Andrew to take the piss but for once his brother was showing no sign of his usual sarcasm.

'So this is something serious for you?'

'It's not,' Jacob said and then sighed. He took a swig from his bottle of beer. 'It's not because she doesn't want it to be.'

'But you'd like it to be.'

Jacob didn't speak for the longest time. 'I really like her. But she's locked that part of her heart away and I don't think she's ready to open herself up to that again. Part of me wants to help her deal with that grief properly. She never talked about it when her husband died, kept it all bottled up and then tried to forget all about it. I want to help her move on and find happiness again, even if that happiness isn't with me.'

Andrew sighed. 'You've been down this road before with Ella and it didn't end well for you.'

Jacob flicked the bottle top he was holding into an empty bowl. It bounced off the side and landed on the floor.

Ella Bradley. Christ, it had been a long time since he had thought of her. They had been best friends in their early twenties and she would come to him with all of her problems. He had been there for her through everything, including numerous failed relationships with boyfriends. He would hold her when she cried, patch her back up and give her some advice on how she could win her man back. He had been in love with her, but she had never looked at him in that way. Jacob would often tell himself, it didn't matter, he just wanted his friend to be happy. But really it did matter. When she'd got married, it had broken his heart. And if he was honest with himself that was a big reason he'd avoided all emotional connections with women ever since.

'This is different,' Jacob said.

'I'm not sure how, but OK.'

Jacob wasn't sure either. He was not going to get what he wanted out of this. The more time he spent with Ruby, the more he knew he was falling for her. But the closer they got, the more she looked like a deer in the headlights of a car. His feelings for her, and her feelings for him, were scaring her away.

Andrew took a swig of beer, contemplating this issue. 'When Willow first moved to Happiness, she didn't want a relationship either after just coming out of a crap one. But our connection was just too strong to ignore. If you two are meant to be together, it will happen.'

'Thanks for that oh so wise cliché,' Jacob said.

Andrew laughed and raised his beer. 'I can get it printed on a t-shirt if you like.'

Jacob sighed. 'I think the big difference between Willow and Ruby is that Willow pretty much fell in love with you from the first time she met you, no matter that she tried to deny it. Ruby, as far as I can tell, is still hung up on her husband. If she loved me, or had any feelings for me, surely it would be worth the risk.'

Andrew shrugged. 'Maybe you just need to give her some time to realise that.'

Jacob nodded. If time was all she needed, he would give her as much of that as she wanted. He just had to hope that was enough.

CHAPTER 11

Ruby looked round the shop to check for the twentieth time that everything was in its place. Every surface gleamed and sparkled, the fairy lights twinkled, the baubles and decorations shone. Willow had even given her some Christmas-scented candles to light in her shop. Currently she had a Christmas-cookie-scented candle burning happily in the doorway and a toffee-apple-scented candle burning near the back of the shop. She had homemade mince pies, gingerbread men, mulled wine and hot chocolate to give out to any customers who might come through the door. She even had chocolate gold coins for any children, although they probably wouldn't come until after school.

Everything was ready.

She looked up and saw Jacob watching her, leaning against the archway between the two shops.

'Does it look OK?' Ruby asked.

'It looks great.'

She looked around again. 'I was so excited about having my own shop but now I'm just terrified. What if no one comes? What if I don't sell anything?'

'Firstly, everyone will come. I had the villagers coming in droves into my shop when I first opened.'

Ruby wondered if that had anything to do with Jacob being ridiculously good-looking and most of the women fancying him.

'Secondly, before the merry throngs come crashing through the door, I will be your first customer.'

Jacob pulled out his wallet from his back pocket and looked around.

'Stop it,' Ruby laughed. 'As if I'm going to let you buy anything. I'll give you whatever you want.'

'No, I want this to go through the till,' Jacob insisted. He moved around the shop and picked up a small giraffe with a Santa hat on. It was quirky and actually one of her favourite pieces. 'This little chap would be perfect in my shop.'

'Jacob, you don't need to buy it. You can have him.'

'No, how much is he?'

Ruby smiled at his insistence and walked over to the till. 'Two pounds fifty please.'

He handed her a fiver and she gave him the change then placed the giraffe in a little paper gift bag and passed it back to Jacob. She looked at this wonderful man and reached up and kissed him on the cheek. 'Thank you.'

He grinned. 'It was my pleasure. Now, what time is everyone coming?'

Her heart dropped into her stomach. Should she have arranged an official grand opening? 'Well… I… just thought that I would open and people would come in throughout the day.'

He rolled his eyes. 'You need to tell people, make it all official. I'll put something out on the forum. Go and open the door, I'm sure we'll have people coming shortly.'

She moved over to the door as he grabbed his phone from his pocket and started tapping away at it. She unlocked the door and peered outside into the cold, blustery street. It had been cold when she had walked to work earlier that morning but in the last few hours the wind had really got up. Although not as heavy as the day before, the snow was still falling and the wind was blowing the flakes in gusts across the street. An icy blast ripped through the houses and shops, rattling the shutters and bending the plants and bushes at odd angles. There was not a single soul in sight, everyone was probably tucked up in their homes and shops. No one was going to come all the way down here today.

She closed the door and sighed. So much for the grand opening.

She grabbed a gingerbread man and bit off one of his legs just as Jacob came back into her shop.

'Hey, don't eat all of them, the villagers are on their way.'

Ruby took another bite. She might get one or two customers later on if the wind dropped but she certainly wasn't going to get a big influx.

'It's OK,' she shrugged. 'At least I had one sale.'

She moved over to her desk and started getting out a few paints to decorate some of the glass baubles.

She was halfway through painting a holly leaf when she heard the shop door open and she smiled when she saw Julia wrapped up against the cold. She'd brought Dorothy and Liz with her, Roger was close behind and, as the door closed behind him, Tabitha and Connor from the pub pushed it back open again.

Ruby stood up and looked over at Jacob, who was grinning at her.

'What on earth did you write on that forum?'

'Only that it was your big opening and that everyone should come along.'

She watched as Mary and Ginny arrived in the shop, followed by a few others.

She looked back at Jacob, her heart filling up a little bit more for him. Whatever he'd written, it had worked.

She focussed her attention on her customers, offering them drinks and mince pies – anything to avoid the overwhelming feeling in her heart.

RUBY COULDN'T STOP SMILING. The place was heaving, it seemed like everyone in the village had turned up at some point that morning. The villagers had stayed, drank the wine and hot chocolate, ate the snacks and chatted like it was a party, with so many turning up at the start of the day that some of them had to stand in Jacob's shop. But amongst the party atmosphere, everyone had been genuinely interested in her baubles and decorations. Well, everyone except Lucy, who had walked in with a face like she'd sucked a lemon as she moved around Ruby's shop and looked at the different decorations.

Ruby still couldn't help wondering if something had happened between Lucy and Jacob, as Megan had said. She knew she had no right to care or be jealous but she did wonder why Jacob would go with someone like that. He was fun and kind and Lucy didn't look like that sort of person at all. Surely he wouldn't go to bed with Lucy just because she was attractive. Ruby shook her head. What did it matter who he slept with and why? They were friends, she had no claim to him beyond that.

But … as his friend she wanted the best for him, someone nice who would appreciate how amazing he was and see him as more than just another notch on the bedpost. Someone like Megan perhaps. She ignored the punch of sadness she felt at the thought of him with *anyone* else.

She decided to bite the bullet and go and talk to Lucy. She'd been kind enough to come to her opening, after all.

Ruby walked over. 'Hi Lucy, thanks for coming. Has anything caught your eye?'

Lucy laughed and not kindly. 'I think the same thing that has caught the eye of most of the women in here.'

She gestured to where Jacob was holding court in the middle of a gaggle of women of all ages. There was even a little girl of around six years old staring at Jacob like he was a god.

Was that really the reason why most of the women had come that day, so they could fawn over Jacob? Ruby had kind of hoped that the excitement of a new shop and interest in her unique, handmade decorations would be enough of a lure. She felt her bubble of happiness at the success of the day slowly deflate like a balloon.

But she decided to play along in the interest of getting some information from Lucy.

'He's easy on the eye, isn't he?' Ruby said.

'He is that. And amazing in bed.'

Oh well, if Lucy was going to get straight to the point then so could she.

'So you knew Jacob before you moved here. Were you and he a thing?'

'Oh, I know Jacob very well,' Lucy said, with a smug smile, which wasn't exactly answering the question. 'I bet you think all your Christmases have come at once being put next door to him.'

There was something very blunt about that question.

'Jacob's lovely,' Ruby said.

'I wouldn't get your hopes up. I think a man like Jacob has very particular tastes, the sort that will drink the finest wines. He could have any woman he wanted, so he's only going to pick the crème de la crème.'

Ruby was astonished that someone could be so blatantly rude.

'Well, that's very flattering, isn't it Ruby,' Julia said as she squeezed past them to get to some gold baubles painted with glittery red poinsettias. 'He slept with Ruby several times in the summer, so if Jacob only indulges in the finest wines, that must make Ruby Champagne.'

Ruby smiled and she had to bite her lip to keep from laughing out loud. Lucy was obviously less than impressed.

'You and Jacob slept together?' Lucy said, aghast, just as Jacob walked past.

'Yes, and let me tell you, she was the best sex I've ever had,' Jacob said as he helped himself to another cup of hot chocolate.

Ruby smirked. God she really bloody liked this man.

'Did you want a hot chocolate, Lucy?' Jacob asked.

'I'm fine thanks.'

'Pity,' Jacob said. 'You look like you could use something sweet.'

Oh wow, he'd totally just called her out on her bitchiness.

He turned his attention to his hot chocolate for a moment, spraying squirty cream on the top before taking a long sip. He moved back towards his shop but he had cream on the top of his lip.

Ruby stopped him and without thinking leaned up and wiped the cream away with her thumb. His eyes darkened at her touch as he looked down at her.

'You had cream on your lip,' Ruby said.

He slipped his tongue out and licked round his lips.

Oh god.

'All gone?'

She nodded, because right then there were no words in her head at all.

'Come up to my flat tonight, once you close. I think we should celebrate your first day,' Jacob said and Ruby was aware of Lucy and Julia standing nearby watching and listening to their every word. Jacob must have been aware of it too.

She smiled. 'Just the two of us?'

'All the best celebrations are with two people; you don't need more than that.' He surreptitiously winked so that Lucy wouldn't see him and Ruby smirked.

'Sounds good.'

He gave her shoulder a squeeze and moved off through the crowds of people.

Ruby cleared her throat and looked at her small audience. Julia was standing there obviously absolutely delighted with this new turn of events. Lucy had a face like thunder.

She didn't want to break it to either of them that she would probably go up to Jacob's flat for a glass of wine and would more than likely be tucked up under a blanket on her own sofa, wearing her snowman pyjamas by six o'clock, probably reading her new book. Alone.

'Ladies, is there anything else I can help you with?' Ruby smiled brightly.

They both shook their head and Ruby turned and left them to it.

RUBY LOOKED up from rearranging some of her displays. It was getting a bit quieter now, although there was still a good number of customers browsing her stock. She glanced over at Megan who had been hovering in her shop and Jacob's for the last few hours. It was lovely that Megan wanted to be so supportive, but the length of time she'd been here led Ruby to think she might have an ulterior motive. Ruby watched her as she glanced over in Jacob's direction as he chatted to some of the villagers. Her heart sank. After Ruby's meddling the day before, Megan was clearly here waiting for Jacob to ask her out and that wasn't going to happen.

Ruby took a deep breath and walked over to her. 'Hey Megan, how you doing?'

'Good. Good, thanks,' Megan said, eyeing Jacob again.

He wasn't looking at Megan at all and Ruby felt awful. She suddenly wanted Jacob to ask Megan out, even if that would make her green with jealousy. Jacob looked over and flashed Ruby a big smile.

Megan looked between the two of them and her shoulders slumped, her cheeks flushing bright red.

'He's not going to ask me to the Christmas Eve ball, is he?' Megan asked quietly, staring at her feet.

Ruby snagged her arm and pulled her to the back of her shop out of earshot of the other customers. 'I'm so sorry, Megan. This is all my fault. *I* told Lucas that Jacob was going to ask you to the ball.'

Megan stared at her. 'Why would you do that if it's not true?'

'Because I was hoping it might encourage Lucas to ask you instead.'

Her shoulders slumped even more. 'Lucas doesn't like me that way.'

'He does, anyone can see that. Why do you think he was so upset about Jacob asking you to the ball?'

Megan shrugged. 'Pete sees me as a little sister. Lucas probably feels the same. He was just being protective.'

'There was a lot more to it than that.'

'I thought if Jacob asked me to the ball Lucas would finally see me as someone who is desirable. I have this gorgeous dress and I thought if Lucas saw me in it, he'd finally see me as something more than just Pete's little sister-in-law.'

'The way he looks at you, I promise you there is nothing sisterly about that,' Ruby said. 'Look, if you like Lucas, why don't you ask him to the ball?'

'I couldn't do that. I have to see him at all

the family events and get-togethers. If he says no, it would be so awkward.'

'But what if he says yes?' Ruby said.

Megan shook her head. 'If he liked me, he'd ask me out.'

'He probably thinks it would be awkward too, for the reasons you mentioned,' Ruby said.

Megan sighed. 'Why is it so complicated?'

Just as Ruby was trying to think of some way out of this. Jacob walked past. He saw them huddled into the corner and came over. 'Is everything OK?'

'We're just complaining about men and why they're so bloody hard to read,' Megan said.

'Ah, I see, I apologise for my gender,' Jacob said.

'I don't think you have anything to apologise for, you're pretty much an open book,' Megan said, with exasperation. 'You see something you want and you go after it.'

Ruby smirked. That was true. Jacob had

made no secret of his feelings for her since she'd come back.

'Is this about Lucas?' Jacob asked.

'Oh my god, am I that obvious?' Megan said, her cheeks flushing bright red again.

'No, but he is. He came in here earlier and told me in no uncertain terms that I was to keep my hands off you and if I was lucky enough to go to the ball with you then I was to treat you like a queen. He told me if I broke your heart, there'd be hell to pay.'

Megan stared at him. 'Are you serious?'

Jacob nodded.

Megan clearly thought about this for a moment. 'Well, that's pretty significant.'

Both Ruby and Jacob nodded encouragingly but then Megan sighed. 'We're not even speaking right now. How can I tell him that it's him I want to go to the ball with when he won't even talk to me?'

'Well, the cookie-decorating competition is tomorrow,' Ruby said. 'Maybe I should pull a few strings and make sure you're both on the same table. You'll have to talk to each other then. Even if you don't declare your feelings for him or ask him to the ball, at least you might spend enough time with each other to be friends again.'

Megan nodded. 'I'd like that. Look, I should go. I did actually come in here to buy something for my tree.' She moved forward into the shop and plucked a decoration off one of the shelves. She showed it to Ruby. It was of two snowmen hugging. 'I saw this but wasn't sure if it would be too optimistic.'

'Take it,' Ruby said. 'Give it to Lucas if you can't face telling him how you feel. He might actually get the hint.'

Megan smiled. 'Thank you. But let me pay.'

'No, I insist, after the damage I did interfering, it's the least I can do.'

'Thank you,' Megan said. Tucking the ornament carefully into her bag, she left the shop.

Ruby turned to Jacob. 'Did Lucas really say those things to you?'

'Yeah.'

'What did you say?'

'I told him, if he was so worried about me taking her to the ball, maybe he should ask her himself. He stormed off at that though, saying I didn't understand.'

Ruby frowned. 'I hope we haven't got this all completely wrong and sent Megan off to make a fool of herself.'

'He likes her. I can see it in his eyes,' Jacob said. 'Whatever reason he is holding himself back, it's not because he doesn't have feelings for her.'

Ruby sighed. She should never have interfered.

'And she was right about one thing,' Jacob went on. 'When I want something, I go after it.'

She smirked. 'Doesn't mean you'll get it though.'

He grinned. 'We'll see.'

RUBY TURNED THE 'OPEN' shop sign to 'Closed' and locked the door. She'd had the most successful, profitable day ever with her till ringing almost non-stop. Her shop was looking more than a little depleted now and she would have to spend some time making and sourcing some more decorations, but she didn't care. Almost everyone in the village had turned up at some point in the day. Willow and Andrew had chosen all their tree decorations together, so they could decorate their first tree in their home. Even Kitty and Ken had turned up and bought decorations for all the tables for the Christmas Eve ball.

The day had been a huge success.

And now she was going to celebrate.

She jogged upstairs to Jacob's flat and found him pouring out two glasses of champagne. He looked up and watched her with a smile as she did a little excited jig on the spot, then she ran over and hugged him. He immediately wrapped his arms around her and hugged her back.

What had purely been a celebratory hug seemed to quickly escalate into something more. Even though neither of them had moved, there was this… spark between them. Truth be told, that spark had been there since she had arrived back in the village. She stood there listening to his heartbeat, relishing the warmth and comfort of his arms. She had firmly drawn a line under what happened between them in the summer, laid down the rules, but she had no desire to step away and neither, it seemed, did he.

After the longest time, she looked up at him and he was smiling at her.

God, she wanted to kiss him so much right then.

He brushed a hair from her face. 'I'm glad you've had a good day.'

'Thanks to you.'

'Not thanks to me at all. The villagers are all very welcoming and supportive, you'll learn that. All I put on the forum was that your shop was now officially open and it would be lovely to see everyone here.'

Ruby wasn't totally sure she believed him but, regardless of what he had said to get them there, and even if many of the women had come purely to see him, the villagers had bought the decorations of their own free will.

'Well, thank you,' Ruby said. He was still holding her and her arms were still wrapped around his back. 'For everything.'

'For what?'

'For being a great friend since I've been here. For listening to me, for helping me un-pack, for making me dinner, for... just being there.'

'Always.'

'And thanks for the compliment too. Downstairs, with Lucy,' Ruby explained when Jacob clearly didn't know what she meant.

'Oh, well it sounded like Lucy needed taking down a peg or two. Besides, I was only speaking the truth.'

Ruby gave a bark of a laugh. 'I'm the best sex you've ever had?'

'Yes.'

'How many women have you slept with?'

He pulled a face. 'A lot.'

'And I'm the best?' Ruby said, incredulously. 'I bet you say that to all the women.'

'Ruby, we had something special. I know you don't want to admit that but we did.'

Panic fluttered in her heart and she stepped away, shaking her head.

'And there it is,' Jacob said.

'There what is?'

'The look of fear you get every time you try to pretend you don't have feelings for me.'

'God, you're so arrogant, I don't have any feelings for you,' Ruby said, fear clawing at her throat. She couldn't face this. She moved away.

'I wish this was just my arrogance, because I could walk away from that very easily. But there's something between us and it's not just one-sided.'

She shook her head.

'I'm trying to help, I'm trying to fix this, but I feel every time we take a step closer, you take three steps away from me,' Jacob said.

'I don't need your help, I don't need to be fixed,' Ruby said, turning back round to face him.

'You think hiding away from any emotional connection for the last twelve years is perfectly normal. You think that being scared to fall in love again, pushing away the people you care about, is a healthy way to live?'

Ruby had no words to defend herself.

Jacob took a step closer. 'Last night, in the snow, we nearly kissed, but then you panicked and ran away.'

'I did not panic. I just didn't want to kiss you.'

'You're scared of letting me in, of getting close, you're scared to kiss me or sleep with me because you know that all those feelings you're keeping locked inside would come tumbling out.'

'That's rubbish. I could kiss you without feeling anything,' Ruby said, knowing the words were a complete lie.

'Really?' Jacob said.

'Yes, absolutely.'

Jacob bent his head and kissed her.

CHAPTER 12

SHE HESITATED FOR JUST A SECOND BEFORE SHE was kissing him back. The kiss was angry at first but it quickly turned to something passionate and needful. She ran her hands down his shoulders, running them over the strong muscles in his back. His hands were at her waist where he suddenly hauled her closer.

God she wanted this man so much. She found her hands on the buttons of his shirt, desperately tugging them open as the kiss continued. He shuffled her back into his bedroom. Holy shit, they were really going to do this and there was not a single part of her that didn't want this. Greedy hands explored each other's bodies. He pinned her against the wall next to his bed, his shirt fell to the floor and still the kiss continued. She caressed his arms, his chest, his stomach. With one swift movement, he pulled her dress over her head and let that fall on the floor too. She reached for the belt on his jeans and fumbled to undo it. He kissed her again and she desperately pushed his jeans and his shorts down as he made quick work of the rest of her clothes so they were both naked.

'Condom,' she muttered against his lips.

'Not yet,' Jacob said.

She let out a groan of frustration but that groan quickly turned to one of pleasure as he placed kisses across her breast.

He slipped his hand between her legs, stroking and touching, that feeling was there but just out of reach.

'God, Jacob, please.'

But he was not to be deterred, he kept on stroking and slipped her nipple into his mouth. She cupped the back of his head, that feeling spreading inside of her so she felt like her whole body was on fire. She shouted out his name, trembling in his arms as he held her there against the wall.

She lifted his head and kissed him and she heard him fumble in his bedside drawers for a condom.

He pulled away from her for a few seconds while he slid it on and then he was kissing her again.

He lifted her and she wrapped her legs around him. He pulled back slightly to look at her.

'Are you sure you want this, Ruby?'

'It's not possible for me to want you more than I want you right now.'

'Is that a yes?' he teased.

'God, yes. Hit me with it.'

He laughed, loudly, and she could feel the vibrations of it through her body. 'I'm not going to hit you with it. I'm not sure what kind of sex you've been having, Ruby

Marlowe, but that's not how this thing works.'

She giggled against his lips. 'Show me how it works.'

'My pleasure.'

He slid inside her in one exquisite move.

'God Jacob.'

He moved against her slowly, taking his time as he pinned her to the wall with his weight.

Nothing compared to this. Nothing ever would.

'I missed you so much,' she whispered.

'It's OK, I'm here now.'

She arched into him, pulling him tighter against her, and that glorious feeling started building in her again.

'I need this, I need you,' Ruby said, letting all her emotions tumble out.

'I'm here, always.'

She felt herself fall apart around him, as he moved against her harder and faster. She shouted out all manner of words and clung to him barely able to catch her breath as he carried her to the bed and collapsed down on top of her. He carried on moving against her, his eyes on her the whole time. She stroked down his back and he kissed her as he moaned against her lips.

He pulled back to look at her, his breath heavy, and as she stared into his beautiful blue eyes, she didn't think she had ever felt so complete in her entire life.

JACOB STROKED his hand down Ruby's back. She was lying on his chest, presumably asleep or at least dozing.

He wasn't sure how he had ended up here, with this incredible woman in his arms. He had reconciled with himself that it was never going to happen again and yet here they were.

She stirred and looked up at him. They hadn't said a word since they'd had sex and he had no idea where he stood with her now or what would happen between them next. He didn't think he could handle just being friends again but he knew she would hardly be willing to jump straight into a proper relationship just because they'd had amazing sex.

'Hey beautiful,' he said, stroking her hair.

Something like fear flashed in her eyes and she scrambled out of bed.

'I should go. This was a mistake.'

He felt that like a punch to his gut. She thought sleeping with him had been a mistake when he had been so blissfully happy about it moments before.

She started gathering her clothes from where they were strewn around the room.

He swallowed. Nothing had changed. Yet it felt like everything had. She still liked him and during sex she had been unguarded with her feelings. She liked him a hell of a lot more than just two people having casual sex. But she was still running away. She wasn't ready to face those emotions yet.

'Why are you going?'

'Because we shouldn't have done this,' Ruby said, seemingly looking around for some item of her clothes.

'But we did and running away isn't going to change that,' Jacob said, carefully. He felt like he was dealing with a frightened animal.

'But this means more to you than it does to me. I can see that. This wasn't what that was. This was just two friends having incredible un-complicated no-strings-attached sex, this was never going to be the next big love story of Happiness.'

He sighed. 'I know you would like to be-lieve that was what it was but we both know it was a hell of a lot more than that.'

'I'm sorry, I really am. I never wanted to hurt you Jacob, that was the last thing I wanted, but I'm not looking for a relationship or love.' Ruby pulled her bra on.

'Just because you don't want to fall in love doesn't mean you can simply push those feel-ings away.'

'I don't have those feelings for you. I don't,'

Ruby said and Jacob got the feeling that she was trying to convince herself more than she was trying to convince him.

She reached for her knickers and he put a hand out to stall her. There was no way in hell he was going to let her go now that he had her.

'Look Ruby, I like you a lot, probably a lot more than I should. But if you just want no-strings-attached sex then that's absolutely fine with me.'

She paused for the longest time as if she was weighing it up. He used the opportunity to gently pull her back onto the bed and she didn't resist.

'You and I both know that being just friends wasn't working,' Jacob said. 'We wouldn't have ended up in bed together with the first kiss we've had in months if that was the case. It was torture for me to work along-side you and not be able to kiss you or take you to bed and I think you felt the same. Don't you think we should at least try the no-strings-attached route for a while?'

He had no idea why he was suggesting this. The last thing he wanted was casual, meaningless sex with her. But he couldn't walk away from her either. He knew she was scared of what she felt for him. Maybe the more time they spent together, the more willing she might be to take a risk on them.

'I don't want to hurt you,' Ruby said.

'I'm a big boy, I can look after myself. If we have no-strings-attached sex for the next few weeks and it comes to an end, or we have no-strings-attached sex for the rest of our lives with no emotional attachment or commitment, I'll be absolutely fine.'

She arched an eyebrow in amusement. 'No-strings-attached sex for the rest of our lives?'

He shrugged. 'If you want.'

'Exclusively?'

'Yes.' There was definitely not any room for negotiation on that point.

'That kind of sounds like a relationship,' Ruby said.

'Nope. Two friends having sex. That's it.'

She looked doubtful.

'Look, you end this whenever you want,' Jacob said. 'You call the shots.'

He placed a kiss on her shoulder and he felt her melt against him.

'I'm in charge?' Ruby said as he placed another kiss on her throat.

'Definitely.'

She shifted round and straddled him. 'And I can do whatever I want with you?'

'You have my full permission to use me however you see fit.'

He slipped her bra from her shoulders and then placed kisses over her breast.

She let out a sigh of contentment. 'Well, I could definitely get used to this.'

He stroked his hands down her back, caressing her hips, and she moaned softly as he continued to kiss across her breasts. She reached over to the drawers and grabbed another condom and ripped it open with her teeth. She rolled it on him, her touch almost unravelling him. She shifted over him and the next thing he was deep inside her. She kissed him hard as he moved his hands to her hips, holding her close. She wrapped her arms round his neck, stroking the hair at the back of his head. They moved in perfect sync with each other, stroking and caressing in the exact places where they knew the other liked to be touched.

He felt her breath change on his lips and he pulled back to look at her. The adoration for him in her eyes floored him. There was no way this was just sex for her. And he was prepared to wait for however long it took for her to realise it too. He would be there for her in any way she wanted, he would slowly whittle away at her defences so her wall came tumbling down and maybe, just maybe, he could make her ever after a happy one.

JACOB WOKE WITH A START, his heart hammering against his chest, a cold film of sweat coating his body. It was dark and for a few panicky seconds he wondered where he was.

'Hey, are you OK?' Ruby said, gently, stroking his chest.

God, she was here and she was exactly what he needed right then.

He pulled her into his arms and held her tight while she stroked his back soothingly.

'I am now,' he muttered, feeling his heart rate slow.

It had been years since he'd had that dream, water pounding over his head, being dragged along the sea bed, fighting to get to the surface, his lungs screaming for much needed air and then finally breaking the surface and trying to get to the shore but being pulled further and further out to sea. The land disappearing from view and that desperate feeling of hopelessness that he would never be found. He shuddered in Ruby's arms and held her tighter.

'Are you sure you're OK?' Ruby said,

stroking the back of his head. 'You were moaning in your sleep.'

'Just a bad dream,' Jacob said.

God, maybe Andrew was right. Maybe he shouldn't do this Polar Bear Plunge. Maybe his first reintroduction into the sea should be on a calm summer's day, not in the middle of a snowy cold winter. If he explained what had happened to Ruby, she would understand. He pulled back to look at her and saw nothing but affection and concern for him shining from her eyes. He couldn't pull out now. He had to do this for her, not just to raise money for the British Heart Foundation, which he knew was important to her, but also to encourage her to face her own fears.

It was ridiculous for him to get so worked up over something that had happened nearly twenty years ago and it was time he got over that once and for all. He only hoped that one day Ruby would be able to move past her fears too.

CHAPTER 13

RUBY WOKE THE NEXT DAY TO THE SOUND OF someone moving around the flat. As Jacob was wrapped tight around her, she wondered who it could be. Andrew maybe? Who else would just let themselves into Jacob's flat? Although it was hardly likely to be a burglar in the sleepy village of Happiness.

Ruby disentangled herself from Jacob's arms, and started getting dressed. She watched Jacob sleeping as she pulled on her clothes. He was lying there, naked, with a huge smile on his face. She didn't know whether to be delighted or terrified by this 'no-strings-attached' arrangement. He was right, they couldn't just be friends; they'd tried it and it hadn't worked. But was friends with benefits going to work either? The last thing she wanted was to hurt Jacob and if he really started to fall for her she would have to end things between them before they went too far. If he was hoping she would fall in love with him, then he would be sadly mistaken. She liked him a lot but she was never going to fall in love with him. She touched the snowflake necklace Harry had given her. She had learned her lesson there.

She walked out into the living area of the flat, to find Jacob's sister Lottie and his niece Poppy busily decorating Jacob's flat for Christmas. Poppy was draping garlands of tinsel over everything and Lottie was tying baubles here, there and everywhere. As someone who liked things very minimalist in terms of décor, Jacob probably wouldn't be a huge fan of what they were doing now. Ruby couldn't help but laugh at this.

Lottie whirled round to see where the noise had come from and her eyebrows almost disappeared into her hairline at seeing Ruby standing there. Ruby had met Lottie a few times in the summer as she lived in the next town to Happiness and, while she'd probably not made the greatest first impression, Jacob's sister had started to warm to her towards the end of Ruby's stay.

She wondered how Lottie would take finding her here.

'Ruby, sorry, we weren't expecting anyone to be here. Jacob always goes over to Penzance early on a Tuesday, so we thought we'd surprise him with redecorating his home,' Lottie said.

Ruby felt a little kick of disappointment that Jacob wouldn't be there today if he was going off to Penzance. The Christmas Cookie Competition was taking place that afternoon and she had wondered if he would take part and maybe even if they could be a team. Although was that activity too... *cosy* for two people not in a proper relationship?

Lottie's eyes drifted up to Ruby's hair, which was probably showing the signs of a night of passion. 'I have to say, when Jacob mentioned you were working next door and living in the village now, I did wonder if you two would get together again.' She paused. 'He really likes you.'

Ruby didn't know what to say to that.

'I hope we didn't … interrupt anything?' Lottie said.

'No, Jacob's fast asleep,' Ruby said honestly. There was no point lying about what she was doing there. Lottie certainly wouldn't appreciate that if and when she found out the truth, but Ruby didn't need to go into specifics about what she'd spent the night doing with Jacob. She'd leave that to Lottie's imagination.

Although she didn't know how she was going to explain her presence to Poppy. She glanced over at the little girl, who currently had no idea that Ruby was standing there.

Lottie followed her gaze and must have read her mind. 'I'm sure you can make something up.'

Lottie moved over to Poppy who was laying tinsel around the room in gay abandon and tapped her gently on the shoulder.

Poppy turned round and jumped a little to see Ruby standing there. Poppy waved hello and Ruby returned the gesture.

Poppy started signing, her little hands flying at a hundred miles an hour.

'She wants to know what you're doing here?' Lottie said, smirking.

'Yeah, I gathered that. I, umm… learned to sign. I understand a lot more than I can sign, so I might need a bit of help, but I can probably communicate fairly well with her.'

Lottie looked at her in surprise. 'You learned to sign?'

Ruby nodded. She turned her attention back to Poppy and carefully signed to her. '*Me and Jacob were working very hard and very late last night on my Christmas shop downstairs and I ended up sleeping here.'*

Poppy nodded.

'Your Christmas shop is beautiful,' Poppy signed, seemingly accepting that excuse completely.

'Thank you.' Ruby signed back. *'Are you here to make Jacob's home more festive?'*

Poppy nodded eagerly.

'Can I help?' Ruby signed and the little girl nodded again. *'I have more decorations downstairs in my shop. Give me a few minutes and I'll grab some stuff.'*

Poppy clapped her hands together excitedly and Ruby hurried off downstairs, selecting the brightest, craziest pieces she could get her hands on.

She returned to see Jacob had emerged from his bedroom wearing only his jeans, looking all sleepy and dishevelled and sexy.

He was chatting away to Poppy and obviously amused by the whole redecoration that was going on.

Jacob looked over at her as she walked back in and his whole face lit up. 'I thought you'd gone.'

'And miss out on a chance to Christmassify your home? Not a chance,' Ruby said, dumping her wares on the table. She turned back to Poppy and signed. *'Where shall I start?'*

'The kitchen,' Poppy replied.

Ruby nodded and then realised Jacob was watching her in awe, which wasn't good. She didn't need to give him any more ammunition to fall in love with her.

'When you told me you could sign a few words, I wasn't expecting this,' he said.

'I may have played it down.'

Jacob stared at her and then broke into a huge smile. 'Did anyone ever tell you, you're pretty bloody amazing?'

She smiled and picked up a brightly coloured string of Christmas stocking bunting and turned away. He made her feel so warm inside. This friends-with-benefits malarkey was going to get very complicated.

Jacob passed Poppy her hot chocolate with extra cream, marshmallows, sprinkles and even a flake on top and she plopped down on the sofa to drink it. He watched as she got cream on the end of her nose and smiled. Ruby would certainly appreciate a hot chocolate like that, it was a shame she'd had to rush off after they had finished decorating. He went back to the kitchen to get his and Lottie's drinks and then sat down next to his sister.

'Thank you for this,' Jacob gestured to his flat which now impossibly looked more Christmassy than Ruby's shop.

Lottie grinned at him. 'It was my pleasure.'

'Are you two going to hang around here for a few hours? There's a cookie-decorating competition this afternoon,' Jacob said, taking a sip. Poppy was focussing her attention on finding all the tiny marshmallows amongst the big dollop of whipped cream.

'Poppy will love that.'

'And we have the Angel Festival tomorrow. Everyone has to make a sculpture of an angel, using whatever you wish to use to make it, cardboard boxes, toilet rolls. I'm sure Poppy would enjoy doing that too.'

'Are we allowed to take part; we don't live here?' Lottie asked.

'Of course, the more the merrier, and we're raising money for charity so we want as many participants as possible. It was all Ruby's idea.'

'Along with the Polar Bear Plunge,' Lottie said.

He sighed. 'Andrew told you about it.'

'Yeah, I can't believe you're doing it.'

'It's not a big deal, not really, is it? It's just a ten or twenty-second splash in the sea. It's only an issue because of what happened in the past but maybe it's time I got over that.'

Lottie stared at him. 'While I applaud your *get back on the horse* mentality, is there another reason you're doing this after twenty years of never going in the sea?'

'It's for charity,' Jacob shrugged.

'You're doing this for Ruby, aren't you?'

He paused. 'I guess so.'

'You really like her, don't you?'

'We're… just casual. No strings attached. You know me.'

'I do know you, that's why I'm worried. I see the way you look at her and I don't think you're going to get what you want out of this.'

'You're probably right, but if it ends, it ends, I'll cope.'

He ignored the ache in his heart that said otherwise. He would be gutted if this thing didn't work out between him and Ruby. Was he setting himself up for a fall?

'I've seen how much hurt it can cause when one person is more into a relationship than the other,' Lottie said.

'Are you talking about your mystery man?'

Lottie smiled. 'He's not a mystery man.'

'But you won't tell me his name.'

'That's because he's a bit of a celebrity and you're about as discreet as a washerwoman when it comes to gossip. I'm sure he wouldn't appreciate anyone finding out he slept with some random woman who worked in the hotel he was staying at. I'm sure my boss wouldn't appreciate finding out I slept with one of the guests either.'

'From what you told me, it was a lot more than a one-night stand, at least for him,' Jacob said.

'It was more than that for me too and, yes, I think I broke his heart when I pushed him away and that kills me.'

Jacob knew Lottie was still hurting after her ex-husband had left and because of that she had been scared when she got involved with her mystery man. She had ended up pushing him away and he knew she had regretted it ever since.

'All I'm saying is, if this really is a casual arrangement between you and Ruby, then you can't let yourself fall in love with her, because you'll end up getting hurt. If you do feel something more for her, then I think you have to be brave enough to end it before it gets too far.'

Jacob sighed and nodded. He knew his sister was right.

RUBY SPRINKLED flour on the unit top and rolled out the biscuit dough so it was the same thickness all over. She had been busy making biscuits all morning and her arms were starting to ache from all the stirring and rolling.

Almost everyone in the village had signed up for the Christmas Cookie Competition that afternoon. It was lovely that everyone was so supportive but the logistics of doing such a big competition were not something she had thought through when she had offered it to the village. Kitty and Ken had agreed to using the great hall at the castle as they wouldn't be setting up for the ball until the afternoon the next day, but now Ruby had to provide all the cookies and they needed to be big enough to be decorated by the villagers too.

Ruby carefully cut out the biscuit circles and placed them on the baking tray.

Making the cookies did have the added advantage of not having to face Jacob. She just wasn't sure how to handle being around him right now. They hadn't kissed or even touched since the night before when they had agreed to this bizarre arrangement so he was keeping to his side of the bargain. They were friends who would have sex, nothing more. But even she could see this plan had flaws. Great big gaping ones. Could they really work alongside each other during the day, have no-strings-attached sex every night and not develop any feelings for each other at all? In reality she knew it wouldn't work like that. Her feelings for him had definitely intensified over the last few days. Sleeping with him on a regular basis would cement them in place.

They had spent an hour that morning with Lottie and Poppy making his flat look like a grotto. And despite her anti-romance rule, she had enjoyed being with his family and laughing and joking with him. He'd even asked her if she wanted to join him, Andrew and Lottie for Christmas Day and she'd said yes, though she wasn't sure why. If she was honest, the whole thing with Jacob was terrifying her. The thought of letting herself fall in love with this man and then losing him like she did Harry made panic grip her heart. And though the rational part of her brain said lightning wouldn't strike twice, she couldn't let go of that fear.

She sighed. This whole thing was a mess and she blamed Harry completely. If he hadn't upped and left her, she wouldn't be the emotional mess she was now.

She focussed her attention back on the cookies.

The other advantage of making the cookies was that she had something to share on her Instagram. She had created her profile, 'The Christmas Fairy', a year or so before and would share photos almost daily of the different baubles she had been making or any other Christmas activities she was doing throughout the year. Since coming here she had managed to post lots of photos; of her shop, of Jacob's metal Christmas tree, of the ginger-bread men, the mulled wine, the tall Christmas tree outside the castle, some of the more … *appropriate* Christmas lights in the village. It all helped to direct people to her website where people could buy decorations online. Earlier that morning she had posted photos of the cookies she was making, explaining that it was for a Christmas Cookie Competition to raise money for the British Heart Foundation. She'd said that she needed to make two hundred cookies and had finished the post with *Send help* and *Send icing sugar, Smarties and sprinkles.*

She opened the oven and took out the biscuits that were golden brown, replacing them with the ones she had just rolled and cut out. Then she started mixing up a new batch of dough.

She had definitely bitten off more than she

could chew with the Christmas Cookie Competition, the Angel Festival the next day and the Polar Bear Plunge on Christmas Eve. It didn't leave much time to actually be in her shop in her busiest time of the year. Maybe she should cancel something, the Polar Bear Plunge ideally. She thought back to the night before and Jacob's nightmare. Had that been related to the Polar Bear Plunge? The thought that this silly swim for charity was affecting him so badly made her heart sink. She hated the idea that he was worrying so much about this that he was having bad dreams. She could put a note on the forum that it was cancelled because of lack of interest. That was plausible. But she didn't want Jacob to think she was calling it off for him. And she got the feeling he needed to do this to conquer his demons once and for all.

There was a knock on the door and she sighed and dusted her hands down her apron and went to answer it.

Jacob was standing there and she couldn't help the flutter of excitement at seeing him.

He raised two bulging carrier bags. 'You said, send help, so I'm here to help.'

He stepped inside without waiting to be invited and kissed her on the cheek by way of a greeting, then moved through to the kitchen.

She stood there in shock for a moment, touching her cheek where his lips had been. Had they progressed to that now with their friends-with-benefits arrangement? She wasn't sure if she liked it. No, actually she knew she liked it. Too bloody much.

She closed the door and followed him through to the kitchen, still confused about what he was doing there. She hadn't told him she was going to be making cookies this morning. And wasn't he supposed to be in Penzance?

'What do you mean, you're here to help?'

'On your Instagram post, you said send help and send icing sugar, Smarties and sprinkles. So I brought them all.'

She blushed at the thought of him looking at her Instagram. She was always quite candid in her posts and she wouldn't be surprised if she'd put something up there about working next door to a sexy artist. She wracked her brains trying to remember. She'd certainly took a picture of him working away at the Christmas tree when he wasn't looking, but she wasn't sure if she'd got round to posting it yet.

'You've seen my Instagram?'

'You left it on my computer the other day, I've been cyber stalking you ever since. I like the idea of you being a Christmas fairy, sprinkling your Christmas magic over everything and everyone. Anyway, I saw your post about making cookies today so I thought I'd come and give you a hand.'

'I thought you'd be heading over to Penzance today?'

'It can wait for another day.' He moved over to the sink and washed his hands. 'What do you need me to do?'

She found herself smiling at him. He was here for her. As a friend. There was no agenda, he just wanted to help her out.

He grabbed some kitchen towel to dry his hands and she walked over and hugged him, her face against his back, her arms around his stomach.

'I really bloody like you, Jacob Harrington.'

He squeezed her hand. She wondered if he would say something back about how much he liked her but he didn't. Although he'd already proved that by coming here.

'Come on, shall I make the icing? After years of cupcake-making with Poppy, I reckon I know my way around a batch of buttercream or glacé icing.' He stepped away from her and started taking out the bags of icing sugar. 'Which one are we making?'

She watched him for a moment, that ache in her heart for him getting bigger. She cleared her throat.

'Buttercream, I think. You can pipe that on

and get some good effects or spoon it on and it won't run,' Ruby said.

'I bought food colouring too so we can make different colour batches.'

'Good idea. You do realise you're going to have to make a ton of it?'

He shrugged. 'I have time.'

They worked together in silence for a while, though it wasn't uncomfortable. It was just two friends working side by side. Maybe they would be OK after all.

CAL PHONED JUST after Jacob had left to deliver a car full of biscuits and icing to the castle. Ruby was busy cleaning the kitchen; the icing sugar had seemingly got everywhere. She put the call on loudspeaker as she wiped around the kitchen.

'How's it going out there, Cal?' Ruby asked, keen not to get onto the subject of her and Jacob again.

'All good. But I'm nearly done here. If I can get a flight out, I was thinking of coming down and spending Christmas with you.'

Excitement over seeing her brother again mixed with nerves at the thought of having Cal there interfering with her love life. She didn't need him there sticking his oar in, she could cock everything up quite well on her own. But she did want to see him again and it would be lovely to spend Christmas with him.

'That would be great.' She winced a little over what she was going to say next. 'I'm actually spending Christmas with Jacob and his family, but I'm sure you'll be very welcome to come along too.'

There was silence from Cal for a second and she thought the connection between there and the States had dropped out.

'You're spending Christmas Day with Jacob, a man who you have feelings for but refuse to let anything more happen between you? That doesn't sound like you're keeping your distance to me.'

'Well, actually we've made a bit of progress there.'

'Really?' Cal said, eagerly.

'We're trialling a friends-with-benefits arrangement,' Ruby said, knowing how pathetic that sounded.

Cal didn't say anything for a while. 'Right.'

'I thought you'd be pleased.'

'Pleased? How can I be pleased that my little sister is having meaningless sex with the only man who has meant something to her in twelve years?'

Ruby sighed but she knew that her brother was partly right.

'Look, we're both happy with this arrangement,' she tried. 'We're good friends, we get on well, we have great sex. It doesn't need to be more than that.'

'Maybe not for you.'

'This was Jacob's idea,' Ruby said.

'I think I might have to have words with Jacob Harrington.'

'Cal, I love you, I'm looking forward to seeing you at Christmas, but stay out of this.'

Cal was silent again but eventually he spoke. 'Ruby, when you were a kid, you were completely fearless. You'd climb the highest tree, ride your bike down the hill the fastest, learn all those scary skateboard stunts, do somersaults on the trampoline, stand up to the school's biggest bully. You were tremendous. What happened to that brave little girl?'

'She discovered what it was like to really get hurt, she discovered what real pain felt like,' Ruby said.

'And you've been hiding away ever since. It's time to be brave again, to take a risk. To live the life you want because this half-life is not the life you imagined when you were conquering dragons and fighting pirates. And this is not the life Harry would have wanted for you either. You might as well have died that day too if this is the life you're going to lead.'

'Cal, that's an awful thing to say.'

'I'm sorry but I hate to see you waste your

life like this. If you don't want me to interfere then I promise, I won't say another word, but please just think about what I've said.'

'I will,' Ruby said, quietly.

'I'll keep you posted regarding flights and dates.'

'OK.'

'I love you, kid.'

'I love you too.'

And with that Cal was gone.

Ruby sighed. She remembered that euphoric feeling she'd got as a kid, when she did something daring and bold, the wind in her hair as she raced her bike down the steepest hill. And although the risks of getting hurt were high, the sheer joy she got from those escapades always outweighed those risks.

Cal was right. After Harry's death she had closeted herself away, afraid to take those risks anymore. She had built a wall around her to protect herself from ever getting hurt again.

But Jacob had been pulling that wall down brick by brick, he had worked his way in. And sometimes, when she was with him, she would have those wonderful feelings of joy again and she liked that.

If she wanted that life she just had to reach through the wall and take it. But she had to find a shedload of courage first and she wasn't sure that brave little girl was in there anymore.

CHAPTER 14

Ruby was delighted by how many people had turned up for the Cookie Competition. She'd figured it would just be something families with young kids would want to do, but it seemed that the whole village had turned up. Even Lottie and Poppy had hung around to take part.

The great hall in the castle wasn't quite set up for the Christmas ball yet apart from some of the beautiful Christmas decorations that adorned the ceilings and walls. Andrew had been working hard all morning to set up tables for the villagers to use for their cookie-decorating but there were so many groups now waiting to take part that many of them would have to share a table.

Ken was busy directing operations, doing what he did best. Jacob was running round giving everyone a jam jar so that people could put pennies in the jars of their favourite cookie, which would help to declare the winner and raise money for charity too. Willow was delivering bags of coloured icing to the tables and Ruby was collecting money at the door in return for a plain cookie and directing people to their places.

Lucas arrived at the door and handed over his money. She wasn't sure where things stood between him and Megan right now, whether they'd made up after their little spat or not, but as promised she was going to place Lucas with Megan so at least they could talk.

'Let me see where I can squeeze you in,' Ruby said, pretending to consult her clipboard.

'Would you mind sharing with the person on table eight?'

Lucas looked over and let out a little sigh, but he didn't protest and went over to join Megan. Megan glanced up as he arrived and then looked back down again at her cookie as if planning out what she was going to do. Obviously the air hadn't been cleared between them, but maybe this would give them the chance to at least become friends again.

When everyone seemed to be in their designated areas, Ken came over to Ruby with a microphone.

'These events are a wonderful idea,' Ken said. 'The Cookie Competition and the Angel Festival are something the families can all get involved in. Although I think the one event everyone is looking forward to the most is the Polar Bear Plunge on Christmas Eve. Everyone wants to see Jacob get wet.'

Ruby smiled, uneasily. This was such a big deal for Jacob and the thought that everyone was going to get a good laugh out of watching him do something that terrified him made her feel sick.

'I don't think he's looking forward to it,' she said, carefully.

'I'm not surprised, it's bloody freezing out there.'

Ruby couldn't tell him that it was so much more than that.

'Are you all ready to start?' Ken asked.

She looked around and nodded.

'Do you want to say a few words and explain any rules?'

'Sure,' Ruby said.

'Well, I'll introduce you and then pass the microphone over to you.'

He switched on the microphone and tapped it a few times to get everyone's attention. Silence fell over the great hall.

'Thank you all for coming to our first annual Christmas Cookie Competition,' Ken said. Ruby couldn't help but smirk that he had decided it was to become an annual thing rather than just a one-off, even though the event hadn't even kicked off yet. 'I'm going to pass you over to Ruby and she will explain how the whole thing is going to work.'

The villagers gave a small round of applause and Ken handed over the microphone.

'Thank you,' Ruby said to the villagers. 'You all have half hour to decorate your cookies, only using the sweets, sprinkles and coloured icing on the tables. Please do share the bags of coloured icing with other tables. We couldn't make every colour for every table – that would have been a lot of icing.'

Everyone laughed.

'After the thirty minutes is up, you will be able to walk around and see what everyone has made and you can put pennies or as much as you can afford in the jars next to your favourite cookie. As many of you are aware, we are raising money for the British Heart Foundation. Heart disease is one of the biggest killers in the UK and I myself lost someone close to me to a heart attack, so this charity is very important to me. So dig deep but have fun too.'

The villagers clapped loudly this time and Ruby passed the microphone back to Ken.

'Thanks Ruby. OK, without further ado, I declare the Cookie Competition open. You can start your cookies in three, two, one, go.'

There was suddenly a hive of activity as families, friends and couples all started working on their own cookies, making plans, squeezing the bags of icing, the children surreptitiously eating the sweets. Ruby didn't hold out any hope that any of the cookies would be great works of art but at least everyone was having fun.

She looked round and saw that Andrew and Willow were working together at one table and Lottie and Poppy were busily beavering away next to them.

She glanced over at Megan working alongside Lucas. Although they were working on their own individual cookies, it was evident they were at least talking, as something that Lucas said made Megan laugh.

Ruby looked around to see if there was a table spare so she could have a go but Jacob caught her eye and waved her over to join him.

She smiled and walked across to his table where there were two cookies waiting for them.

'Come on, I need a Christmas expert on my team if we stand any chance of winning this thing,' Jacob said.

'What about a little competition between ourselves?' Ruby said, moving to his side. 'You're an artist, I'm an expert in all things Christmassy, let's see who gets the most coins in their jar.'

He grinned at the challenge. 'OK, you're on. And what do I get when I win?'

She leaned up and whispered in his ear and took great pleasure in watching his eyes widen to comic proportions.

'Bloody hell, that's some incentive.'

'You won't win though, so don't get too excited,' Ruby said.

'What do you want *if* you win?' Jacob asked, picking up one of the bags of green icing.

She thought about this for a moment and decided to knock another brick from the wall, although it suddenly felt like a very big brick.

'I want you to make me a new necklace. Something Christmassy. I've had this snowflake for a while and maybe it's time I had something new.'

He stared at her for a moment. Had he detected a quiver in her voice when she'd suggested it? There was no way she was throwing Harry's necklace away, but maybe she could vary it with something different some days.

'You have yourself a deal,' Jacob said, seriously, but then he nudged her. 'You're not going to win though.'

'We'll see about that.'

'Twenty-five minutes,' Ken said over the microphone.

Ruby quickly grabbed a bag of brown icing and started carefully piping it onto the biscuit as Jacob got to work himself. She did the outline of the robin first of all and then coloured it in with long strokes so it looked like feathers.

She picked up the red icing and started creating the red breast. She glanced over at Jacob, who was clearly taking his time to get his design of a Santa just right.

'You're taking this very seriously,' Ruby said.

'There's a lot at stake.'

She laughed and picked up a bag of white icing as Jacob reached for it too, laughing and holding it out of his reach.

'Oh, is that your game, trying to hinder my creative process,' Jacob said. 'Well we'll see about that.'

He grabbed her around the waist with one arm, hauling her against him as he reached for the bag with the other. She squealed and tried to wiggle from his grasp. But then he was suddenly tickling her in the ribs, touching her in the exact spot that made her go weak. She brought her arms down in an attempt to protect herself and he swiped the bag from her hand and released her.

'That's not fair,' Ruby laughed.

He shrugged. 'If you can't take the heat, get out of the kitchen.'

'Oh, I can take the heat,' she said.

He fixed her with a dark look that gave her a punch of desire. 'Is that right?'

She shook her head with a smile and took a step away from him.

'Just get on with your biscuit.'

She turned her attention back to her own design, applying icing around the outside and then a pattern of sweets while she waited for him to finish with the white icing.

He passed over the bag and she carefully piped the white feathers at the bottom of the robin's belly. She had painted this design on baubles many times, so it wasn't really that different using icing instead.

Jacob started adding sweets round the outside as Ken began doing a countdown to the end of the competition. Everyone started joining in and there was a last-second flurry of activity from many of the tables.

'That's it everyone, your time is up,' Ken said, over the microphone.

Ruby licked a blob of icing off her thumb and wiped her hands down her jeans. She looked over at Jacob's cookie. It was surprisingly good. Although she shouldn't have had her doubts, he was a brilliant artist.

'That's very good, Ruby Marlowe,' Jacob said, studying her robin. 'But I don't think it will beat my Santa.'

'You're so cocky.'

He shrugged. 'We'll let the people decide.'

'Make sure your names are written on the jars so we can identify the winner,' Ken was saying over the microphone. 'And now please give donations in the jars next to the cookies you like the most.'

Jacob pulled his wallet out. 'Damn, I only have a twenty, I didn't bring any change.'

'Well, twenty pounds is a very generous donation,' Ruby teased. 'I'll put in for you if you tell me which cookie you like the most.'

'Thanks.'

People started walking around and Ruby moved between the tables, dropping a few coins in the jars here and there. Some of the designs were amazing, some were... more fun than artistic.

She moved to Willow and Andrew's table and smiled at the snowman cookie that kind of looked like the Stay Puft Marshmallow Man.

She turned around and bumped into Julia, who was eyeing her beadily.

'Julia, how did your cookie-decorating go?' Ruby asked, even though it was quite clear the postmistress wasn't there to talk about cookies.

'I was walking Colin and Rufus around the village last night around eightish and I noticed your cottage was in complete darkness. And then when I walked them later around ten, it was still in darkness and I thought perhaps you might have stayed at Jacob's last night to celebrate your first day in style.' Julia waggled her eyebrows mischievously.

Ruby wasn't exactly sure how to respond to being put on the spot like that.

'No, I—'

'And then I saw you leaving your shop around nine this morning wearing exactly the same clothes as you were wearing yesterday and my suspicions were confirmed.'

'Wow. That's… some good detective work,' Ruby said, not wanting to say that it was actually more than a little creepy.

'So are you two… making whoopee again?'

Ruby cleared her throat. 'Julia, sometimes a lady likes to be a bit mysterious and keep her secrets to herself.'

Julia looked delighted. 'That's a yes if ever I heard one.'

Ruby smiled and, as Julia looked around for Dorothy or Liz to spread the joyous news, she slipped away. She was sure that piece of gossip would be round the whole village within an hour. She really didn't have a chance of hiding something that momentous in a village so tiny it didn't show on any maps.

After Ruby had moved around all the tables, Ken came back on the microphone. 'Have you all now had a chance to put your money in the jar next to the cookie you like the most?'

There were murmurs of agreement from around the hall.

'Great. So can we have all the jars up here on the stage and we will count the money.'

Ruby grabbed a few nearby jars, bringing them over to the stage, and everyone else did the same.

'Well, it seems like we have a winner,' Ken said after a few seconds, which surprised Ruby. They couldn't possibly have counted all the money in all the jars already.

He held a jar aloft which quite clearly had a twenty-pound note stuffed inside, along with a few pennies. Ken tipped the jar into his hands and he quickly counted the coins.

'With twenty pounds and thirty-six pence,

our winner is actually our very own Ruby Marlowe.'

Everyone clapped but Ruby frowned in confusion. There was no way she should have won; the robin was good but there were some real masterpieces out there. And then, suddenly, comprehension dawned on her. She whirled around to find Jacob and saw him standing by their table. He caught her eye and gave her a wink.

She made her way to the stage to collect the tin of chocolate biscuits which was her prize. Considering what she had promised Jacob if his cookie won out of the two of them, it would have been the obvious choice to stick his twenty pounds in his own jar, but he hadn't. He had made sure she'd won, which meant she was now going to get a new necklace.

She shook her head. This man really was going to be her undoing.

CHAPTER 15

JACOB WATCHED RUBY AS SHE LAUGHED WITH Willow up at the crowded bar. He couldn't drag his eyes away. She made him feel things he'd never felt before and he had no idea what to do about it. He wasn't sure whether this friends-with-benefits arrangement was going to be a great idea or a terrible one, though pessimistically he didn't think it was going to end well.

Andrew came over to join him, handing him a pint.

'Why the long face?' his brother said, sitting down on the sofa opposite him.

Jacob took a long sip of his beer. 'I think I've made a terrible mistake.'

'Well, rumour has it that Ruby stayed over at yours last night. Is that your terrible mistake?'

Jacob let out a heavy breath. 'Sleeping with Ruby was not the mistake. Suggesting that we could have a no-strings-attached-sex kind of relationship was probably one of the stupidest things I've ever done.'

Andrew stared at him for a few seconds. 'And why on earth would you suggest that when you like her so much?'

'Because it was that or nothing and I couldn't face nothing again.'

Andrew sighed. 'I don't think you're going to get what you want out of this. This is going to be like Ella all over again.'

Jacob nodded, knowing his brother was right. He had hoped that by being there for Ella

319

she would eventually turn her affections in his direction, but she had never seen him that way and ultimately broke his heart. He thought Ruby had feelings for him but maybe he was only seeing what he wanted to see. As far as she was concerned, this arrangement could purely be about sex with a friend and nothing more.

'What do I do?' Jacob asked.

'I suppose you give her time initially. She likes you – anyone can see that –and she might eventually realise she likes you a hell of a lot more than friends. Although she might not. I guess, ultimately, meaningless sex can only last so long and at some point you're going to have to be honest with her about how you feel and hope she feels the same way. And if she doesn't I think you have to be brave enough to end it or it will only end in heartbreak for you.'

Jacob nodded and then let out a little laugh. 'I never thought I'd see the day when me and you have a proper serious conversation.'

'Ah, I'm practically a married man now, I suppose I had to grow up sometime.'

Jacob smiled. 'Well I think we better get back to telling fart jokes and talking about beer before our reputations are completely ruined.'

Andrew grinned. 'I'll do my best.'

RUBY LOOKED AROUND NERVOUSLY. The pub was pretty packed so doing what she was about to do was a big risk. But when she'd returned from the bar with their drinks, she'd tucked herself away in the corner. Earlier she had enlisted Willow and Andrew to help her and Jacob. She had also changed Jesus's costume so no one would be on the look-out for a doll dressed as a reindeer. He was now dressed as an elf instead.

Andrew, Willow and Jacob were largely blocking her from view as Ruby sat Jesus on a bar stool, next to the pint she had just bought for Jacob. She quickly looked around and then took a picture, before bundling poor Jesus back into her rucksack again.

She looked around again to see if anyone had seen and locked eyes with Lucy. Her heart leapt. Had she seen, could she have seen Jesus from where she was sitting? Ruby had no idea but, judging from the smug smile slowly spreading on Lucy's face, she had definitely seen something.

God, if anyone could make trouble for Ruby, it would be her. She just had to hope Lucy had some kind of sense of humour.

RUBY PULLED her coat around her tighter as she waited for Willow to unlock the door to her house later that night. Being stylish at Christmas with her purple velvet coat was one thing but being warm when living in a coastal village was probably more important. With the icy winds that were blowing in from the sea, Ruby thought she might need a coat made for Arctic explorers at this rate. Willow and Andrew's house was right on the cliff tops looking out over the sea, which made for some stunning views, but at this time of year it must be colder for them than if they lived a bit more centrally in the village.

Willow had invited her and Jacob round to watch Christmas movies, which was obviously code for Willow wanting to find out what was going on between her and Jacob. Ruby was happy to oblige though; Willow was sure to find out soon enough and Ruby would rather her friend heard it from her.

Willow pushed the door open and stepped back to let them in, Ruby rushed in and started building a fire, although it was very clear that the heating was on as well.

'Mulled wine OK for everyone?' Willow asked, shrugging out of her coat and heading for the kitchen. 'Or I can do hot chocolates. I'm having a hot chocolate so it's no bother.'

'Mulled wine is fine for me,' Ruby said, closing the log burner door.

'And me,' Jacob said.

'Mulled wine for me,' Andrew said, hanging all the coats up near the door.

'Ruby, why don't you give me a hand,' Willow said, meaningfully.

Ruby smirked as she ditched her coat and walked into the kitchen. Jacob winked at her as he flopped down on the sofa. He knew she was about to get the third degree.

Ruby watched as Willow poured the bottle of mulled wine into a saucepan. Where Ruby preferred to make her own from red wine and different spices, Willow had found a bottle of pre-spiced mulled wine that took away all of that hassle. She bought a few bottles of the stuff every year and Ruby had to admit the stuff was good, potent but delicious.

'So tell me everything,' Willow said eagerly.

Ruby smiled. 'There are certain things that even I don't want to share.'

'Ah come on, just give me a little bit. Did you...?' she trailed off, waving her hand in some kind of vague gesture. 'I heard lots of people say you had and although Lottie didn't say anything to anyone else, she did confide to me that she kind of walked in on you both this morning,' Willow said, as she started making herself a hot chocolate.

Ruby laughed. 'That makes it sound like she walked in on us in the middle of the throes of passion. She came into Jacob's flat early this morning when we were both fast asleep. I walked out of his bedroom with extreme bed hair and she made up her own mind about what me and Jacob had been doing all night. Although I'm sure whatever conclusion she came to was completely accurate.'

Willow turned around so fast she spilt hot chocolate powder all over the floor and didn't even notice. She let out a little squeal of excitement.

'Look, don't get too excited, we're not together, not in that sense.'

Willow frowned. 'What sense are you together?'

Ruby grabbed a dustpan and brush and

started clearing up. She threw the chocolate powder in the bin and checked where Jacob was, but he was busy in conversation with Andrew.

Ruby took a deep breath. 'Casual, a friends-with-benefits arrangement.'

Willow couldn't have looked more disappointed if Ruby had told her Christmas was cancelled.

Ruby was starting to think it was a terrible idea too, not least because feelings were bubbling to the surface that she didn't want to face.

'This spark has been bubbling between us ever since I got here and I just thought, maybe, if we scratch that itch the need for each other will go away.'

'And did it work?'

Ruby shook her head. She sat down at the table, all the fight going out of her.

'I just need some time to get my head round all this. It feels so new and scary and terrifying. There's a huge part of me that wants this with Jacob, to say to hell with it and dive head first into a proper relationship. But then I remember Harry and…' she swallowed and touched the necklace he'd given her. 'We were supposed to be forever and then I lost him.'

Willow nodded and sat down at the table with her, holding her hand. 'I can't begin to imagine the pain you went through losing the only man you've ever loved. The thought of losing Andrew is enough to bring me to my knees. And I know this is easy for me to say, but you have to continue to live your life. You can't be too scared to get on a plane because it might crash, you can't be scared to go to Australia because you might get bitten by a poisonous spider and you can't be scared of falling in love again because you might get your heart broken in the worst possible way. Because getting on a plane or going to Australia could lead to the most amazing, beautiful adventures and falling in love, being loved in return, is one of the most glorious, wonderful, deliriously happy adventures we can ever go on.'

Ruby smiled at how happy Willow was with Andrew and she nodded. 'I know you're right. And Cal said pretty much the same thing, that I need to be brave. But I just can't rip the plaster off in one quick yank, I have to do it slowly. I need some time and I only hope Jacob is prepared to wait.'

Willow stood up and poured out three glasses of mulled wine, then added hot water to the hot chocolate. 'I think you two are perfect for each other, but just take it slow. I don't want to see either of you get hurt.'

Ruby nodded. 'I know. I don't want to hurt him either.'

Willow added some milk to her hot chocolate and then grabbed a can of squirty cream and sprayed a big dollop of that on the top.

'Why are you not drinking the mulled wine anyway, you love that stuff?' Ruby asked just as Andrew walked into the room.

Willow blushed furiously. 'I just… fancied some hot chocolate.'

Andrew stared at her. It was her reaction to

the question which made it obvious there was more to it than that.

'Oh my god, are you pregnant?' Ruby asked.

'No... I don't know,' Willow said.

'You're pregnant?' Andrew said.

Shit. Even he didn't know. Well this had suddenly got a little awkward.

'I don't think so. I'm not sure,' Willow said.

'Why didn't you tell me?' Andrew said.

Ruby wanted to leave them alone. This conversation was private but her friend suddenly looked close to tears and Ruby wanted to make sure she was OK.

'I wanted to be sure before I said anything. I'm a few days late, I don't think it's a big deal. I stopped using that new pill last month because it was giving me headaches and we've been super careful ever since then so it's really unlikely that I am. My body is probably still trying to sort itself out so it makes sense that I'd be late. But it's still too early to tell for sure and I didn't want to get your hopes up if it's just a… hormone thing.'

Andrew moved into the kitchen. 'Are *your* hopes up?'

Willow dashed tears from her eyes and laughed. 'A little. I mean, it's not the best time, we're not even married yet and I don't want to be the huge pregnant bride, but we have spoken about having children and I know it's something we are both looking forward to when the time is right. But yes, I am a little excited about the prospect I might be carrying your child.'

'Then why wouldn't you share that with me?' Andrew said.

'I only realised I was late this morning and, yes, I got stupidly excited for a few minutes when I thought about what that could mean. But it felt like buying a lottery ticket and then getting excited about what I'm going to spend the money on before the numbers had even been drawn. It felt silly to tell you I might be pregnant when the chances are I'm almost definitely not.'

'We made a deal, that we would always share our hopes and fears, our sadness and our triumphs.'

'OK, then. There is a very teeny tiny chance I might be pregnant. How do you feel about that?'

Andrew stared at her for a few moments and then took Willow in his arms. 'I feel… really excited.'

Willow groaned. 'But that's why I didn't want to tell you. I don't want you to be disappointed if I'm not.'

'But we'll share that disappointment together. If you didn't tell me, then when you found out in a few days' time that you're not, you'd be disappointed on your own and I don't want you to ever feel like you're alone in this relationship.'

Willow nodded and wrapped her arms around Andrew, leaning her head against his chest. 'OK.'

Ruby took the glasses of mulled wine and walked back into the lounge, leaving them to it.

'Is everything OK?' Jacob asked.

She passed him a glass of mulled wine and sat next to him on the sofa, cuddling into his side.

'I think it is now,' she said, leaning her head on his shoulder. He wrapped an arm around her and kissed her head.

Being part of a couple meant going through the good and bad times together, knowing you always had someone there to watch your back. Could she really have that with Jacob? Did she and Jacob really have that longevity to weather the storms, not just celebrate the sunshine? He had been there for her so much since she had arrived, but if she was going to enter into a proper relationship with this man, she had to trust that they would have that.

She looked up at him and he gave her a sweet kiss on the lips. She wanted to believe in that more than anything.

THEY HAD CHOSEN to watch *The Holiday*. Not that Ruby had seen most of it. Willow and Andrew had come out of the kitchen, looking happy and loved-up. They'd sat down with Willow on Andrew's lap and probably ten minutes after the movie had started Willow was fast asleep, with her head on Andrew's shoulder and his arms tight around her. It was probably only another ten minutes after that that Andrew had fallen asleep too. Ruby and Jacob had spent most of the rest of the film kissing like teenagers on a first date. There was something gloriously wonderful about spending her evening like that, just kissing, because she really did like this man and it was quite obvious he was pretty keen too.

She was vaguely aware the film had finished and she pulled back to look at him.

She stroked his face, relishing the feel of his stubble against her fingers. 'I think we should go.'

He fixed her with a dark look. 'I think so too.'

She smiled and stood up. She watched Willow and Andrew for a moment; they looked so sweet together. 'Should we wake them?'

'Yeah, they'll be stiff tomorrow if they sleep here all night.'

Ruby moved over to them and gave Willow's shoulder a little shake. She opened her eyes blearily.

'Hey, we're off now.'

Willow looked around in confusion and at the credits rolling on the TV and Andrew snoring softly.

'Oh god, did the movie finish already? I'm so sorry, we're terrible hosts.'

'It's OK, I had a lovely evening.'

Willow stood up and Andrew carried on sleeping. She gave Ruby and Jacob a hug and then followed them to the door.

'I'll see you tomorrow,' Ruby said, as they pulled on their hats and coats.

Willow nodded sleepily and, as they stepped outside, she closed the door behind them.

Snow was still falling and the whole outside world was glittering under a layer of soft, white powder, making the night much lighter to walk through. The snow crunched under their feet and their breath escaped in small billows of steam.

'So Willow might be pregnant?' Jacob said.

'I didn't think you'd heard.'

Jacob laughed. 'The kitchen is right there.'

He linked hands with her as they walked up the little track back towards the village.

Ruby looked down at their joined hands. This seemed a bit too familiar for their friends-with-benefits arrangement but she liked it so she didn't pull away.

She focussed back on what he'd said.

'I'm sure they don't want anyone to know yet until they can at least confirm it,' Ruby said.

'You have nothing to worry about with me,

but the whole village will know once she buys a pregnancy kit. In fact, I wouldn't put it past Julia Dalton to know already, she knows everything.'

Ruby laughed. 'I might have to buy one for her.'

'Oh great, then everyone will think I've gotten you pregnant just a few days after you've arrived,' Jacob said dryly.

She laughed. 'It will at least keep the attention off Willow and Andrew for a few days.'

'True.'

'So how do you feel about possibly being an uncle again?' Ruby asked as they followed a set of animal tracks through the snow. They looked like they might belong to a fox.

'Oh, I'm more than ready to play that role again. I love hanging out with Poppy, she's the funniest person I know. Besides, it would be good for Poppy to have a cousin to grow up with.'

They cut through an alley that took them to the village high street.

'I had Poppy quite often when she was little, took care of the stinky nappies, endured the sleepless nights,' Jacob said. 'Alex, Lottie's ex-husband, wasn't always around when Poppy was born, he was away a lot with work. Lottie found it hard to look after Poppy on her own so me and Andrew took her as often as we could. I'd do it all over again for Willow and Andrew.'

Ruby smiled. 'Does it make you think about having your own children?'

He grinned down at her. 'Is that an offer, Ruby Marlowe, because I'm not sure our casual sex arrangement covers that.'

She laughed.

'I never thought children were in my future,' she said. 'I never thought a serious relationship was in my future either but now...' she trailed off because it was unexpectedly sounding very serious and scary. 'Maybe... one day.'

God, that was a very big step all of a sudden for her to admit that she wanted that.

She decided to try to lighten the mood a little.

'With the right person, obviously,' she teased.

Jacob was quiet for a while. They reached the main high street and they walked down it towards the shop.

'Oh look, someone else has built a snowman,' Ruby said, pointing to a strange-shaped snowman further down the street.

'That's outside Megan's house,' Jacob said.

Ruby looked up at him. 'Do you think it's from Lucas?'

'It might be.'

They drew closer and her heart leapt as she realised it was two people hugging.

'It's just like the tree decoration Megan bought from my shop yesterday. I bet she gave it to Lucas and he's done this.'

'Maybe, or Megan did it herself maybe as a massive hint for Lucas,' Jacob said.

'Well, let's hope he takes it. I really want those two to get together.'

'For someone who doesn't believe in the fairytale ending, that surprises me,' Jacob said.

'Maybe I'm coming round to the idea.'

She could see their snowman standing sentry by the shop door. Jacob had given her that. He had also given her a lot more than she'd ever dreamed possible.

'Why did you make sure I won the Christmas Cookie Competition? Why did you want to make me a new necklace rather than what I offered you?'

Jacob was silent for a while as he unlocked the shop door and then ushered her inside out of the cold.

'Harry gave you that necklace, didn't he?' Jacob said, rubbing his hands down her arms to get her warm.

She nodded.

'I thought as much. Every time you talk about him, or sometimes I can see you think about him, you touch that necklace. But I think it reminds you of the pain you felt when he died rather than the good times you shared.'

Wow, that was very insightful.

'And I never want to take away what the two of you shared, but maybe it's time you made some good memories for you to focus on instead. A new necklace could be the start of that.'

She smiled and reached up and kissed him. He held her against him, so she felt safe in his arms.

She pulled back to look at him. 'Take me to bed, you big beautiful man.'

He grinned and took her by the hand and led her up the stairs. He kissed her gently as he slipped her coat from her shoulders and she stroked his face and then started undressing him too. It wasn't fast and hurried this time, there was no desperate rush. Jacob was taking his time to treasure her, kissing her every-where as he slowly removed her clothes. He moved his mouth to her neck and placed a kiss right where her pulse was hammering against her skin. It was so gentle and so completely unexpected it stalled her. He placed another soft kiss on her shoulder and another on her collar bone that was almost a whisper. He trailed his mouth to the other side, caressing her with his lips. She felt… adored.

He lifted her and laid her down on the bed as she removed the last of his clothes too.

He stroked her face. She ran her hands over his shoulders. He leaned forward and kissed her, wrapping his arms around her and bringing her close to his body. He didn't stop kissing her as he caressed her all over, stroking his fingers across her breast, down her ribs, over her stomach, and then slipping his hand between her legs.

God, this man. She loved his touch, his familiarity, the way he knew her body better than she knew it herself, the way he could bring her to the very edge with the simplest of touches. She moaned against his lips, felt her body shudder against his and still the kiss continued, his other hand in her hair stroking her, soothing her.

He reached out for a condom from the bedside drawers, shifted back a bit to put it on before he rolled back on top of her, settling himself between her legs. He stared down at her as he slid inside her and she felt her body almost sigh with relief.

He moved against her slowly, not taking his eyes from hers for a second. She wrapped her legs around his hips, bringing him closer as she stroked his face. That glorious feeling started spreading inside of her and she wanted to tell him how important he was to her. Words failed her as she stared up at this brilliant man. Her heart was full for him.

But instead, she kissed him. As she fell apart around him, as he moaned against her lips, shaking in her arms, she knew she wanted a chance at love again and she had to find the courage to take it.

CHAPTER 16

JACOB BENT TO PICK UP ANOTHER SHELL FROM the beach and put it in his bag.

He and Ruby had agreed they were going to make their angel for the festival later that day out of shells so he'd left her in bed and gone down to the beach to collect some. He was studiously ignoring the sea as it crashed onto the shore a few metres from where he stood. The tide was in but there was still enough beach left to collect the shells.

Fortunately, he had something else to focus on. He couldn't get the night before out of his head. Sex with Ruby had been magnificent because for the first time in his life it hadn't just been sex. It had been two people who cared about each other a great deal making love.

He'd never thought he would ever utter those words to describe sex. He had described it in many ways, sometimes in the crudest terms, but he'd never *made love* to a woman before. But he knew, in his heart, that he couldn't describe what he'd shared with Ruby any other way.

He had to believe that she felt that too. He just had to give her time to realise it as well.

He looked in his bag. It looked like he had enough shells to make a smallish hollow sculpture with perhaps chicken wire or paper and cardboard on the inside. He made a move to go back up the steps that would take him to the cliff tops but he hesitated.

He turned and faced the waves. Two days from now, on Christmas Eve, was the Polar Bear Plunge and he was going to go in the sea for the first time in around twenty years. He felt sick at the thought and he hated that it scared him so much. He had loved the sea as a child – growing up in Newquay he had been on the beach and playing in the waves almost every day of his life – and then one day had taken away that love completely. He needed to get past this and he needed to do this for Ruby.

He stared at the waves, watching as they crashed onto the shore and then were sucked back into the sea. He stepped closer, feeling the spray on his cheeks.

Suddenly he felt a hand in his and he turned to see Ruby standing next to him, all wrapped up against the cold. She looked adorable.

He leaned down and gave her a kiss on the lips, the taste of her a punch to the gut.

He pulled back to look at her, wondering if the night before had meant as much to her as it did to him. She smiled at him and stroked his face.

She gestured to the waves. 'Are you psyching yourself up for the plunge?'

He smiled, weakly. 'Something like that.'

'You don't have to do it, you know. You don't have anything to prove to me or to the villagers.'

'I am doing it. How much money have you raised for the Polar Bear Plunge?'

She hesitated. 'Eight hundred and forty-six pounds.'

'That's eight hundred and forty-six reasons why I will be doing it.'

She sighed. 'Jacob, I'm sure they would all still pay that money if I did it alone. And if they don't then they don't. I set up these charity events in the hope that I would raise a few hundred pounds and I've already raised a hundred and eighty from the Christmas Cookie Competition yesterday. I'm more than happy with that. I don't want you to do anything you don't want to do.'

Jacob shook his head. 'I need to do this.'

'Why?'

He studied her face but he couldn't tell her.

'I just do, but having you there, by my side, that will make all the difference.'

'I'll be here.'

He smiled and kissed her on the forehead. 'Come on, we have an angel sculpture to make.'

RUBY LOOKED at the materials that Jacob had laid out for them on his desk ready to start making their angel sculpture. It didn't look promising. She had specifically banned him from using any metal as that was his specialist material and she didn't want him to have too much of an advantage over the children of the village using toilet rolls. Eventually she'd relented and let him use chicken wire, but she didn't think that really counted.

As per the instructions she had put up on the forum, the villagers could use whatever material and tools they wished, and they could spend as much time on the sculptures as they wanted, but all the finished angels had to be placed in the village by noon. Ruby had been busy in her shop all morning, replenishing the stock and getting ready for any last-minute shoppers who might pop in today and to-morrow before the big day, so with only one hour until their sculpture had to be placed out on the street, she didn't have much hope.

Jacob brought out two steaming mince pies with brandy ice cream drizzled over the top and passed her one. 'To help inspire us.'

She grinned and took a bite; it tasted divine.

'Come on, let's get started with our master-piece,' Ruby said, swallowing another mouthful and then putting her plate to one side.

Jacob rubbed his hands together. 'This is where I shine. I'm definitely going to win this one.'

She smirked at his confidence. 'What did you have in mind?'

'Are we going for the typical angel image, long flowing dress, feathery wings?' Jacob asked.

'Yes, I guess so.'

'OK, so I suggest we use this plasticine to make the basic shape. I use this sometimes to make little maquettes of the sculptures I make, kind of a rough model, before I start. We'll get the basic shape from that, add the chicken wire around the outside of the wings, then we can add the shells to the wire to get that feathery look.'

'OK, sounds good.'

Jacob opened a large box with creamy white plasticine inside and plonked a large blob on the table. 'This is the fun bit.'

They started squeezing the plasticine between them, moulding it into the shape of a dress and the top half of the angel with the arms, head and wings.

'This is nothing like building our snowman,' Ruby protested. Whereas Jacob was shaping something beautiful, Ruby was seemingly creating an angel that had been hit by a bus, several times. Jacob was having to do her parts of the sculpture again, though he didn't seem to mind.

'Our snowman was something special,' he said. 'We should have made our angel sculpture out of ice and snow instead.'

'I think sadly our angel would have melted in here if we'd done that.'

'Yeah, you're probably right.'

They worked alongside each other in silence for a while as their angel slowly took shape. Watching Jacob sculpt, shape and smooth was fascinating.

'What made you become an artist?' Ruby asked, as she watched him work. 'When did you decide you were going to be Phoenix Blade?'

'I just loved making stuff as a child. This kind of thing would have been right up my street when I was young, making things out of cardboard boxes or clay or papier-mâché. I always had little models everywhere when I was growing up. I used to make aliens and monsters because with them there was no limit to my imagination. An alien could be any shape, size or colour. It could have five arms or twelve eyes and no one could say it was wrong. When other kids were out on the street playing football, this was how I wanted to use my spare time.'

'So the hobby turned into a job?'

'My mum always wanted me to be a doctor; I think she was a bit disappointed when I told her I wanted to be an artist.'

He paused for a moment and Ruby didn't know whether he was focussed on the sculpture or whether he was trying to find the right words for what he wanted to say next. He looked suddenly uncomfortable.

'I had a bit of a near-death experience when I was a kid.'

Ruby knew he was talking about the day he nearly drowned but she couldn't tell him she knew. 'What happened?'

He was silent as he smoothed out a bit of

the wing and then he shook his head. 'It doesn't matter. But I realised that life is short and fragile and I had to get out of it what I wanted, to do the things I love the most. So I pursued this life. Not the life my mum wanted me to take or the life that my teachers encouraged me to follow. I never wanted to look back on my life and wish I'd done things differently. You have to seek out the things that make you happy and then fill your life with them.'

She smiled. 'I think those are very wise words. Do you think you have everything you need in your life to make you happy?'

He stared at her for a moment. 'I'm working on it.'

Her breath caught in her throat and she wondered if he was going to say something else, but whatever it was slipped away.

Jacob focussed his attention back on the angel. 'I think maybe we should just use the chicken wire around the outside of the wings so we can attach the shells and leave the rest of the angel as it is.'

'OK, but she needs hair.'

'Yes, we can do that too.'

Jacob had already cut some of the chicken wire into strips and they set about securing it around the wings and then fixing the shells on with tiny strips of wire thread through the holes he had drilled through the shells earlier.

'So tell me, what is it about Christmas that you love so much? I mean, a lot of people love Christmas but to make it your job, that's a whole other level of love for the season,' Jacob asked.

She smiled. 'I don't know really. I loved it as a child and I suppose I never really grew out of that. I always hated it when the Christmas lights and decorations came down and that joy and celebration was forgotten for another twelve months. I vowed that when I grew up, I would keep the magic of Christmas alive all through the year. I think for me that magic was the thing that I loved the most. I used to love hearing the story of Santa Claus, travelling around the whole world in one night, and it seemed like that magic cast a spell over everyone. It felt like, at that time of year, anything was possible.'

'I like that.'

She focussed her attention on the shells for a moment. 'When I got married to Harry, we talked about our plans for the future and although it had been my dream to have my own Christmas shop, I thought practically that maybe I should do something else that had a bit more of a reliable income. But Harry encouraged me to follow my dreams and do it. When he died, I knew it was something I had to do. I went to university to study business studies so it wasn't just a hobby but something I was taking seriously. And I suppose all the festive activities and increased custom helps to keep my mind off our anniversary too, it gives me something else to focus on.'

She looked up at Jacob and he was watching her.

'I can understand that. And I don't think you should ever give up on your dreams. In fact, I wanted to talk to you about one of your dreams—'

They were both distracted for a moment by shouting and laughter outside as some kids walked past the window outside, struggling under the weight of a six-foot angel. It looked like it had been made out of their mum's clothes and stuffed with newspaper, with a football for a head and a tinsel halo glued onto it.

Ruby giggled and turned her attention back to Jacob. 'What were you saying?'

He shook his head. 'It doesn't matter, let's get this finished, we haven't got much time.'

They finished off their angel as quickly as they could and stepped back to look at it.

It had actually turned out really well, with longer shells towards the bottom of the wings and the smaller ones towards the top so it really did look feathery.

'She's beautiful,' Ruby said.

Jacob nodded. 'We make a pretty good team, Ruby Marlowe.'

She smiled. 'Yeah, we do.'

They bundled themselves into coats and Jacob carefully picked up the angel and carried it outside. They walked up the high street where there was quite a crowd gathering, some people placing their sculptures around the village, some walking around and admiring each other's.

Jacob placed their angel in between a sculpture made from cardboard boxes and another made from plastic bottles. It was quite obvious that some of these sculptures had taken hours to make.

Ruby noticed Willow and Andrew placing a small sculpture that looked like it might be made from wax. Lottie and Poppy were standing near what might have been their sculpture, made entirely out of tinsel and other Christmas decorations.

She looked around and saw Megan and Lucas putting a sculpture outside the pub, this one made from hay and straw like some kind of bizarre wicker man that looked a bit sinister.

They were chatting and laughing together. Ruby didn't know if they'd plucked up the courage to ask each other to the ball yet but the important thing was they were at least friends again. Ruby had meddled enough there and it had made things worse so she wasn't going to try it again.

'Look, I have to go to Penzance for a few hours. Sneak this ten-pound note into Poppy's jar for her sculpture, will you?' Jacob said.

Ruby smiled and nodded.

He bent his head to give her a kiss on the cheek but she moved to hug him and he caught her on the corner of her mouth instead.

He pulled back slightly and smiled, his eyes going dark, and he leaned forward and kissed her properly in full view of everyone else. For a second, she worried about what people would say but with his mouth on hers she found she suddenly couldn't care less. His mouth was warm and sweet, his stubble soft as she stroked his face.

He pulled back and his smile was even bigger. 'I'll be back this afternoon.'

He gave her another quick peck on the cheek and moved off through the villagers.

Ruby cleared her throat and straightened her hair and then turned round to see how many people had noticed their very public display of affection. Sadly it seemed quite a lot, as Andrew, Willow, Lottie, Poppy, Julia, Dorothy, Kitty, Ken and several others were all staring at her, mostly with delight at this new turn of events.

Ruby decided she'd brazen it out and move around the village to look at the sculptures as if nothing had happened.

She moved over to Kitty's sculpture. She too had used chicken wire to get the basic shape but she'd also used holly leaves and poinsettias woven into the wire to decorate it. It looked stunning and was certainly getting a lot of attention from the villagers, judging by the amount of money that was in the jar. Ruby slipped a pound coin into the jar and moved on to Lottie and Poppy's sculpture. She could see Poppy walking around the village with Andrew and Willow but Lottie was hanging back as she was replying to an email on her phone. As she finished and shoved her phone back in her bag, she looked up at Ruby and smiled.

'This is great,' Ruby said, admiring their sculpture that really did look like an angel, through all the glitter and sparkle.

'Thank you, and your sculpture looks amazing,' Lottie said.

'Oh, you know I can't take any credit for that. It was pretty much all Jacob, he's very talented.'

'He is,' Lottie said, proudly.

There was silence then and Ruby got the sense that she wanted to say something else.

'He really likes you,' Lottie said.

'Oh no, it's not like that,' Ruby said automatically, knowing that it probably was exactly like that.

'No, he does. I've never seen him like this

with anyone before.'

Ruby shook her head.

'Listen, there was a guy I met about six months after Alex walked out and left us. He was staying at the hotel I was working at in Penzance. We just clicked. He was funny and brilliant and great with Poppy. We spent a few days together and, god, I think I fell in love with him. But when his stay came to an end, I pushed him away. I was still hurting after Alex left and I wasn't prepared to risk my heart again. So he left and I never saw him again. I have always regretted that. Don't make the same mistake I did. Jacob won't hang around forever waiting for you. He has a whole life in Penzance, his shop is there, he has friends, women who he used to date. It would be very easy for him to move back there unless he has a really good reason to make him want to stay.'

Ruby stared at her. The thought that Jacob might leave hadn't even occurred to her. She'd thought that she had time to get her head and heart used to the idea of being in a relationship again but it wasn't fair on Jacob to drag this out forever, making him wait while she came to a decision about whether she wanted a relationship or not.

'I know this is scary for you, but you don't want to look back on your life and regret the things you didn't do. I see the way you look at him and I think letting Jacob walk away would be the biggest regret of your life.'

Ruby swallowed down the lump of emotion that was caught in her throat. She put the money that Jacob had given her in Poppy's jar. 'That's from Jacob.'

Lottie smiled. 'He's a good man.'

'I know. Look, I better go and...' Ruby waved with her hand '...circulate.'

Lottie nodded and Ruby moved away.

Maybe she needed to talk to Jacob about all of this, ask him to be patient and give her more time.

Or maybe it was time she was brave and took this chance once and for all.

CHAPTER 17

SITTING IN THE PUB LATER WITH ANDREW, Willow, Lottie and Poppy, and enjoying the general buzz of happiness from the other villagers, Ruby couldn't help but smile about how everything had turned out in the last few days. The Angel Festival had been a big hit with over a hundred sculptures dotted about the village. Everyone had enjoyed making the angels and seeing everyone else's sculptures. Kitty had won with her holly leaf and poinsettia angel and generously matched all the money raised that day. Ruby didn't know what the final total would be, but she knew they had raised over a thousand pounds for the British Heart Foundation.

The villagers had welcomed her with open arms and she felt she had really brought something to the village and spread a bit of Christmas magic. She felt like she could really make a home here and not leave after a year, as had been her original plan when she'd first moved here. Regardless of what happened with Jacob, she knew she wanted to stay.

Although Jacob was another great big plus point. Things were going great between them and for the first time in twelve years she thought she might even be ready to have a proper relationship. He was good for her, in so many ways.

Suddenly everyone's phones started beeping at the same time and all the villagers fell quiet as they looked around at each other in confusion. Then Ruby noticed Lucy climbing on a chair and banging a glass to get everyone's attention.

'I've just sent a video to you all via the village forum. It's something you all need to see. I'm sure we all would like to know who cruelly stole Jesus from the nativity and has then been mocking us with these photos of Jesus all round the village.'

There was stifled laughter; obviously a lot of people found this a lot funnier than Lucy did. But unease settled into Ruby's stomach. If there was a video of the event, would it show her manhandling the poor sheep?

'I had my suspicions that it was Ruby Marlowe, as Jesus went missing the same night she arrived.'

Other people started nodding but again not taking this remotely seriously. Even Julia was nodding and Ruby wondered if she had known all along.

'So as my company supplied the webcam for the animals, I did a bit of digging. Fortunately we had recorded the night of the theft. I expected to find evidence of who had stolen

Jesus, but what I found instead was truly horrifying and I wanted you all to see it.'

People started pulling their phones out of their pockets and bags and clearly began watching the video. There were sudden gasps around the room.

Ruby quickly grabbed her phone, found the video and pressed play to see what everyone was watching. The camera didn't show the nativity scene at all, it was just focussed on the little paddock. Ruby didn't come into shot until that fateful moment when the sheep started choking, but it was painfully obvious that it was indeed her. Ruby watched as she approached the sheep, stood behind it, wrapped her arms around it and started squeezing its belly. There were gasps around the room as Ruby smacked the sheep between the shoulder blades and more gasps of shock as Ruby lifted the back legs up in the air and got kicked in the leg herself as soon as the sheep stopped choking.

Ruby was then seen running away and the video stopped.

Crap. That looked awfully damning. Ruby knew the reasons why she had been abusing the sheep, but no one else did.

Ruby looked up at the villagers who were all staring at her aghast. The only ones not finding it horrifying were Andrew and Willow who were giggling quietly as they watched the video but their giggles faded as they realised how everyone else was reacting to it.

Willow stood up quickly.

'Wait! Although many of you believe this to be Ruby, the video is not of good enough quality to prove it was her without any reason-able doubt—'

'It's OK, Willow, everyone knows it was me.' Ruby stood up too, ready to defend her-self, but who was going to believe that she was trying to do the Heimlich manoeuvre on a bloody sheep? It sounded ridiculous even to her own ears.

'Well, I'm sure Ruby has a very good explanation for what we've all just seen,' Willow went on.

Ruby cleared her throat. 'It is true that I stole Jesus from the nativity and I've been the one responsible for taking photos of him around the village and all the posts on the fo-rum. But it was never my intention for it to be cruel or malicious, I was just having a little joke.'

'What about the poor sheep?' Lucy shouted.

'While I was there, I gave some carrots to the donkey and the sheep, and one of the sheep started choking on the carrots and... well, I was trying to help it,' Ruby finished, lamely.

'A likely story,' Lucy said, who was obvi-ously in full swing now and enjoying every moment of her discomfort.

The villagers started muttering between themselves.

'There you go, Ruby was trying to help one of the sheep,' Willow said, over the noise of the villagers. 'I'm sure none of us would have liked to have seen Minty die and we all would have done the same thing in Ruby's shoes.'

The villagers didn't seem convinced at all.

Well, the perfect day had suddenly turned out to be not so perfect after all.

Ruby grabbed her bag and pulled out Jesus, who was dressed in a snowman outfit for some more photographs she'd planned to take later on. She placed him on the table. 'I'm really sorry.'

And with that, she left the pub and no one tried to stop her.

JACOB WAS on his way back from Penzance and had just stopped to get some petrol when his phone beeped with notification of the video. As he got back in the car he clicked on the video. He watched in surprise as Ruby gave one of the sheep the Heimlich manoeuvre and was impressed that she would go to those lengths for a sheep. He was also pretty impressed she knew how to do it. But then he realised that it was Lucy who had posted the video and he doubted somehow that she had done it to share Ruby's heroic actions with the rest of the village. Lucy could very easily twist this somehow. Many of the villagers probably wouldn't recognise Ruby's actions as the Heimlich manoeuvre and would be less than happy to see what she was doing to the sheep. God, he didn't want to give Ruby any ammunition to run, their relationship already felt tentative enough as it was, with Ruby looking like she was set to flee at any moment. If the villagers turned against her because of this, that could be all the reason she needed to pack her bags and go.

He quickly started the engine and drove down the road to the village. As he approached, he saw Lucas fixing one of the fences and he had an idea. He pulled over and wound down his window.

'Lucas, I need your help, will you come with me?'

Lucas looked at him suspiciously. 'Is this to do with Megan?'

'No, but if you come with me, I'll make it worth your while in that regard.'

Lucas clambered in.

Jacob drove off before Lucas had even put on his seatbelt.

'Look, I was never going to ask Megan to the ball.'

'Then why did Ruby tell me that you were?'

'Because she was hoping it might prompt you to ask Megan instead.'

Lucas flushed. 'Why would I do that?'

'Because you like her, anyone can see that, and she's crazy about you. So put the poor girl out of her misery and ask her. I guarantee she will say yes. In fact, I'll put my money where my mouth is and pay you a thousand pounds if you ask her and she says no.'

Lucas was silent for a moment. 'What did you want help with?'

Jacob decided to let the subject go. He'd done enough and he had more pressing things to attend to.

He handed Lucas his phone. 'Watch that video.'

Lucas was silent for a moment as he watched it. 'Christ, she saved Minty's life.'

Jacob had no idea how Lucas could tell the difference between the two sheep but he was just glad that Lucas had recognised the scene for what it was.

'Yes, Poppy made me watch a video once on how to do a Heimlich manoeuvre on dogs. That's what Ruby was doing, wasn't she?'

'Yes, thank god she was there.'

'Anyway, I doubt anyone in the village would understand what she was doing. Lucy posted it on the forum and you can bet it wasn't for nice reasons.'

'God, that woman is a cow,' Lucas muttered.

'Exactly. I need you to help me do some damage limitation here, explain to the villagers what Ruby was really doing.'

'I don't do public speeches.'

'Ruby saved Minty's life,' Jacob said. 'Are you really going to hang her out to dry?'

Lucas paused for a moment and then nodded. 'OK, fine.'

Jacob pulled up outside the pub, hoping there would be some villagers in there he could talk to. Otherwise he had every intention of marching Lucas round every house and shop to make sure everyone knew the truth.

The pub was quite full but there was no sign of Ruby. Or Willow and Andrew for that matter. But Lucy was holding court at a packed table.

'I think it's disgusting,' she was saying. 'And certainly not the kind of behaviour we want in our village.'

'I'm sure there is some reasonable explanation for all of this,' Kitty said. 'What did Ruby say?'

'Some rubbish that the animal was choking, a likely story.'

'It's true,' Jacob said.

'Of course you would say that,' Lucy said.

'No, it is true,' Lucas said. 'Trust me, when you work with animals long enough, you learn all sorts of ways to help them.' He flicked through his phone. 'This is a video on YouTube on how to give the Heimlich manoeuvre to dogs. You'll see a striking similarity to what Ruby was doing to Minty.' Lucas showed the phone to Kitty and then passed it round the table for others to see.

Lucy's face fell.

'Well there you go,' Kitty said, folding her arms and looking at Lucy. 'I have to say, *this* is certainly not the kind of behaviour we want in our village. You deliberately posted this video on the forum to turn people against Ruby. Why would you do that?'

'I... I didn't. I just thought people had a right to know what she did to the sheep. I didn't realise she was helping it.'

'Well you could have asked her first, instead of humiliating her in front of the whole village,' Julia said.

'But that wouldn't have had the same effect, would it?' Jacob said. 'What was this, revenge because I asked her to the ball and not you?'

Lucy's cheeks flushed. 'Of course not.'

Jacob looked around the table. Everyone had seen the truth of it, despite her denials.

'I would never have asked you, Lucy,' Jacob said. 'As you said before, I only go out with the finest, most attractive women. And while you might be quite pretty on the outside, there is certainly nothing attractive inside.'

'I agree,' Kitty said. 'What you did was ugly. And if that kind of attitude continues I will be looking for someone else to fill your house once the year is up.'

Lucy stared at them in shock. It was safe to say her cunning plan had totally backfired and everyone knew it.

Jacob had seen enough. He nodded his

thanks to Lucas, who was busy uploading the dog Heimlich video onto the forum for everyone else to see, and turned and left.

'COME BACK TO THE PUB, I'm sure we can sort it all out,' Willow said.

'I'm not exactly winning any popularity contests right now,' Ruby said, grabbing some baubles to paint. She needed to focus on something else right now. She had ruined everything.

'It was quite obvious to me you were trying to help the sheep, I'm sure everyone else will see that too,' Andrew said.

'This is such a mess,' Ruby sighed. 'I shouldn't have stolen Jesus, none of this would have happened.'

'It was just a joke,' Willow said. 'People found it funny.'

The door was pushed open and in walked Julia and Kitty.

Ruby stood up from where she was working, wondering if this was it and she was about to be asked to leave.

'Julia, I'm so sorry,' Ruby said.

'What are you sorry for?' Julia asked.

'For stealing Jesus and—'

'I knew it was you – as soon as I saw that picture outside the post office, I knew,' Julia said. 'Biggest laugh I've had in ages watching these photos of Jesus pop up in various costumes around the village. I'm not sure which was funnier, that or the bizarre penis candles that Willow arranged to be hung over the village.'

'And the Y-fronts,' Kitty added.

'What, wait, you saw they looked like penises too?' Willow said.

'Yes, of course, the whole village has been talking about it for weeks. The whole thing is hilarious. But we didn't tell you because we didn't want to upset you after you went to all the trouble of arranging the lights,' Julia said.

'I thought no one noticed,' Willow muttered.

Julia patted her arm consolingly and then turned to Ruby. 'Now about this sheep.'

'Oh god, Julia, I really was trying to help it.'

'I know.'

Ruby paused. 'You do?'

'Lucas came into the pub not long after you'd left. He'd seen the video and recognised it for what it was. He showed us videos of Heimlich manoeuvres on dogs on YouTube and we all could see that you were doing ex-actly what was in those videos with Minty. You saved his life, you're a hero.'

Ruby stared at them. 'I don't know about that. If I hadn't been stealing Jesus from the na-tivity, if I hadn't given the carrots to them in the first place, none of this would have happened.'

'None of that was done maliciously,' Kitty said. 'It was unfortunate what happened but you dealt with it in the best possible way.'

'Everyone thinks you're amazing,' Julia said. 'There's even talk of erecting a statue in your honour.'

'I think that's a wonderful idea,' Willow giggled.

'I'll get right on that,' Andrew said.

Ruby laughed. 'That might be going too far. Just as long as I can stay in the village, then I'm happy.'

'Of course you can stay, you're exactly the sort of person we want in this village,' Kitty said. 'Now, Lucy on the other hand. I made it very clear to her that that kind of spiteful attitude was not welcome here in Happiness and if she was to continue acting like she did today, she wouldn't be welcome to stay here once her year was up. We have a very long waiting list of people who want to live here and it would be very easy to fill her shoes. I told her to watch her step.'

'I'm so relieved. I think I upset Lucy because I got together with Jacob. I'm sure she'll get over it.'

'That's what Jacob said,' Kitty said.

'Jacob's back?'

'Yes, he's just moving his car to the car park. It was parked rather illegally outside the pub and I told him he needed to move it. But he certainly came into the pub all guns blazing ready to fight for you.'

'He did?' Ruby smiled.

Kitty nodded.

'Now, about you and young Jacob,' Julia started. 'I think we need some kind of clarification of what is happening between the two of you—'

'Oh shush, we're not here for that,' Kitty said.

Ruby laughed as Kitty hauled Julia away before she could grill her with any more questions.

The door closed behind them but actually that was exactly what Ruby wanted to talk to Jacob about too.

RUBY GLANCED over into Jacob's shop. He had come back an hour before with a huge smile on his face, given her a kiss, explained his take on what had happened in the pub with Lucy and then disappeared into his shop where he had been banging, cutting and welding on a very small piece of metal ever since. She wondered if he was making her necklace.

She wanted to talk to him but she couldn't find the right words to even begin to cover all the emotion and worry in her head. She wanted to tell him that she was prepared to give having a proper relationship a go. She wanted to say that she had feelings for him that went way beyond friendship. But the words simply wouldn't come out. Saying them out loud kind of felt like a huge sign to the universe that she was happy again and then it would all be taken away.

Ruby's shop door opened and Willow burst in, pulling Andrew along with her.

'Right, we're doing it now,' Willow said.

'What are we doing now?'

'I'm taking a pregnancy test. It's safe to say that ever since I've declared that I might almost definitely not be pregnant we've thought about nothing else. Now, online information varies saying I shouldn't take a test until one week after I'm late and some websites say I can take it the day after, so I bought three different tests and we're going to find out once and for all.'

'You're doing it here?' Ruby asked in surprise as Jacob wandered into her shop.

'Yes. You two are the only ones that know, so you should be there when we find out,' Willow said.

'Yes, apparently taking a pregnancy test is a group activity,' Andrew said, dryly.

'There are some things I'm quite happy not sharing,' Jacob said.

'Oh shush, it's not like I'm asking you both to watch me do it,' Willow said. 'I just want you there after, for better or worse. And once we're done, we'll say no more about it. I bought these tests from out of town so no one in the village knows and I won't get loads of people coming up to me and saying how sorry they are if I'm not pregnant. Andrew and I have agreed that we're not going to be disappointed if we're not pregnant. It's not really the right time anyway when we're not even married yet and we'd both like a bit more time just for the two of us. If we are pregnant that's great, but if we're not then that's great too.'

It sounded like she was trying to convince herself more than she was trying to convince them.

'Well, my bathroom is free for you to use,' Jacob said, gesturing to the stairs like he was showing off a fabulous prize.

Willow ran up the stairs and they heard the bathroom door close.

Ruby, Jacob and Andrew followed her up and sat on the sofa. Jacob flicked the TV on, presumably to drown out any bathroom noises or maybe just to pass the time.

They all stared at the screen as some TV show demonstrated how to baste a turkey.

'Well it's safe to say this is not how I imagined spending my afternoon,' Jacob said.

'We just need to know,' Andrew said, quietly. 'It's driving us mad. She wanted you there because she didn't want to have to tell you she wasn't pregnant and have to deal with all that emotion a second time. Despite what she says, she'll be really disappointed if she isn't pregnant, we both would.'

Jacob nodded. 'Yeah, I get that.'

Willow emerged carrying three white plastic wands.

'They're clean, I promise, and you don't have to touch them, just look at them. Jacob and Ruby, your tests will be ready in three minutes. Andrew, yours will be ready in five,' Willow said, laying a white plastic stick in front of each of them.

Jacob pulled out his phone and swiped the screen a few times. 'Right, I've set two timers.'

'Now, we're going to talk about something else, anything but this,' Willow said, gesturing to the three tests which held so much weight with the answers they would soon tell.

'OK,' Ruby said. 'Tell me the worst Christmas present you ever had.'

Willow laughed. 'Mine would be from my ex, Garry with two Rs. He bought me a new ironing board cover.'

Andrew laughed. 'But you don't iron. I've not seen you iron a single thing in the whole time we're together.'

'I know, I don't. Life's too short for that kind of rubbish. When I was dating Garry I never told him that I don't iron, I just made up loads of excuses, lack of time, dodgy iron, crappy ironing board cover. I suppose he thought he was doing me a favour by buying me a new cover. I had to pretend to be de-lighted when I opened that on Christmas Day.'

'Well there was me worrying about what to get you for Christmas,' Andrew said. 'But I think anything I buy will be better than that.'

'What's yours?' Willow asked.

'Mine was from Jacob,' Andrew said.

'Of course it was,' Jacob said, dryly.

'When we were kids, Jacob had this cool Millennium Falcon which I always wanted.'

Jacob let out a bark of laughter; obviously he knew where this was going.

'He never let me play with it but he would take great pleasure in playing with it in front of me,' Andrew went on. 'Anyway, one day, our dog Barney found it and chewed it up. After that Jacob didn't want to play with it anymore, but that Christmas I got it in my stocking. This half-chewed, de-formed plastic spaceship. I wasn't impressed.'

'I thought I was being quite generous,' Jacob said.

'What's yours, Jacob?' Ruby laughed.

'I was sort of seeing this girl just before Christmas one year. We'd met up twice before so it wasn't exactly the greatest love story. Anyway, we met up on Christmas Eve and she'd obviously thought she probably should buy me something and made a last-minute dash to the garage. She gave me a toothbrush and a car air freshener.'

They all laughed.

'What did you get her?' Ruby asked.

'I didn't. I'm not sure what was worse, me opening up that crappy present or me not giving her anything in return.'

Ruby got up and moved over to the kitchen area. 'Does anybody else want a drink?'

They all shook their heads. Ruby grabbed a glass. 'Mine was a Secret Santa thing we all did in the market hall where I worked. Except I ended up with someone else's present, at least I think I did. It was a pair of elephant underpants for men, with the trunk area where the… penis goes.' They all roared with laughter. 'I'm not sure what I was supposed to do with that.'

Ruby grabbed a bottle of juice and started pouring just as Jacob's phone went off to indicate that the three minutes were up.

They all fell silent. Ruby moved back into the lounge but she felt too nervous all of a sudden to go round and have a look at her test.

Willow took a deep breath. 'Go on then Jacob, tell me, are you about to become an uncle?'

Jacob looked down at his test and no one spoke, no one even breathed. He didn't say anything for the longest time as Jacob continued to stare at it. He looked back up at Willow and shook his head. 'I'm sorry, it's a negative.'

Willow let out a heavy breath and Andrew put his arm around her. 'Well, it's probably for the best,' she said, her voice shaky.

Ruby moved to sit back down on the sofa, suddenly feeling so disappointed for her best friend.

She glanced at her pregnancy test.

'We have the rest of our lives together to make hundreds of little babies. Now isn't our time, but our time will come,' Andrew said, gently.

'I know,' Willow said, quietly.

Ruby stared at the test, but there was no mistake. 'Um, my test says you *are* pregnant.'

Everyone turned to look at her.

'What?' Willow said.

Ruby passed her the test. 'See for yourself.'

Willow stared at it and showed Andrew. 'It says I am pregnant.'

'Or not,' Andrew said, gesturing to Jacob's test. He turned to Jacob. 'Are you sure you're reading it right?'

Jacob handed it over.

'That definitely says I'm not,' Willow said. 'So which is it?'

'I've heard that pregnancy tests can give out false negatives but not false positives. Although I'm not sure if that's true,' Ruby said.

'I guess the third test will be the decider,' Willow said.

They all stared at the test lying in front of Andrew. Jacob checked his phone. 'You still have one minute to go until it's ready.'

No one said anything. That minute that slowly ticked by was the longest of Ruby's life. She wanted this for Willow and Andrew so much.

The timer went off and Andrew picked it up. He let out a heavy breath but it was the huge smile on his face that confirmed his answer. 'We're pregnant.'

'Oh my god,' Willow said. 'Oh my god. We're going to have a baby.'

'Yes we are.'

Willow hugged him.

'Congratulations,' Ruby said.

'Thank you,' Willow said, wiping tears from her eyes. 'I can't believe this. We're going to be parents.'

'And brilliant parents at that,' Jacob said. 'Congratulations.'

Ruby couldn't help smiling. They had this perfect little future laid out in front of them and, for the first time since Harry had died, she suddenly wanted that future too and she wasn't afraid to take it.

CHAPTER 18

RUBY WAS WAITING FOR JACOB IN HIS FLAT WHILE he got changed in his bedroom. They were going off to the carol service around the tree together. She was sure that everyone in the village would have some thoughts on that but she didn't really care. They could hardly keep their semi-relationship a secret.

Jacob came out of his room, dressed in a thick jumper and carrying what looked like a black watch box.

'I have your new necklace in here. I apologise for the box, but it was the only one I had.'

Ruby's heart fluttered at the prospect of wearing it and what that actually meant. 'You didn't have to put it in a box at all.'

'Well I did, because if you decide to wear it, I wanted you to have somewhere safe for your other necklace.'

She smiled at this lovely gesture. He knew what a big deal it was to take Harry's necklace off and replace it with his.

She swallowed. 'Well, let's see it.'

He opened the box and she stared at the beautiful silver Christmas tree that shimmered in the light. The baubles were made from tiny pieces of coloured metal and on the top was a star that glittered with gold.

'Oh Jacob, it's wonderful, thank you so much.'

'You don't have to wear it tonight,' Jacob said.

She looked up at him. 'I want to.'

He paused. 'Are you sure?'

She nodded.

He moved round behind her and she lifted

her hair. His warm fingers at the base of her neck was an incredible feeling. He unhooked Harry's necklace and Ruby pushed down the feeling of panic that started to rise in her. He moved back to the box, took out the Christmas tree and carefully laid the snowflake inside. Then he came back to her and fastened the Christmas tree around her neck.

She admired how it looked in the long mirror near the door. It was beautiful. 'Thank you.'

'It looks good on you. I've never made any jewellery before, so this one was a bit of a challenge.'

'Well you did a wonderful job.'

She carefully closed the lid on Harry's necklace. Baby steps.

'Let's go and sing our hearts out,' Jacob said, pulling his coat and hat on.

Ruby did the same. 'You'll regret saying that when you hear me sing.'

They went downstairs and left the shop. They started walking up the high street and

Jacob slipped his hand into hers. She looked up at him and smiled. This felt so right. Tiny snowflakes were falling, the Christmas lights were twinkling and she was holding hands with the most wonderful man she had ever met.

She was scared, of course she was. She had successfully avoided all relationships for the last twelve years, only ever seeing men casually, and now she had been in Happiness for only a few days and was on the verge of starting a proper relationship. They had something special and running away or denying those feelings was not the answer. She didn't know whether she'd be any good at being in a relationship but if they were really going to do it, she was going to give this her all.

They came to the end of the high street and there, on the grassy slopes leading up to the castle, villagers were gathering around the tree. It looked like something out of those old-fashioned Christmas cards with everyone bundled up in hats and scarves, the big tree in the middle, the snow glittering on the ground, children running around and chasing each other, the adults all holding their song sheets. The only anachronism in the scene was that Julia had wheeled out a large electric keyboard and a small generator and was currently practising a few chords while everyone got themselves ready to start. She spied them as they drew close and waved them over, holding out the song sheets.

'Come along, we're just about to get started,' Julia scolded.

Ruby reached out for the song sheet when Julia caught her hand.

'So you arrive here holding hands, you've spent the last two nights at his flat, we saw you kissing at the Angel Festival yesterday – are you two a thing now?' Julia waggled her eyebrows.

Ruby blushed, horribly aware that the villagers had fallen silent behind her. They all wanted to know too. Was nothing private in this place?

She looked at Jacob. They hadn't talked about whether or not they were going to tell people about their new 'friends-with-benefits' arrangement and things seemed to have moved on quite a bit since then, although they hadn't properly discussed that either. She didn't want all the villagers sticking their oar in – this was still so new for her and Jacob and they were quite capable of cocking it up on their own without outside interference. But there was a part of her that was very excited about this development and she wanted to shout about it. Jacob still wasn't saying anything, he was leaving it up to her.

'We're... trying it out,' Ruby said, lamely.

'Trying it out?' Julia said.

'Yes, like buying a new jumper or a pair of shoes,' Jacob said. 'If we don't like it we can take it back to the shop and exchange it for a different pair.'

The villagers tittered and Jacob took the song sheet and moved over to the villagers, disappearing to stand near the back.

Crap. Ruby had clearly pissed him off with her answer.

She took the song sheet and made her way over to the tree. Should she join him, should she not? God, this was all so complicated all of a sudden. She was saved from making that decision by Willow snagging her arm and pulling her into her side.

Her friend gave her a hug and Ruby held her tight.

'Are you OK?' Willow whispered in her ear before stepping back to look at her.

Ruby nodded. 'I really am.'

Willow smiled and linked arms with her as Julia started playing the first few bars of 'Silent Night'. The villagers turned their attention to their song sheets and started singing.

'So are you and Jacob…?' Willow said over the sound of the music.

'I'm not sure how you could define what we have right now. It seems more than what we had before but we're not there yet,' Ruby explained, knowing they weren't there because she wasn't quite ready yet. 'And evidently I'm making a huge success of it,' she gestured to Jacob grumpily staring at his song sheet.

'I shouldn't worry, he always has that face on,' Andrew said.

'You're out of practice,' Willow said. 'And what were you supposed to say when standing in front of the whole village like that?'

'I don't know,' Ruby sighed. 'I should go and see him.'

She kissed Willow on the cheek and walked over to Jacob. He glanced at her and she nudged him playfully. He smiled and wrapped an arm around her shoulders, kissing her head.

Well it seemed she was forgiven. She leaned into him and listened to the villagers sing their hearts out, some of them had wonderful voices.

The song ended and Julia moved seamlessly into 'We Wish You a Merry Christmas'.

Jacob started singing and she looked up at him in surprise. He had a beautiful voice, all deep and theatrical. He gave her a little nod of encouragement. He certainly wasn't going to be impressed in a minute.

She took a deep breath and, as the villagers started singing about figgy pudding, she joined in with great gusto. His eyes widened as he registered just how bad her singing voice was and then he laughed. Ruby carried on singing and Jacob hugged her closer to him.

'I really bloody like you, Ruby Marlowe,' Jacob said.

She smiled. She had a feeling that this Christmas was going to be a good one.

RUBY WOKE up with a huge smile on her face the next day. There was glorious sunshine outside the window, the snow had stopped falling but it had settled nicely in the street and on the roofs opposite. The sun made it sparkle and shimmer. It looked like a Christmas card scene outside. But the thing that was making her smile was Jacob Harrington wrapped around her; it really was the best possible way to wake up. However, much as she wanted to stay there with him for the rest of the day, there was probably tons to be done.

As she became more awake she realised what day it was. December 23rd. There was maybe two or three seconds when she didn't make the connection, when she was thinking of the day ahead, making some more decorations just in case there was some last-minute shoppers coming in before the big day, the Polar Bear Plunge the next day. And then as she woke up more fully, it hit her like a ton of bricks.

Today was her anniversary. Today, thirteen years ago, she'd got married to her best friend and the love of her life. She had woken up wrapped in Harry's arms on the morning of the wedding because they'd not held much stock in the superstition of not seeing the bride before the ceremony. They'd known they were forever; they didn't need to worry about silly little things like spending the night before the wedding apart. He'd kissed her, told her he'd loved her and then they'd made love. And then after, as he held her in his arms, he'd told her of his plans for their honeymoon – she'd had no idea what he'd been planning. They were to fly out to New York late that night to see the big tree at the Rockefeller Center and, after she stopped squealing in delight, they'd made plans to see all the big trees of the world. God, it still hurt when she thought about him and everything they had missed together.

It didn't feel right waking up with another man today, almost as if she was betraying Harry's memory, which was ridiculous.

She wanted that future with Jacob but suddenly all those memories of the pain she went through when Harry died came flooding back, and that fear and panic of letting herself fall in love with Jacob and losing him slammed into her hard.

Jacob stirred next to her and she tried to push all these feelings away.

He smiled sleepily when he saw her and leaned over and kissed her.

'I love waking up next to you,' Jacob said. 'I love that kissing you is the first thing I do in the morning and the last thing I do at night. You make me smile so much.' He frowned as he stared at her. 'I never wanted forever before but I want that with you. I know we agreed no-strings-attached but I have to tell you, I love you.'

Panic ripped through her at those words.

'I was going to wait until Christmas Eve to give this to you as you're my Secret Santa, but I'd like to give this to you now,' Jacob said.

He leaned over and pulled out an envelope from the bedside drawers and handed it to her. She sat up in bed to open it. She slid out the contents and stared at them.

'It's two tickets to Italy. I thought you might want to finally go and see the largest Christmas tree in the world on Mount Ingino. We fly out on Boxing Day.'

God, it was happening all over again, the

declaration of love, the trip to see the Christmas tree. What if what happened next was losing him just like she lost Harry?

'I need some air,' Ruby said, scrambling up from the bed.

She started throwing on some clothes and then moved out into the living area of the flat.

Everything was happening so quickly and she didn't like it. She had arrived in Happiness not wanting another relationship and Jacob had got right under her skin. They had progressed from friends, to friends with benefits, to… whatever this was and she wasn't ready. Cal had said she was living this half-life, but she'd been relatively happy, she certainly hadn't had to deal with all this kind of emotional stress when she'd been free and single. She'd been content in her little bubble and at least she'd never get hurt.

Jacob followed her into the lounge.

'What's going on?'

'You, this,' she waved the tickets in the air. 'We agreed that we would have no-strings-attached sex, be friends with benefits, nothing more, and now you're telling me you love me and want to whisk me off to Italy,' Ruby said.

'We have something special Ruby, you know that. There are strings whether you want them or not.'

Ruby shook her head. 'No, I don't feel that way,' she said, knowing that she was saying things she didn't really mean out of panic.

But that was the problem. There *were* strings, tying his heart to hers, she could feel that and she knew how much it would hurt if those tethers were to snap.

He stared at her for the longest time.

'God, I'm so stupid,' Jacob said. 'I should have let you walk away the other day when we first slept together, when you said sleeping with me was a mistake. That hurt but letting myself fall in love with you and knowing you don't feel the same hurts even more. It hurts that you won't risk your heart on me, that I'm not considered worth the risk. I'm good for sex but not a lot else. I thought you might start to see things differently, that with time you might fall in love with me too, but that's not going to happen, is it?'

'I just…' Ruby trailed off, struggling to find any words to defend herself. She wanted to ask for more time but was that fair? What if she could never give him that? She glanced over to the watch box which currently held Harry's necklace and she felt that pain and fear slam into her again.

'Jesus Ruby, I can't do this again.'

'What does that mean?'

'I've been here before, falling in love with someone who only ever saw me as a friend. I waited and waited and she never saw me like that. If you genuinely don't see us going that way, then I need to get out now before I fall in love too deeply.'

He was breaking up with her. She felt one of the tethers tying him to her break, and god that hurt. She was going to lose him and she couldn't help the sob that escaped her lips. But maybe it was better this way. Better to watch him walk away now than fall in love with him completely and lose him so cruelly again. Maybe this was the out she needed. She had been on an emotional rollercoaster since she'd arrived in the village and she suddenly wanted to get off.

'If you want that life, marriage, children, the happy ever after, then you need to find someone else,' Ruby said. 'I thought I could have that life, I tried, I really did, but I can't do it. You need to find someone that can.'

She ran from the room, went downstairs and out onto the street. She leaned against the wall, sagged to her knees and burst into tears. What the hell had she just done? She was supposed to feel free, relieved. She hadn't wanted a relationship and now she'd got what she wanted. But why did her heart feel like it had been smashed into smithereens again? She had been scared of losing him but she had lost him anyway. She put her head in her hands and sobbed. She didn't love Jacob, she didn't. So why did it hurt so much?

CHAPTER 19

RUBY KNOCKED ON THE DOOR OF WILLOW'S cottage. Snow swirled around her. It wasn't the slow dance of soft gentle snowflakes, but angry flakes of ice that whipped against her face.

Andrew opened the door, wearing only his jeans as he pulled a jumper on. It was clear he had only just woken up.

'Oh god, I'm sorry. I didn't mean to disturb you.'

'You didn't, you're fine. I need to get up anyway, I was just being lazy,' Andrew said.

She looked at her watch to see it was only half eight in the morning, hardly the greatest lie-in.

He gestured for her to come in and closed the door behind her. 'Willow's out, I'm afraid. She had some last-minute Christmas shopping to do, so she got up early and went to Penzance.'

'Oh,' Ruby said, feeling disappointed that her best friend wasn't there to hold her hand.

Andrew put a gentle hand on her arm. 'I can offer a shoulder to cry on if you need it.'

She smiled weakly.

'Let me make you a cup of tea,' Andrew said. 'And I could rustle up some pancakes if you're hungry. And if you feel like pouring out your heart to me, then I'm a good listener.'

Ruby nodded and followed him through to the kitchen. She wasn't sure if she should talk to Andrew or not. It didn't seem right talking to him about his brother. Although maybe he was the perfect person to talk to.

'So how's the shop going?' Andrew asked

as he started making the pancake batter and mugs of tea. She smiled because she knew he was making polite conversation, to distract her.

'Good, the villagers seemed to like it. How are the renovations in the old shop going?'

'We're doing OK, but it will still be a couple of weeks before you can move back in.'

Ruby nodded. God, that was going to be awkward having to be next door to Jacob for the next few weeks now that whatever they'd had between them had ended so badly.

Andrew started cooking the pancakes and she felt the tears well in her eyes again.

How had it come to this?

Thirteen years ago today she was marrying the man of her dreams. Twelve years ago today she had been in pieces over Harry's death and now she was crying over another man.

She had thought she'd gotten over Harry's death – she certainly hadn't cried over him for many years – but being with Jacob made all these feelings and emotions bubble back to the surface. She knew that was because Jacob was the first man since Harry who had made her feel that way again and she remembered feeling that way before and then losing it all.

'Hey, come on,' Andrew said, placing down a plate of pancakes with chopped bananas and fruit on the side. 'Whatever my brother has done, I'm sure it can't be that bad. I'm sure he'll be banging on your door to apologise in the next hour or so.'

Ruby smiled, sadly, at Andrew's assumption that it must be Jacob's fault she was upset.

She pierced a bit of pancake on her fork and ate it. It tasted delicious but she was suddenly not very hungry.

'Your brother didn't do anything, other than tell me he loved me.'

'Ah, I see.'

'And then I told him I couldn't do it anymore, I couldn't be what he wanted,' Ruby said, tearfully.

'Oh crap.'

'Exactly. What kind of idiot says things like that to a wonderful man like Jacob when he tells her he loves her?'

'You're not an idiot, Ruby. You're just… broken. It takes time to heal and Jacob needs to realise that.'

'It's been over twelve years since Harry died. And the thing is, I can't even say that I'm still in love with him, even though a piece of my heart will always belong to him. It's just the pain of losing him I remember the most and that fear of letting myself fall in love with Jacob and it happening all over again.'

'That fear is not going to stop you falling in love with him, it will only stop you acting on it. But running away is not going to change those feelings for him,' Andrew said, kindly. 'And what happens if you keep pushing Jacob away and one day he starts going out with someone else, marries them, has children with them? You would have lost him anyway and it has nothing to do with the grim reaper.'

Ruby stared at him, knowing what he said

made total sense. She'd lost Jacob now and it hurt so much.

'I'm not saying you should declare your love for him now and whisk him off to the nearest registry office this afternoon. You need time to get used to the idea of being in a relationship again and Jacob needs to be patient enough to give you that. But if you feel even half what he feels for you then you need to give this a chance.'

'I don't want to hurt him.'

'But isn't it better to hurt him because you both gave it your best shot than hurt him because you gave up on him before it even started?'

Ruby pushed a piece of her pancake around her plate as she thought about this.

'That fear is never going to go away until you face it. It's like being scared of spiders or snakes or clowns, you can avoid them but the only way you can get rid of that fear is to pick one up and hold it in your hand.'

'I'm not holding a clown in my hand.'

Andrew laughed. 'No, fair point.'

'What if that fear never goes away? What if I hold the snake every day for the rest of my life and that fear of it biting me is with me every day?'

'It will get easier; I promise you that. It doesn't mean you won't worry about him, but surely a life with the man you love, if you do feel that way about him, has got to be better than a life without him.'

Ruby stared at her pancakes for a moment. She had lived most of her adult life without the man she loved. Over the last few days she had glimpsed what it could be like being in a relationship with Jacob and she didn't want to lose that. She couldn't. In many ways it would be like losing Harry all over again.

She stood up. 'I need to talk to him.'

'Go,' Andrew gestured.

'I'm sorry about the pancakes,' Ruby said, knowing that even if she stayed she still couldn't eat them.

Andrew picked up her plate and slid the

pancakes onto his own. 'I am eating for two now.'

She laughed and bent down and kissed him on the cheek. 'Thank you.'

'It's my pleasure.'

Ruby smiled and left the house.

JACOB DROVE his car down the winding narrow lanes. He'd needed to get out so he didn't have to stare at the walls of his flat and replay that fateful conversation over and over again. Except now he was sitting in his car feeling sorry for himself and still replaying that bloody conversation.

He was an ass. He'd pushed her and she'd bolted like a frightened animal. He should have known better than that.

But the way she had easily thrown their relationship away hurt. When times got tough her answer was to run rather than face it and talk things through. How could they ever make a relationship work with that attitude?

Although what had she been supposed to say when he'd told her he needed to get out of their relationship now? That hadn't exactly been a loving and supportive attitude either.

He had no idea what he was going to do now. He wanted to fight for her but if they stood any chance of making this work she had to fight for them too.

He came to a stop at a little roundabout. He could go straight on towards Penzance or turn the car round and go back to Happiness.

He was still hurting because the sad reality was she didn't want him as much as he wanted her.

He put the car into first and drove straight on.

CHAPTER 20

RUBY LEFT HER HOUSE AND MADE HER WAY DOWN towards the beach ready to do the Polar Bear Plunge the next day. It was Christmas Eve but she wasn't feeling remotely festive. Tomorrow was Christmas Day and although Cal was coming later she couldn't get excited about that either. She had been looking forward to spending the day with Jacob but that wasn't going to happen now.

The day was bitterly cold, the wind hadn't abated from the day before, the clouds were a slate grey. It was not a good day to go swimming in the sea. But there were lots of villagers walking towards the beach ahead of her so she knew she had to do this. Entertainment was clearly thin on the ground round here and they all wanted to watch Ruby freeze her arse off in the cold sea.

She had spent most of the day yesterday looking for Jacob but when Julia had told her she'd seen him leave the village in his car, Ruby had returned to her shop to wait for him. She knew that even if he went straight up to his flat, he'd have to walk through his own shop to do that and she'd see him. But he hadn't come back. She had called and texted him but he hadn't returned any of her messages. Kind of ironic that she had done the same to him a few months before. And now it was looking pretty likely he wouldn't be there for the Polar Bear Plunge either and, after the way she had treated him the day before, she couldn't blame him. He hadn't wanted to do this Polar Bear Plunge anyway so he was probably as far away from here as possible right then.

She couldn't be angry at Jacob, none of this was his fault. He'd told her he loved her and bought her tickets to Italy to fulfil her dream to see the world's largest Christmas tree and she'd thrown it back in his face. She had to try and fix this but she had no idea how. The thought of entering into a proper relationship with him thrilled her and terrified her in equal measure but the part of her that wanted this now far outweighed the part that didn't.

She wrapped her coat around her tighter. The Mrs Claus costume she was wearing was skimpy and quite honestly completely ridiculous. Thankfully she was wearing her bathrobe and her coat over the top which she was only going to take off just before the swim, but she was still cold.

Ruby made her way down the steps that led to the beach, her heart heavy.

When she reached the bottom she could see that it was fairly crowded for a cold winter's day. The waves were crashing on the shore, big white foamy horses thundering onto the sand. Definitely not the best day to take a swim.

She looked around for Willow and found her next to Andrew, Kitty and Ken. Ruby wandered over to join them. Willow smiled at her as she reached them.

'Hello Ruby,' Kitty said. 'Are you ready to throw yourself into the icy waves?'

'Not really,' Ruby forced a laugh. 'But at least it will be over relatively quickly.'

Ken leaned round Willow and Andrew to talk to her. 'I've screened off the cave over there so you can get changed straight after into something warm. I've put some large towels in there too.'

Ruby nodded and held up her bag. 'Thank you. I have some spare clothes in here.'

'Why don't I go and take that into the cave for you,' Kitty said, taking the bag and walking off to a large cave cut into the cliff face

'Oh, there's Lucas. I'll just go and see if he managed to get me a loudspeaker,' Ken said, hurrying over to the steps where Lucas had just arrived.

Ruby turned her attention back to Willow and Andrew.

'Are you OK?' Willow said, giving her a hug. 'Andrew told me you and Jacob ended things.'

'We had a fight; it was my fault. I overreacted because yesterday was mine and Harry's anniversary.'

'I know, I told him that. His timing was awful.'

'You spoke to him? Is he OK?' Ruby asked.

That was the worst thing about all of this, that she had broken his heart with her stupid fears and inability to move on.

'Yes, I spoke to him about five minutes ago,' Willow gestured to the sea.

Ruby looked where she was pointing and her heart leapt.

Jacob wasn't hard to spot. Probably around six foot five and dressed in a bright green elf outfit with candy-striped socks, he actually stuck out like a sore thumb as everyone else was bundled up against the cold. He was standing near the sea, staring out over the waves.

God, he was here and he'd come for her. After everything she'd said and done and knowing how much he hated and feared the sea, he was really going to do this just for her. He was an incredible man. Her heart filled with love for him. And then it hit her with the force of a bus. She was in love with this amazing man and it wasn't just this moment of clarity that made her love him. Truth be told, she'd had these feelings for him all along, she'd just refused to acknowledge them before.

But today Jacob was facing his fears, so it was about bloody time she faced hers too.

She started moving down towards the shore. Several people wished her good luck as she passed and she nodded and smiled, but her eyes were fixed on Jacob who was still staring out over the waves.

He was an impressive sight in his skin-tight

costume. He hadn't lost any of his grandeur because of the ridiculous green jacket and shorts he was wearing. His strong back muscles stood out across his shoulders and the arms of the jacket bulged. The shorts were especially tight across the bum, something she couldn't help but appreciate as she drew closer.

She reached his side and he glanced briefly at her before returning his attention to the sea.

'I'm sorry I took so long to come back. Getting this elf costume was a lot harder than I thought.'

Oh god. Was that really what had kept him away?

He turned to face her. 'I'm very sorry about yesterday morning.'

'Please don't apologise, you didn't do anything wrong.'

'I did. You were very clear about having a friends-with-benefits arrangement. I shouldn't have tried to move the goalposts. And I was an insensitive ass. I forgot it was your anniversary. I should have been there to support you and instead I just made things even more difficult for you.'

'I'm the one that needs to apologise. I overreacted. I woke up and remembered my anniversary, remembered how happy I was that day marrying the love of my life and how much it hurt when it all came to a crashing end. And I got scared. Everything has been so lovely and perfect between us and I got scared of losing it all over again. Of losing you.'

'You'll never lose me, Ruby. I will always be here for you. As a friend.'

As a friend. Christ, that wasn't good.

He turned to look at the sea. 'Right, let's do this before I chicken out completely.'

And before she could say anything, he was suddenly running into the waves.

'Crap,' Ruby muttered.

He didn't hesitate as the sea crashed around him, he dived head first into the water and then started swimming through the surf, his powerful body pulling him easily through the waves.

Ruby watched him in awe for a moment.

She quickly ditched her coat and bathrobe on the sand and this caused a small cheer from the onlookers. She toed off her shoes and ran out into the sea, the icy waves crashing over her and knocking her backwards. The water was so cold, it actually hurt. She waded up to her waist, her legs going numb. The waves were so big she couldn't see Jacob at all, which was more than a little worrying.

Jacob's elf hat floated past her on the top of a wave and she grabbed it and looked around. Where the hell was he? It was ridiculous to suddenly feel scared for him but the thought of something happening to him out here filled her with dread.

A huge wave came thundering towards her and she tried to jump over it but mistimed it. It hit her hard in the stomach and sent her staggering backwards, she lost her footing and the wave crashed over her head. She fell back and landed on her bottom on the sand.

She coughed and spluttered and wiped the water from her eyes. She looked up and saw Jacob wading back out the water towards her and her heart soared with relief.

And although he was wearing a silly elf costume, he looked like a Greek Adonis, with his curly black hair and his ill-fitting clothes clinging to him *everywhere*, showing him in his magnificent glory.

He frowned when he saw her and knelt in front of her.

'Are you OK?'

She reached out and stroked his face. 'I am now.'

She needed to tell him how she felt, but not here, in front of everyone.

'How was it out there?' Ruby asked, playing for time and because everything she wanted to say was a jumble in her mind.

'It's a bit rough out there today,' Jacob said, running his hand through his hair but a small smile appeared on his face. 'It was actually really great to be back in the sea again after all this time.'

She grinned. 'I'm so glad you're OK. Are you going back in?'

He shook his head. 'I think we've done enough for one day.'

He stood back up and offered out his hand. She took it and he helped her to her feet. She scooped up her bathrobe and wrapped it around her. She offered out her coat to Jacob and he laughed and shook his head.

'I think that will fit me even less than this ridiculous costume.'

They walked back up the beach and people stopped them to congratulate them. They became separated and Ruby hurried up into the cave to get changed. She slipped behind the screen and started undressing and was standing there completely naked trying to get her clothes out of her bag when Jacob stepped inside the cave.

'Crap, sorry,' Jacob said, turning away slightly.

'Don't be daft. You've seen me naked before.' And hopefully would again.

Ruby grabbed one of the big towels and draped it around his shoulders. He turned to watch her. She shivered a little and he caught the ends of the towel and wrapped them around her, bringing her into his arms and holding her close against him.

'They say, if you're exposed to the cold, you're supposed to share body heat,' Jacob said.

She could feel his heart thundering against his chest.

'Is that what this is?' Ruby said, wrapping her arms round his back.

'I have no idea what this is. Are you wanting to go back to the friends-with-benefits arrangement again?'

'No, I definitely don't want that,' Ruby said. She swallowed and slid her hands up to his face. 'You are the most amazing man I have ever met. That you just dived into the freezing cold sea, when you haven't been in there for twenty years, and you did that for me...'

'You know about that?' Jacob said.

'Yes and I just...'

She had no more words to describe how he made her feel so she leaned up and kissed him briefly on the lips. She watched the spark of desire ignite in his eyes. He bent his head and kissed her hard.

The taste of him was sublime as he kissed her. He wrapped his arms around her tighter and a tiny moan of need fell from her lips. The noise seemed to spur him on, and he slid his tongue into her mouth, caressing his hands down her naked body. The towel fell to the ground and she wrestled his wet top from his body. He shuffled her back against the cave wall, barely taking his mouth from hers for a second. She hooked a leg around his hips, kissing him, touching him.

A child's laughter from outside brought the

world back into focus again and she suddenly remembered where she was.

She put a hand to Jacob's chest and he stopped kissing her, searching her eyes intently.

They needed to talk but not here where people could hear them, not here where they couldn't celebrate their love for each other properly.

'Why don't we go back to mine to warm up?'

Jacob looked round the cave and nodded. 'I think that's an excellent idea.'

They quickly got dressed, which seemed slightly counterintuitive considering her plans for getting warmed up.

They grabbed their things and left the cave only to be met with a big cheer. Ruby blushed, knowing what the villagers would have heard if she hadn't stopped it from going any further. She suppressed a smile when she saw Jacob holding his costume and towel discreetly in front of his jeans.

'Well done, you two,' Ken said. 'You've both raised a lot of money for a very worthy cause.'

'I think those congratulations are mainly for Jacob,' Ruby said. 'But I'm just very grateful to everyone for sponsoring us.'

'Well shall we all go off to the pub to celebrate? We have mulled wine and hot chocolate ready to warm everyone up,' Kitty said and there was another collective cheer of approval from the villagers and many of them started making for the steps, Ken leading the way.

'That sounds lovely...' Ruby said. Jacob cleared his throat. 'But I think I'm going to have a shower first to warm up.'

Jacob nodded his approval. 'That sounds like a good plan.'

Kitty's eyes slid between her and Jacob and she smiled. She obviously knew what was going to happen between the two of them. 'Well maybe you can come along later.'

Ruby nodded and Kitty gave her a squeeze on the shoulder.

They followed the villagers up the steps but it was very slow progress and she couldn't help looking at Jacob and giggling at how frustrated he was getting.

They reached the top and started making their way up the hill but the villagers in front of them were certainly in no hurry and many of them wanted to talk and congratulate them. She could see her house now ahead but it still seemed like a million miles away as they tried to circumnavigate around the villagers.

Finally they got there. She walked up to the front door and opened it, moving inside the warmth of her house. She held the door open and, without a second's hesitation, Jacob stepped inside and closed the door behind him.

CHAPTER 21

SHE QUICKLY MADE A FIRE AND THEN SHE TURNED round to face him.

There were two seconds, maybe even three, when they stood and stared at each other before she stepped forward to kiss him. Or maybe he moved forward to kiss her. It didn't seem to matter because they were kissing, his large hands spanning her back, her arms round his neck, his body against hers.

She pushed his coat off his shoulders while he made short work of the buttons on her coat, dumping that on the floor too. She ran her hands down his sides, caught the hem of his jumper and t-shirt and slipped them over his head.

He yanked her jumper off and then he was kissing her neck, her shoulder, stroking his hands down her body.

He kissed her again. There was something so utterly wonderful about kissing this man. An immense sense of this was where she belonged.

He suddenly snatched his mouth from hers and groaned. 'Christ Ruby, I can't do this with you. I *really* wish I could but I can't have no-strings-attached sex with you anymore. You were right, it means more to me than it does to you and I can't do it. I thought about this a lot yesterday and I know I was a complete dick but breaking up was for the best. You got it right when you first came to the village, we really are better off being friends.'

God, this wasn't going at all to plan. She had to tell him how she felt.

'Wait, no, you don't understand. I love you.'

Jacob went very still.

'I love you Jacob Harrington. I think I always have. From the first moment we met, you got under my skin and I couldn't let you go. I wasn't ready to fall in love again but that didn't mean I didn't have those feelings for you. I kept pushing them away, told myself it was lust and nothing more. Told you nothing could happen between us. But you got it right, you knew. I was scared of how I felt and I was trying to run away from that. And yesterday I freaked out because it was my wedding anniversary, because I remembered what it was like to be so blissfully happy and then to have all of that snatched from me. But I'm not scared anymore. A life with you has got to be better than a life without you. You make me happy, Jacob, and I want that life with you. I want to fulfil our dreams and then make new ones together. I love you so—'

His mouth was on hers hard and she

couldn't help the tears that were falling as he continued to kiss her. Clothes were removed in quick succession, his, hers, until they were both naked and he was shuffling her back onto the rug. She had enough time to snag the box of condoms that Julia had forced her to buy a few days before and threw it onto the rug and then she was on the floor and he was over her, kissing her again, touching, stroking, caressing everywhere until she was humming with need for him. He grabbed a condom from the box and tore his mouth from hers for just a second while he ripped it open and slid it on and was inside her a second later. He pulled back to look at her, trembling as she held him.

'I love you too, Ruby Marlowe. I probably should have mentioned that back there,' he gestured to the door where they'd been a few minutes before.

She giggled. 'Timing is everything.'

He moved against her slowly and she wrapped her arms and legs around him.

'I love you,' Ruby whispered against his lips.

She kissed him, stroking her hand round the back of his neck. She had never felt so blissfully happy before. Every fear, every doubt that this was the wrong thing, faded away. She had been given a second chance at happiness and this time she was going to take it.

JACOB WALKED up the high street towards the castle hand in hand with Ruby. He looked down and she flashed him a beautiful, happy smile. God, she filled him so much he felt his heart was going to burst. The Christmas Eve ball was something everyone was looking for-ward to, but the thing that he was most excited about was spending the rest of his life with the woman he loved.

They approached Megan's house and he

could see Lucas waiting outside dressed in a tux. The door opened and Megan was standing there in a red velvet dress. Jacob felt Ruby slow down as they passed so she could watch. They heard Lucas say Megan was beautiful and suddenly Megan stepped forward, tugged the lapels of Lucas's jacket and kissed him. Ruby gave a little squeal of delight. Jacob hurried her on before she could stand there and gawk some more but he couldn't help looking back as Lucas hustled Megan back inside, his lips still against hers and kicked the door closed behind them. It seemed someone else was going to get their happy ever after tonight.

'I'm so happy they've finally got together,' Ruby said.

'I think when two people are meant to be together, love finds a way,' Jacob said.

Ruby grinned. 'Or tenacity.'

'That too.'

She leaned up and kissed him on the cheek. 'Thank you for being tenacious.'

He smiled. 'My pleasure.'

'I still feel bad that I never got you any-thing for the Secret Santa,' Ruby said as they walked past lanterns lighting their way to-wards the castle entrance. 'Everything has just been so busy the last few days.'

'You gave me your heart, Ruby Marlowe. Of all the crappy gifts that were being given out this afternoon at the Secret Santa, I defi-nitely got the best one. Probably the best present I've ever been given.'

She smiled. 'I'm sure I can make it up to you later tonight.'

He grinned, feeling the punch of desire at that thought. He didn't think that need for her would ever go away.

'I'm looking forward to you meeting Cal tonight as well, he will love you,' Ruby said. 'His plane got in this afternoon, so he's on his way here now.'

'I'm looking forward to meeting him too,' Jacob said. 'I hope he approves.'

She looked up at him with a laugh. 'How

could he not approve of someone who makes me so happy?'

He smiled.

They walked into the entrance and were met with an actual butler who offered to take their coats. Jacob knew that Kitty and Ken only had one housekeeper to cook and clean their tiny living quarters, so this butler was a step up, although he suspected it was just for tonight, along with all the other staff who were busy moving around, handing out champagne flutes and making everything run smoothly.

Ruby shrugged out of her coat and he got the chance to admire her dress again. She looked magnificent, wearing an emerald-green ball gown that clung in all the right places.

They moved down the corridor and stepped into the great hall, which really did look magnificent. There were several ornate-looking chandeliers dotted around the room that had been festooned with lots of holly, berries and other festive greenery. A large tree in one corner was dressed all in gold and a holly berry garland was draped across the spectacular fireplace, which had a huge log fire burning away. The tables, all covered in white tablecloths, looked spectacular with beautiful decorations in the middle that Jacob knew Kitty and Ken had bought from Ruby's shop.

He was well aware that many of the villagers were watching them as they walked hand in hand across the room to their table and he didn't care. Nothing could take away his happiness right then. They could stare and talk and whisper and point and his smile was still going to be permanently on his face.

He noticed Lucy in the corner with her friends. Clearly her date, if there ever had been one, was a no-show. Lucy looked well and truly fed up. While everyone was wandering around the tables and mingling happily, they were all giving Lucy's table a wide berth. But it was no wonder when she had a face like she'd just been told Christmas was cancelled. Jacob hoped that Happiness would thaw her out, and she would relax into having the kinder and more generous attitude that the rest of the villagers had, but he wouldn't hold his breath.

Julia came barrelling over before they'd even reached their table.

'It's nice to see you put that silly argument behind you,' she said. 'Are you two…' she gestured vaguely as if a simple gesture could even begin to cover what Jacob felt for Ruby Marlowe. Despite wanting to shout about their relationship from the rooftops, he would leave it up to Ruby to decide if she wanted to tell people about their new status or not.

'We're together,' Ruby said, proudly. 'Properly. He's my boyfriend and I love him.'

Jacob smiled and leaned down to kiss Ruby on the forehead.

Julia looked like she was about to burst with excitement. She immediately leapt forward and pulled them both into a big hug and then ran off to no doubt tell the entire village this exciting news.

'So it's official then, Ruby Marlowe?'

She grinned. 'I guess it is.'

He glanced over her shoulder and spotted Cal walking into the room, wearing a tux. He was a confident man, but not cocky, just someone who was very happy in his own skin.

He gestured to Ruby that her brother was here and she let out a little squeal and ran across the room to greet him. He watched her as she threw her arms round Cal's neck and he picked her up and swung her around.

Ruby linked arms with him and brought Cal back over to introduce them. This was it, the time he had to impress a Paralympian.

Ruby was whispering something to Cal as they drew near and Cal was smiling hugely.

'Cal, this is Jacob,' Ruby said. 'Jacob, this is my big brother.'

Cal squared up to him, which wasn't what Jacob was expecting at all. 'I need a word with you, Jacob Harrington. Is it true you're sleeping with my little sister?'

Jacob had no idea how to respond to that.

But then Ruby giggled and Jacob noticed the smile playing on Cal's lips.

'I'm totally messing with you,' Cal laughed, offering out a hand to shake. 'It's nice to finally meet the man who has put such a big smile back on my sister's face.'

Jacob sighed with relief but before he could speak, he heard a voice behind him.

'Cal?'

Jacob turned round to see that Lottie was standing there staring at Cal as if she'd seen a ghost.

Cal's face erupted into a big smile. 'Lottie.'

'Do you two know each other?' Ruby asked.

Jacob looked at the two of them, registering the way they were staring at each other, and suddenly he knew. This was the man his sister had told him about, the one she had pushed away because she'd got scared.

'Well, it seems I might need a word with you, Callum Marlowe. Did you sleep with my little sister?'

Cal laughed uneasily.

The band started to play and, because Lottie and Cal were still staring at each other, Jacob snagged Ruby's hand and whisked her onto the dancefloor.

'My brother and your sister?' Ruby said, watching them as Lottie moved towards Cal and gave him a tentative hug. Then Poppy came over and hugged his leg and Cal picked Poppy up and gave her a proper hug too.

'So it seems.'

Ruby leaned her head against his chest as he moved around the dancefloor with her in his arms.

'I love you,' Ruby said, looking up at him. 'You gave me a future that I never thought possible, you made dreams come true that I stopped hoping for a long time ago.'

He bent his head and kissed her in full view of everyone else, not caring who saw or what they thought.

'You have given me happiness that I never knew I was looking for,' Jacob said, against her lips. He looked up for a moment at the tall Christmas tree and then back at Ruby and smiled. 'I think I've finally found what makes my perfect Christmas.'

CHAPTER 22

RUBY WAS FEELING COMPLETELY STUFFED. SHE'D had her fill of turkey, parsnips and roast potatoes and somehow still managed to find room for two mince pies with cream and numerous chocolates.

She looked around the room at the people she loved: Jacob, Cal and Willow and of course Andrew, Lottie and Poppy. The game of charades was well underway with Willow currently taking centre stage and prancing around waving her hands in the air. Andrew was watching her with complete love in his eyes as if her terrible rendition of *Mary Poppins* was the greatest thing he'd ever seen. Snow was falling steadily as it had been all morning. There were several snowmen outside their shop that they'd all spent the morning making.

It really was the perfect Christmas Day. But not for any of those reasons, but because she was spending it with the man she loved with everything she had. She was snuggled up against Jacob on the sofa, his arm around her shoulders. She looked up at him and watched him laugh at whatever Willow was doing. God, she loved him so much and, right then, she couldn't have been happier.

He noticed her watching him and looked down at her, his face lighting up into a beautiful smile.

'I love you,' Ruby whispered, although everyone was shouting out their guesses of what Willow was trying to act out so no one was really interested in what they were talking about. 'Have I told you that today?'

He grinned. 'Many times, but I don't think

I will ever tire of hearing you say it.' He stroked a finger down her cheek. 'And I can't wait until tonight when I can show you how much I love you.'

She smiled. 'I'm so excited about going to Italy tomorrow. I know seeing the world's largest Christmas tree might not be your thing, but there'll be lots of other things we can do while we're there.'

'Ruby, your dreams are my dreams now. I will be more than happy watching you fulfil your dreams. Plus it's Italy, it'll be snowing, that sounds pretty damned romantic to me.'

'I think I'll have to give you that.'

'I knew I'd be able to change your mind about snow being romantic,' Jacob said.

She smiled. She wasn't going to admit that anywhere she was with him would be romantic in her eyes.

She turned back to watch Willow and decided to put her out of her misery. *'Mary Poppins.'*

'Yes, finally,' Willow said, flopping down on the sofa next to Andrew, exhausted.

Ruby stood up. 'Does anyone want a hot chocolate?'

There were nods of approval all around the room.

'Cal, why don't you give me a hand.'

He grinned and shifted Poppy off his lap, signing to her slowly where he was going. He had done the sign language course with her a few months before. It was funny to think they'd both been doing it to communicate with the same little girl.

Ruby walked into the kitchen and Cal followed her. She'd still not had a chance to talk to her brother properly yet since his arrival the night before. He'd spent most of the ball sitting with Poppy and Lottie and talking to them. They had slipped off early and arrived together at Jacob's flat a few hours before so something was definitely going on between them.

Ruby poured some milk into a jug and put

it into the microwave. She turned round as Cal was getting mugs out the cupboard. She looked into the lounge and could see the game of charades was still going, with Lottie taking to the floor this time.

'So what's going on between you and Lottie and why did you never tell me about her before?' Ruby said.

Cal started adding hot chocolate powder to the mugs. 'I didn't tell you because it ended almost straight after it started so it was hardly a good advertisement for getting you back into the relationship saddle. And as to what's going on between us now... I don't know. We have a connection, I felt that the first time I met her. You know when you meet someone and you just know your life is going to change because of that person? That's what I felt when I saw her. We had chemistry. A ton of it. But it was so much more than that. That connection is still as strong now. She says she regrets pushing me away, I haven't been able to stop thinking about her since I left. And Poppy, I adore her.' He shrugged. 'Maybe we can make it work.'

Ruby grinned. She wanted that life for her brother. Now she'd had a taste of the fairytale, she wanted that for everyone. 'I hope so.'

'And what about you and Jacob?'

'I love him,' Ruby said, without a moment's hesitation.

He broke into a huge smile. 'You don't know how happy that makes me.'

'Thank you for pushing me, for helping me to be brave again.'

'I don't know if I can take any credit, you had to choose to take that step yourself in the end.'

'And he's one hundred percent worth it. There's not a single doubt in my mind that he is my forever.'

The microwave pinged and Ruby grabbed the jug and poured out the hot milk into the mugs while Cal added squirty cream and marshmallows to the top.

They took them out into the lounge and for

a moment the game ceased as everyone snuggled up in their chairs and sofas to drink them.

Ruby sat next to Jacob and he put her arm around her. She looked around the room at Andrew cuddled up with Willow, his hand on her belly. She looked over at Cal, one arm around Lottie, the other wrapped around Poppy, and she couldn't help but smile. This really was the little village of Happiness.

EPILOGUE

RUBY HURRIED INTO THE GREAT HALL TO CHECK everything was ready for her best friend. A Valentine's Day wedding for Willow and Andrew couldn't be more romantic and Ruby wanted to make sure that everything ran smoothly.

All the guests were waiting for the wedding to start, sitting in a big circle around the room. There were no 'his and hers' sides, no aisle, it was just going to be a day to celebrate their love for each other. Willow and Andrew had gone against almost every wedding tradition possible. She would not be given away, they were going to enter the circle together, equal partners in every way. Ruby liked that. Andrew had already had the wonderful delight of seeing Willow in her dress earlier that afternoon, a beautiful gold gown that sparkled and shimmered whenever she moved.

Purple flowers adorned the room, entwined with gold candles and fairy lights as Willow hadn't wanted the traditional red associated with Valentine's Day. They were making up their own rules today.

Ken had obviously got the memo about the colour scheme. He was waiting in the middle of the circle ready to perform the marriage dressed in a splendid purple satin waistcoat which actually matched Ruby's own dress perfectly.

Lottie snagged her hand as she walked past. Cal was sitting next to her, holding her other hand with Poppy on his lap. The two of them had danced around their attraction for several weeks after Christmas, with Cal coming and going on several occasions, but eventually Cal had rented a flat just down the road from Lottie and now they were apparently taking things slow, although Ruby knew that their version of taking it slow was Cal spending almost every night round Lottie's place. They both seemed deliriously happy with this arrangement, as did Poppy. Ruby was enjoying having her brother so close again too.

'How's Willow doing?' Lottie asked.

Willow's morning sickness had started with a vengeance a few weeks before, but it seemed to have slowed and almost stopped over the last few days. Whether that had anything to do with Julia's secret recipe of ginger tea and peppermint biscuits, or whether it had just stopped on its own, no one knew, but it seemed that she would at least get some kind of reprieve from it today.

'I think she's OK, she's stocked up on those peppermint biscuits and she says she's doing fine. I think she's just too excited to even have time to be sick today.'

'And how's Andrew doing?' Cal said.

'I left them cuddled up on the sofa together and Andrew had the biggest grin on his face I think I've ever seen.'

'So we're all ready?' Lottie said.

Ruby looked around. 'I think so.'

'You better go and get Jacob, he's outside,' Lottie said, suppressing a tiny smirk.

Ruby moved to the door. Outside, snow was falling heavily, making the night seem so much brighter and magical. Little daffodils and tulips had already flowered and their heads were bowed against the unexpected snow. A large oak tree stood in the courtyard outside all lit up with tiny lights, glowing in the darkness. Jacob stood underneath its great boughs, holding what looked like a blanket. Her heart leapt at the sight of him.

She moved across the courtyard towards him and, as she got close, he wrapped the furry blanket around her shoulders.

'What are you doing out here? The wedding's about to start,' Ruby said.

'We have time.' Jacob gathered the blanket together and tugged her gently towards him, so he could kiss her. She melted against him and he held her in his arms.

'I love you,' Jacob said, against her lips.

She smiled. 'Jacob Harrington, you have changed my life completely. You make me so utterly happy every single day. I love you so much.'

'You're kind of stealing my lines here,' Jacob said, kissing her again.

And then she knew. Willow sending her downstairs to 'check everything was OK'. Lottie sending her outside. Jacob waiting for her in the snow, underneath the fairy lights with a blanket to keep her warm when in reality they both should have been inside waiting for the bride and groom. Her heart soared with happiness, as Jacob stroked her fingers and placed little kisses on her wedding ring finger.

'Ruby Marlowe. I wanted to do this somewhere Christmassy but I'll be damned if I'm waiting until Christmas. I thought that here with the snow and the fairy lights, it would be a close second.'

He took a deep breath and his hands shook as he held her.

'Jacob, if it's any easier, the answer's yes.'

He grinned. 'You're so impatient. You have to at least let me ask you first.'

'I just want you to know, there is not one single seed of doubt that this is the right thing for us. I'm not scared of that future anymore.'

'Some might say it's too soon for us,' Jacob said, his eyes clouding with concern.

'And they don't know what we have. We have something incredible; you know that.'

'I do. You are my entire world and I cannot wait to have you as my wife.'

'You have me, regardless of that ring you have in your pocket. What we have is forever.'

He smiled and pulled the ring from his jacket. Despite what she had just said, she couldn't wait to see it.

'Ooops, wrong ring,' Jacob said, pulling out Willow's wedding ring.

Ruby laughed, knowing Jacob had done that deliberately.

He put the ring back in his pocket with a wink and pulled out another ring box. He opened it to reveal a beautiful emerald.

'For all the Christmas trees we are going to see.'

'Oh Jacob, it's beautiful.'

'Shall I put it on?'

She nodded, tears in her eyes as he slid it onto her finger. She stared at it; her heart completely full.

'It's official, I'm going to be your wife,' Ruby said, tears streaming down her cheeks.

Jacob gently wiped them away and kissed her.

A noise above them broke the moment and Ruby turned round to see Andrew and Willow leaning out the window. 'Did she say yes?' Willow said.

'Of course I did,' Ruby said and then laughed to see half the villagers leaning out of doors and windows to watch the proposal too. They all gave a little cheer.

'Come on then, Ruby Marlowe, we have a wedding to watch, we might get some tips,' Jacob said.

He offered out his hand and she took it as they walked back inside.

'We don't need any tips, we've got this.'

And Ruby knew that was true. This was the start of their own happy ever after.

The End

If you enjoyed *The Gift of Happiness*, you'll love my next gorgeously romantic story, *Sunrise*

over Sapphire Bay, out in April.

Website: https://hollymartin-author.com
Twitter: @HollyMAuthor
Email: holly@hollymartin-author.com

A LETTER FROM HOLLY

Thank you so much for reading *The Gift of Happiness*, I had so much fun creating this story and the beautiful village of Happiness. I hope you enjoyed reading it as much as I enjoyed writing it. If you did enjoy it, and want to keep up-to-date with all my latest releases, just sign up here to join my newsletter. Your email will never be shared and you can unsubscribe at any time.

www.subscribepage.com/hollymartinsignup

One of the best parts of writing comes from seeing the reaction from readers. Did it make you smile or laugh, did it make you cry, hopefully happy tears? Did you fall in love with Ruby and Jacob as much as I did? Did you like the gorgeous little village of Happiness? If you enjoyed the story, I would absolutely love it if you could leave a short review. Getting feedback from readers is amazing and it also helps to persuade other readers to pick up one of my books for the first time.

My next book, out in April is called *Sunrise over Sapphire Bay*. It's the start of a new stand-alone series set on Jewel Island.

Thank you for reading.

Love Holly x

JUNIPER ISLAND SERIES

Christmas Under a Cranberry Sky

A Town Called Christmas

WHITE CLIFF BAY SERIES

Christmas at Lilac Cottage

Snowflakes on Silver Cove

Summer at Rose Island

STANDALONE STORIES

Fairytale Beginnings

Tied Up With Love

A Home on Bramble Hill

One Hundred Christmas Proposals

One Hundred Proposals

The Guestbook at Willow Cottage

FOR YOUNG ADULTS:

THE SENTINEL SERIES

The Sentinel (Book 1 of the Sentinel Series)

The Prophecies (Book 2 of the Sentinel Series)

The Revenge (Book 3 of the Sentinel Series)

The Reckoning (Book 4 of the Sentinel Series)

ACKNOWLEDGEMENTS

To my family, my mom, my biggest fan, who reads every word I've written a hundred times over and loves it every single time, my dad, my brother Lee and my sister-in-law Julie, for your support, love, encouragement and endless excitement for my stories.

For my twinnie, the gorgeous Aven Ellis for just being my wonderful friend, for your endless support, for cheering me on, for reading my stories and telling me what works and what doesn't and for keeping me entertained with wonderful stories. I love you dearly.

To my lovely friends Julie, Natalie, Jac, Verity and Jodie, thanks for all the support.

To the Devon contingent, Paw and Order, Belinda, Lisa, Phil, Bodie, Kodi and Skipper. Thanks for keeping me entertained and always being there.

For Sharon Sant for just being there always and your wonderful friendship.

To everyone at Bookcamp, you gorgeous, fabulous bunch, thank you for your wonderful support on this venture.

To Kirsty Greenwood, thanks for answering all my questions with unending patience.

Thanks to the brilliant Emma Rogers for the gorgeous cover design.

Thanks to my fabulous editors, Celine Kelly and Rhian McKay.

Huge thanks to Cora Cade for the excellent job formatting my book.

To all the wonderful bloggers for your tweets, retweets, facebook posts, tireless promotions, support, encouragement and endless enthusiasm. You guys are amazing and I couldn't do this journey without you.

To anyone who has read my book and taken the time to tell me you've enjoyed it or wrote a review, thank you so much.

Thank you, I love you all.